W9-BCL-022

BLOOD COUNTRY

A CLAIRE WATKINS MYSTERY

Mary Logue

WALKER & COMPANY

New York

First published in the United States of America in 1999 by
Walker Publishing Company, Inc.

Published simultaneously in Canada by Fitzhenry and Whiteside
Markham, Ontario L3R 4T8

ISBN 0-8027-3339-5

Series design by Mauna Eichner

for Peter always with love

I would like to thank my writing group: Deborah Woodworth, Tom Rucker, Becky Bohan, Marilyn Bos, Pete Hautman, and two past members—Andy Hinderlie and George Sorenson. Also, special thanks to readers along the way: R. D. Zimmerman, Kate Green, Ruth LaFortune, Dodie Logue, and Mary Anne Collins-Svoboda.

Fort St. Antoine is a fictitious town. The name comes from a fort that was established by the French somewhere along the eastern shore of Lake Pepin in what is now Wisconsin. No character in this book is based on any real person.

She had told her mother most of it. How the dark green truck had roared out of the night, how the wheels had screeched, how her father had been hit, had flown up, and then had landed on the street. She had even told her how Dad had lain there stretched out flat on the black tar and so quiet that it hurt. How the thought that Dad might be dead had come into her mind then and bloomed, and she hadn't been able to stop it from growing. She had told her mother all that but not everything.

A year later, the secret she kept still weighed her down. It rubbed at her and bugged her. It never went away. She thought of the secret every day. She worried. Sometimes her mother would reach down and rub her forehead and say, "Meggy, you are getting worry lines already. You're too young. Go out and play." And Meg wasn't able to tell her mom that she was afraid. All the time. Because she knew her mother was worried too.

But since they had been living in the country, Meg had started to relax. Maybe she had gotten away. Maybe it was all over. Maybe the man didn't care anymore. Meg had started to think that he wouldn't come looking for her.

That's why it was so hard to feel the fear creep up into her heart again. She had felt someone watching her when she left school today. She had purposely dropped a book and bent over to pick it up so she would have a chance to look around. She hadn't seen anything suspicious. A truck was parked way down the street, but that wasn't unusual. Yet her blood was zinging through her veins like it was made of metal. She sat by the window on the bus ride home and watched. But she didn't see anything out of the ordinary.

When the man in the truck hit her father, her mom thought that Meg had stayed in the house and hid behind the curtains. What Meg never told her was that she had run out the front door. After a moment, Meg had turned around and gone back into the house and hidden in the curtains. When her mom came into the room, that's where she found Meg. Because of this, Meg was in danger. Even though her mom was a cop, she couldn't save everybody from everything. After all, her dad had been killed.

For Meg had seen the man. She knew what he looked like. And he had seen her. Meg had watched his eyes light on her and grow larger for a second. He looked through the truck window at her, and then she ran. He knew what she looked like. She knew he was going to come and get her someday.

1

As Claire stepped out of her house into the fading sunlight of an early-April day, she looked back over the roof. The bluff rose up into the pale blue sky like the walls of a fortress. One of the reasons she had bought this old farmhouse was that it had that protection. The bluff was formed when limestone that had been carved away in the ancient bed of the Mississippi River. Its sides were covered with prickly red cedar, slashes of birch, black walnuts, and oak.

Meg, her ten-year-old daughter, tugged at her jacket. "Mom, I'm going to run over to Ramah's. She's standing at her door. I'll be right back."

"Yes, go ahead."

"But watch me, Mom. Watch me until I get there."

"Of course I'll watch you." She ruffled Meg's hair and sent her on her way. Her darling daughter. Probably the most important reason they had moved down to Fort St. Antoine. Meg had been afraid in their old house in St. Paul.

The two of them had lived in Fort St. Antoine for nearly nine months. The town was about an hour and a half southeast of the

Twin Cities, nestled between the shore of Lake Pepin and the surrounding limestone bluffs. It was situated halfway down a natural lake that had formed in the Mississippi River. The town was named after a French fort that had been built in the eighteenth century, although little of the fort remained. The town had peaked around 1910 with a population of 730, having both a railroad station and a ferry. Neither existed now. Where the town had once been a vital transportation center for the farmers in the surrounding area, it was now just a pleasant day-trip destination for tourists from the Twin Cities. The current population was around 180.

She pulled her eyes down from the bluffs and watched Meg wave from Ramah's doorway. Ramah was an older woman who watched Meg for an hour or two when she got home from school.

Claire saw that her other neighbor, Landers Anderson, was sitting out in his garden, so she walked over to chat. "What's up?" she yelled at him as she got closer.

"Pondering," he told her. He sat smiling up at her, his wisps of white hair sticking out from under a green-plaid tam and an old Green Bay Packers sweatshirt snugged over his belly.

"Good thing to do on a night like this."

"Yes, finally winter is letting loose of us. A fine day. It makes me wonder how many more springs I'll see."

"Oh, I'm afraid you'll be around for a while."

"Keeping an eye on you." Landers patted the chair next to him.

"I can only sit for a moment. Meg and I have a big night planned. We rented a video, and we're making popcorn. Since I don't work tomorrow, we thought we'd have a little party. Would you like to join us?"

"No, thanks." He lifted up the tam on his head and plopped it back down, making his white hair fly out at the sides. "I've got a good book going."

"What are you reading?"

Landers laughed silently, his head bobbing up and down as if on a gentle spring, and then told her. "*The Yearling*. Seeing all the deer this year, I remembered that book that I read as a boy. Took it out from the library. It's still good." He paused, then asked, "How's Meg doing at school?"

"She has her ups and downs. Last few days, she has seemed upset about something, but when I ask her, she says it's nothing."

"Meg thinks a lot. It always makes everyday life a little harder when you do it with full consciousness."

Looking at Landers, Claire was surprised by how much she loved this old man. He had been such a help to her when they had first moved down. Cups of tea when she was tired from stripping wallpaper, water when their well pipes burst, a telephone before the phone company put theirs in, and a shoulder to cry on when she felt alone and disheartened and didn't want Meg to know. He was one of those rare people who had taken growing old as a chance to reflect on both his life and others and, in doing so, had grown wise. A simple sentence from him often put the wrangled mess of her life in perspective.

He cleared his throat and folded his hands. She knew this meant he was ready to make a pronouncement. "Someone called me up and wanted to buy my house."

"Oh, what did you tell them?" Claire felt her heart stop. She couldn't bear to think of Landers moving away. He was so much a part of this place that she was sure the sun wouldn't shine as much if he were gone.

"Hey, I'm no dummy. I asked him how much he'd give me."

"Did he tell you?"

"Sure. He said a hundred and fifty thousand. For the house and the land."

Claire was surprised. Landers had quite a nice parcel of land, but the price seemed exorbitant. She had bought her house and one acre of land for forty thousand a year ago. She knew that property values down along the lake were rising much faster than the stock market, but the offer still surprised her. "Wow."

"That's what I thought too. Wow. But I didn't say it. So then he offered a little more. I told him I'd sell over my dead body, and that might not be too far off. He told me the offer would only be good for a short period of time. I wonder if it has anything to do with that new development they are thinking of putting in down here. People get so greedy when there's a little money to be had."

"Are you considering selling?"

"Not really. I don't need the money. But sometimes I do think I should move to one of those senior apartments. Then I wouldn't have to go fussing around in the garden all the time."

This comment made Claire feel better. Landers loved his garden. She didn't think he could live without one. She saw Meg was running down the road and stood up to go.

"You ready to get your hands dirty tomorrow?" he asked her.

"You bet." They had a date to work on his garden. "I'll see you in the morning."

"Don't arrest anyone tonight," he said, and chuckled at his own joke.

LANDERS ANDERSON PICKED up a handful of black soil and squeezed it. The earth formed a soft ball in his hand, like crumbly pie dough. He leaned back on his heels and smiled. Spring filled him with glee. There was no other way to think about it. Anticipation of all that was to come, all the green that would burst out of the ground, all the color that would swirl out of the green. Buds and flowers and leaves spurting out of this black goop he had created. He looked up into the fading blue sky and, in this his eighty-first year, was glad for spring to be here again.

He dropped the dirt ball back onto the garden bed and straightened up. Standing took an effort, joints rubbing together like tools left out in the rain. He wasn't supposed to be out here in his garden. Or rather, he wasn't supposed to be working in his garden, according to the doctor at the Mayo Clinic. Triple bypass surgery ten years ago had not cured him, only pushed the problem off. Although the doctor was a somber man, he had waxed eloquent for a moment when he declared that Landers' heart and arteries were shot, describing his heart as "one of the worst traffic jams I've ever seen." Landers laughed at the description but hadn't been pleased by the prescriptions: no heavy lifting, hardly any walking, lots of tiny pills always handy.

But the way he looked at it, this effort of living, either you enjoyed it or you might as well dig your own grave. He had given up tennis, then he had given up golf, but he'd be goddamned if he'd give up puttering in his own garden. It would hurt him every day to see it neglected and Landers was persuaded that this pain would do him more harm than a few moments of shoveling, a little extra effort bent over weeding.

Besides, he was asking for help. Claire would come over tomorrow morning and help him uncover all his beds and stir up his compost heap and put some manure on the gardens. He could trust her to do it well. Of course, he would watch her and direct her. She didn't know much about gardening, but she was learning, and she had the love of it. She knew that you needed to touch the soil, get your hands dirty, run fingertips over flowertops, pinch the leaves, clip the branches, deadhead the old blooms. The gardening seemed to be good for her, calmed her down. She was so jumpy. Must be hard to be a cop. He looked up again at the sky and was thankful she had moved in next door.

The light was fading. He could see the blue leak out of the sky, the gray trees around him lose the little green they had in buds. He wiped his hands on his pants and was turning to go into the house when he saw what he had been looking for. Bending forward so quickly he almost toppled over, he caught himself on the fence and then leaned in closer. Yes. Oh, yes, it was the first spear of the new tulips he had planted last fall. *Tulipa greigii*. Small frilly plants with purple-striped leaves, long-lived, hardly like what one thinks a tulip to be. All winter he had been looking forward to watching their leaves shoot out of the ground and then the swell of bloom and finally the red blossom. They would probably last more years than he would. He reached over and touched the tip of the new shoot. Then he heard a sound, the gate creaking. He had been caught. Again, he stood and felt unsteady.

As he turned to face his visitor, he heard a whistle in the air and then saw something coming at him. He tried to make it what it wasn't—the wing of a blackbird, a tree branch falling, something natural and explainable—and then the shovel hit him.

THEY WATCHED BLACK BEAUTY, and at the end Meg told her that it was her very favorite movie in the whole world.

"But last week I thought *Charlotte's Web* was your most favorite movie."

"Oh, Mom."

Claire wrapped an arm around her. "Oh, Meg. It's time for bed."

"But it's only eight-thirty. I don't have to go to bed until nine."

"I'm exhausted. So that means you have to go to bed. You can read for a while, though."

Claire followed her up the stairs and tucked her into bed.

She kissed her daughter on the forehead and said a silent prayer to carry her safely through the night. Meg turned the light on by the side of the bed and propped herself up on her pillow. Claire stood in the doorway and gazed at her for a moment. Meg was caught in a pool of light, her dark hair shining. Her eyelashes dipped over her eyes, reading. A beautiful child.

Claire turned into the darkness of the hallway, glad again that they had moved to this quiet community where the most violent act she would do in a day was to bend and pull a weed from the ground. She hoped it would stay that way.

2

There are good things and bad things, Meg thought as she pushed open the back door and felt sunshine on her face. In her mind she kept a list and reviewed it often. This morning would count as a good thing. Mom had made pancakes for breakfast. She had time to make them, because she didn't have to go in to work. She sang, "Honey in the morning, honey in the evening, honey at suppertime. Be my little honey and love me all the time." She even let Meg pour her own maple syrup. Meg liked a lot of syrup on her pancakes. Her mom would tease her and say her pancakes were islands floating in a dark sea.

Meg walked down the driveway, keeping an eye out for agates. Agates were very good. Her dad had taught her how to find them. The bigger the better. They reminded her of jawbreakers split in half, red with thin lines running through them. A bad thing was a dead animal by the side of the road. She tried never to look at them. She didn't want to know if it was a fox or a possum or a deer, but especially not a dog.

She kicked at an ordinary rock and turned onto the main road. Mom told her she had ten minutes before the bus came, so she wasn't in a hurry. School could be either good or bad. Day to day it changed. Yesterday it had been pretty good. Her teacher had smiled at her, and no one had called her any weird name. For one whole week, Brad Peterson had called her "Meggly Peggly." She had tried to do what Mom had said and just ignore him, but it hurt her inside. Then he had stopped.

The worst thing in the world was when Mom cried in the middle of the night. Like last night. Meg woke up and heard her and pulled the covers up to her ears. She'd pretend it was a bird calling in the night, like the owl under the bluff. She and Mom would stand out in the backyard in the dark and listen to the hooting that would rise up into a howl. Her mom told her the owl was trying to find another owl. She wondered if her mom was trying to find her dad in the night, only he had gone too far away.

She was going to cut through Landers' garden. He had said she could. He liked to see her come home from school, and often he would wave from his kitchen window. She pushed open the gate and walked down the stone path. No agates here, only gravel. Landers was a good man. He knew so much about flowers and nature. She remembered the time he told her that hummingbirds could fly in reverse, and then she had seen one do it.

Someone was lying on the ground at the back of the house. Meg slowed her feet. She knew it was Landers, but she didn't want it to be. He never lay down on the ground. But there he was, looking as if someone had pushed him so hard he was never going to get up again. She took two more steps but didn't need to get any closer. She knew death when she saw it. The earth would grow over him. She wondered if God was watching. Looking up in the sky, she saw the sun pouring down from the clouds. It could be God. Then again, she was never sure God was really there. She didn't have a good feeling about God. She set her books down on the ground, because she needed to run. She turned around and looked back at her house. Her mom was coming around the corner. Her mom would take care of it. Her mom would know what to do. Meg opened her mouth and screamed. No words, just a rush of wind like birds howling, like crying in the night, like calling to a god who never answered.

CLAIRE STOOD IN the bare garden, surrounded by a low white fence. She had sent Meg on to school. She hadn't known what else to do with her. She had explained that Landers was old and ready to die. She had knelt down in front of her daughter, taken her pinched white face in her hands, and said, "This is not like your father. Old people die, and it's okay. We're sad they're gone. We will miss him. But he was ready to go. He was getting tired." She hoped Meg had believed some of what she said, though she herself believed little of it. But her real reason for sending Meg off to school was so she wouldn't have to see her mother cry again.

The morning sun slanted through budding oak trees. Claire wore a large white shirt with rolled-up sleeves, jeans cut off at the knees, and red rubber boots. Her dark hair was pulled back from her face with a twisted bandanna. Crouching down on her haunches, she stared at the pale face of the old man.

She had loved him, and she was so angry at him she could spit. Why had he done this? It was easy to see what had happened. He couldn't wait for her, even though she was on her way over right at eight like they had agreed. No, he had to come out with the shovel and start messing around. She could see where he had been digging, fussing around with the little green sprouts that were starting to appear.

The heart attack that had been flying loops around him all

winter long had finally landed. Attack, that was a good word for it. Dropped him like a sack of potatoes. Small man with thin white hair curled into the earth. She hadn't seen him until she was almost on top of him.

She wasn't ready for him to die. He was going to teach her how to grow roses. Pass on to her his secrets—the way to prune dead branches, when to give them the right amounts of fertilizer, how to cut the roses and keep them fresh in the house, and finally how to prepare their beds for winter. He had promised. This summer was to be her time, the time he had left to give her. Hours of talk. Him sitting in the shade with a straw hat. Her in the sun sweating and slathered with sunscreen. His wisdom filling her bones. She wanted to grab his shoulders and shake him, screaming, "I'm not ready. You can't go yet. Only give me a few more days, another week. I'll make you tea. Come back. Why have you gone away?"

When Claire bent down to touch his face again, she noticed a bruise by his ear. Had he hit the shovel when he had fallen? But it didn't look new, it looked at least a few hours old. How long had he been lying here? She touched it and saw that the cut was over the bruise and that the cut extended into his hairline, dried blood coating his hair, turning it brown.

She stood up to get some distance from this and felt her job taking over, the cop in her coming out. Like blood seeping from a deep wound, knowledge of what she was seeing leaked into her mind. Here was a body in an awkward position, lying on the ground, blood dried on his scalp. The blood was old. He was cold. It was obvious to her he had not died in the last hour or two. She knew that if she examined the body, she would find lividity mottling his back from blood settling. The cut was over the bruise. He hadn't fallen on the shovel. It looked more like someone had hit him. The chop of the shovel coming down, cutting into his cheek, bruising the skin underneath. But she couldn't believe that. Who would want to hurt Landers Anderson?

She needed to report this. With all her heart, she wanted to call her old partner, Bruce Jacobs, and have him look at the crime scene—but she didn't live in Minnesota anymore. This death had taken place in Wisconsin, and she needed to call Sheriff Talbert and let him decide who to call next. She was no longer a detective, simply a deputy sheriff.

Landers' door was never locked, so she walked up the steps to use the phone. She was careful to disturb nothing as she moved through the kitchen. Taking an extra precaution, she stopped and opened a bottom drawer. A good guess. She took out a plastic bag and slipped it over her hand. After she punched in the numbers, she waited for the call to go through and slumped into the old nubby couch she always sat in. When she had first moved to town, Landers had let her come and use his phone for a week before the phone company could get around to having her line connected.

Randy answered, "Pepin County Police."

"Sheriff Talbert in?"

"He's just down the hall."

"Get him."

Again, Claire waited. She could hear Randy moving away from the phone. No fancy switchboard for this office. Talbert was probably having a smoke outside.

"Yeah?" His voice snapped on the line like a towel cracking.

"Sheriff, this is Claire. We've got a death in Fort St. Antoine. Possible homicide."

She heard him breathe, then snort. "April Fool's?"

"No. I found Mr. Anderson, my neighbor, dead in his garden."

"Lord forgive him, so early in the morning. I'm only on my

first cup of coffee."

"I need someone down here right away. Secure the place."

"I'll have Paul come right down, and I'll get hold of Tom. Can you hold down the fort until we get there?"

"Of course."

"We'll be right there." He hung up.

Quiet in the room. Claire caved in on the couch. Tears peppered her eyes. Wiping them away only caused more to come. She gave herself a minute. Cry and cry and get it over with. You have a job to do. If someone had killed Landers, she would find them. No more unsolved deaths in her life. But she hoped that, in the end, the earth had simply risen up to greet him.

3

ridget rode hard. She could hear the horse breathing in surges that connected with her own heart pounding in her chest. Was it the wind she was feeling, or were they moving so fast over the field that the air stirred all around them? Would she make it to the edge of woods in time to get to work? She leaned down close to her horse's neck and clucked. Jester did his characteristic skip and then moved into a full-fledged gallop, legs eating up the ground.

Bridget felt her eyes watering from the speed. Run it all out, she thought. Chuck said she ran away from everything. Maybe she did. What was so bad about that? She aimed toward the woods. Sun fell on her shoulders, but she flew away from it. The rhythm of Jester's shoulders rolling under her made sense. The old wintered-over grass lay down over the field like a bad haircut. The woods loomed in front of them, trees holding out branches to the sky, a path that wound back to the house. If she took it fast all the way, she wouldn't be late for work.

Another minute, and she would be in the woods, but suddenly the world tilted, the sun fell down, the trees swarmed through the sky, and her shoulder plowed into the field, her face full of hay. Bridget rolled over onto her back and waited for something to hurt. Her shoulder, no surprise. Then the pain poured down her arm and settled into her wrist. Damn, what had she done now? She raised her head and looked for Jester. He was nowhere to be seen in the field. That was good; at least he hadn't broken a leg. But how the hell was she going to get hold of him?

Taking a deep breath, Bridget sat up. Her left arm hurt like hell. She should never have been riding that fast in this field. Gopher holes. She whistled for Jester, and he whinnied back. She looked toward the sound and found him tucked into the woods, standing right at the entrance to their path. He batted his tail impatiently, and she was glad he was there.

She wanted her arm not to be broken. Everything in her life was falling apart—her marriage, her job, her hopes—not her arm too. Not something so mundane and simple as a limb on her body. Something she'd actually have to face and deal with. She touched her wrist. She could feel her arm pretty easily through the cotton turtleneck she was wearing. "Where does it hurt the worst?" as her dad used to ask her. Actually it was a bit higher than her wrist, maybe a third the way up her arm. Now she needed to remember her anatomy class. The bone that was aching could be either the radius or the ulna.

As she pushed on it, it felt sore but nothing more. She would be careful until she could get it checked, but she needed to retrieve her horse. She stood up, pushing off with her right arm. Jester was still standing, but he was half turned away from her. Catch his attention.

"Hey, Jester, my man. Good boy." She walked toward him. He didn't move. Please, don't let him start with his games. If he ran, she would not be able to catch him. Maybe if he thought she had something for him. She bent down and pulled out a clump of hay. "Come and get it." She waved the wand of hay over her head. He faced her. She was about ten feet away from him. She stood still. Better to make him come to her. "Come on, my sweet boy. My court Jester." At his name, his ears pricked up. She held the hay out at his head level and told him to come. He took a step toward her.

Bridget knew herself, knew she'd make a leap at Jester before he was close enough to catch, and she couldn't afford to do that and scare him away. So she closed her eyes. She held out the hay and kept her eyes tight shut and waited to feel the horse nibbling on the ends of the grass she held out. She kept talking to him, low and gentle, saying his name often. She heard him whinny, and then she felt a tug. The true blue, sweet boy had come back for her.

FIFTEEN MINUTES LATE to work, Bridget ran into the Rexall Pharmacy in Wabasha. She hadn't had time to change, so she was still wearing the navy turtleneck. But the fact of the matter was, she hadn't wanted to try pulling it off over her hand. Her arm throbbed and was starting to feel tight in its skin. She knew she had hurt it.

Mr. Blounder was there. He worked mornings. She took over for him at noon several days a week. At fifty, Mr. Blounder walked as if he was eighty. His skin shone the color of skim milk. He belonged to the old school of pharmacy—you give the customer what they order, you don't tell them anything about the pills because they won't understand anyway, and you take their money. But he didn't own the pharmacy, so he didn't have to approve of her.

"Sorry I'm late."

"Right." He took off his white smock.

"I probably broke my arm."

"Right." He put on his blue suitcoat.

"I'm not sure I can work."

"Right." He walked to the door of their cubicle.

Bridget gave up. He either wasn't listening to her or really didn't care, and she didn't want to know which was true. She picked up her white smock and noticed a red stain blopped near the neck. Must be from the ketchup on the french fries she ate yesterday. Why hadn't she taken it home last night to wash?

"Oh." Mr. Blounder turned back from the door. "Your sister called. She wants you to call her. Said it was an emergency."

No, not Claire. Everything else in her life could be going bad, but not Claire. She needed to get out of here; she couldn't stay and work her shift. So she did the only thing she could think of doing that would stop Mr. Blounder in his tracks. With her good hand, she lifted up the old apothecary bottle that was Mr. Blounder's pride and joy. Written across the bottle in old script was the word *Calendula*. Its solid glass stopper was a perfect orb on top. She held it up precariously high. Mr. Blounder released the door handle and licked his lips nervously.

"I think we need to talk," she told him.

BRUCE JACOBS' CHAIR was driving him crazy. He was ready to go out and buy a new one and pay for it himself. He was no featherweight, but a chair shouldn't break just 'cause a guy weighed over two hundred pounds. Well, closer to two-fifty, but he was also six feet four inches tall. This was the third chair he had destroyed in a month. He wasn't sure Acquisitions would send him another one. After a while the air just seemed to go out of the pneumatic lift, and they wouldn't pop back up to the proper height anymore. So here he was sitting about a foot off the floor. The phone rang.

Reaching up to his desk, he picked up the phone and said politely, "Hello. This is Bruce Jacobs speaking."

"I have to tell you something," a young boy said.

Jacobs guessed the kid was fourteen. His voice was deep but clean-sounding. Nothing had roughed it up yet. "Try me."

"Well, it's really about two things."

"Start with one."

"Which one? One's a killing, and one's a drug deal."

Jacobs stood up from his chair. "That is a hard choice."

"I'll tell you the killing first. Because that's really what started all this. Don't tell my mom I called, though, because she told me not to. I know about you, and I read about you in the paper, how you caught those guys that had taken that money away from the old woman. Well, that was my grandma. So that's why I called. She said you were a very polite man. That goes far with my grandma."

"So who got killed?"

The boy didn't say anything. Jacobs realized he wanted to get a tape on this. "Is it okay if I turn on my tape recorder?"

"Yeah, I guess. Listen to my whole story before you say anything. Don't laugh." The boy started in, "Two weeks ago, my dog died. At first, Mom tried to persuade me it was nothing. The dog was old, she said. Hah! Jack was only ten. That really isn't old in dog years. I mean seventy is hardly old anymore, when the life expectancy of a woman is now eighty-three. Do you think dogs' life expectancies go up as humans' go up? I do. Jack felt fine that morning. When I got home from school, he was dragging his tail. Then he just lay down and died. Of course, I couldn't persuade Mom to do an autopsy, so we had to just bury him. Well, I went and looked in the backyard. See, Jack stays outside while

I'm gone at school. We have a fenced-in backyard. There was this white paper plate next to the fence. I could see the stains of some meat on there. So I think that the neighbor fed it to him."

"Why do you think your neighbor would do that?" Jacobs paced around the room as far as the telephone cord would let him. Hard to work on a phone with a cord these days. Didn't allow for the movement his cordless phone at home did. He paced when he needed to think. As long as he was hitting them up for a new chair, he should try for a new phone too.

"There's this new guy living next door. He rented the place about two months ago. People are kind of coming and going from his house. Jack barks at everybody. I think he doesn't like the way they smell. The guy's name is Red. Don't know his last name. He's kind of a skinny, sleazy-looking guy. Sometimes he's gone for a while. Then, when he comes back, people start coming around again."

Bruce leaned over his desk and wrote *Red* on a scrap piece of paper. He underlined the name three times. "Where do you live?"

"Buchanan, you know where that is. Just off of Hennepin in North Minneapolis."

"Yeah, I know." Marginal neighborhood. Lots of families, but could be pretty rough. "That's over by where they dug up those bodies, isn't it?"

"Yeah, that was pretty cool. Anyways, I figured they poisoned Jack because they didn't want him making so much noise when all these people came over. So I put it together and figured they must be dealing drugs."

"Any proof?"

The boy cleared his throat and then said in a quiet voice, "I heard them."

"You heard them?"

"Yeah, I snuck over there and sat under his dining room window when some people came over. They said they got a big deal going down. Sounds like cocaine. Is that what they make crack out of?"

"Yeah. Right."

"Someone's bringing in a big shipment in a week or two, and they were lining up their dealers to come and get it."

"Okay. I'll check on this." He realized he didn't know this boy's name. "Son, what's your name?"

"I don't know if I can tell you that."

Jacobs could find out by talking to the boy's grandmother. A fine woman, Patsy Lingon. She had made him a whole plate of *lefse* when he told her she would be getting her money back. At first he didn't know what to do with the *lefse*, but she explained, put a little butter on them and some jam and have them for breakfast. The plate had lasted him a week, and he missed having the *lefse*. Maybe he should go back and visit her anyway.

" 'Spose I can tell you. It's Brandon, but my friends just call me Brand."

"Okay, Brandon. We need to make a deal here. I won't say anything to your mother at this time if you promise me that you won't go near that house again, not look at it, not walk near it, nothing. That clear?"

"Yup."

"Do you keep promises?"

"Yes, sir, I do."

"So you promise me you'll stay away from that guy?"

"I promise."

Jacobs got the address and told Brandon he would keep him posted. When he hung up the phone, he sank back down in his chair. Maybe he'd just keep it like this. Sitting a foot off the floor would keep a person humble. He stared at the piece of paper where he had written the name *Red*.

SUCH A LITTLE bird and so full of itself. Claire watched the wren land on the tip of Landers' satellite dish and sing its liquid warble. Its song made the world a better place, which it sorely needed to be this morning. She was standing by the gate at the end of Landers' walk, waiting for reinforcements, as they say.

She wasn't sure what her role would be in all of this. So far on the squad, she had been just one of the guys, ticketing speeders, checking on intruders, supervising parades. But the sheriff knew she had worked on homicide cases. She wouldn't let go of this one if she didn't have to.

As she watched, a car drove up. She knew the car, and she knew the woman who was driving it. What was Darla doing here? Darla Anderson, Landers' sister-in-law, got out of her car. A well-preserved seventy-something woman, she stood in the sunlight adjusting her clothes and holding an aluminum cake pan with a slide-on cover. Her frosted blond hair, probably dyed to hide the gray, shimmered in the sun, a brilliant fluorescent, totally artificial color. She was wearing a pink sweatshirt with rhinestones embedded in it and a matching pair of stretch pants.

In her nine months of living across the street from Landers, Claire had never seen Darla come over to visit, not even when Landers' brother, her husband, Fred, showed up. But she knew Darla, had met her at various functions: the church ice-cream social, the Halloween party at the Fort, and at the election held in the village hall. Darla didn't let an event go by without participating in it. As Claire recalled, she had dressed as Eva Gabor from Green Acres at the Halloween party and had even tried to talk like her. After she downed a couple Tequila Sunrises, the accent had improved.

Claire walked out from the yard to greet her. She didn't particularly want Darla to see Landers, even if Darla wasn't one of her favorite people. Claire felt like Landers wouldn't have wanted Darla to see him either. He had never said a bad word about Darla, but he never said a good one.

"What can I do for you, Mrs. Anderson?" Claire stopped her by the hood of the car.

Darla smiled, and wrinkles creased her face, lining the makeup. The smile stayed on her face after it had died off her lips. "Why, I just brought a little something over to Landers. Is he in?"

"I'm sorry to have to inform you, Mrs. Anderson, but Landers has passed away." Claire hated using the euphemism "passed away"—after all, didn't one pass kidney stones? But, especially in the country, it wasn't thought polite to say someone had died.

"What?" Darla blinked hard.

Claire wasn't sure what Darla hadn't understood, but maybe she was digesting the information. "He appears to have fallen in the garden and maybe had a heart attack."

"Landers? He's in the garden?" Darla moved to step around Claire, but Claire took hold of her arm and turned her away from the yard.

"I think it would be better if you not see him."

"Why?"

Good question, Claire thought. "He has been there overnight, I'm afraid."

"I need to see him."

Now it was Claire's turn. "Why?"

Darla drew herself up and handed the cake tin to Claire. "We were related by marriage. I'm family. Doesn't someone in the family have to see the body?"

"Only if the identification of the victim is in doubt."

"Victim?"

"I meant that loosely."

Darla pressed her eyes with her fingertips. The better not to smudge her mascara, Claire thought. "My poor Landers."

"I am sorry, Mrs. Anderson."

"Claire, you know me, you can call me Darla."

"I like to stay professional."

"Oh, so you're here as a police officer?" Darla looked at Claire's gardening outfit.

"Well, not really. I mean, yes, as it turns out, I am. I was going to help Landers garden, but when I found him, I called the sheriff."

"Well, I need to see him."

"Why?"

"To see if he's really dead. I was a nurse, you know." Darla shook Claire's hand off her arm and sailed past her. Claire went after her, still carrying the cake pan.

"Stay on the path," Claire asked as she came up behind Darla.

"I never thought he'd die. I thought I'd die first." Darla shook her head while staring down at Landers. She made no move to touch him. "He doesn't look so bad. He only looks a little dead. I'm not surprised. He was a walking heart attack the last few years. Ever since his wife died. Now what are you going to do with him?"

"Mrs. Anderson—Darla—can I ask you to go back out to your car? We really can't have anyone in here, just in case we need to check the grounds."

"He would have liked to die in the garden. He spent so much time here."

"Yes, that's true."

Darla reached over and took the cake tin from Claire's hands, then she dropped it on Landers' chest and turned and walked away. Claire reached down and picked up the cake tin and slid back the cover. A whole pan full of yellow squares with powdered sugar dotting them filled the tin.

"Lemon bars!" Darla shouted. "He liked lemon bars. Even if I made them." She got in her car and drove away.

4

Claire found herself standing in what she guessed was an old classroom in the basement of a church. The church had been desanctified, the sheriff had explained, and the upstairs converted into a clinic by a doctor. Sheriff Talbert said that the doctor was a soft touch, and he said it with a slight sneer. "I don't mind he takes care of the kids and the old folks, but when a grown person who can get a job mooches off of him, it gets my goat."

The room held the cool air that settles in basements. She guessed that they didn't heat it much at all, especially when it was being used as the morgue in Durand. Claire didn't quite know where to stand. The coroner, as he was called in this county, was ignoring her, setting out his instruments. Sheriff Talbert had curtly introduced them when he dropped Claire off. Dr. Lord hadn't said much of anything to her, just led her down to the basement.

So she had time to study him. To Claire, he appeared to be aging well. His balding hair was cut short, no nonsense about trying to comb the salt-and-pepper hair over a thinning spot. Dr. Lord wore horn-rimmed bifocals that made him look studious.

At the moment, he was studying Landers Anderson's head. His hands were covered with the thin sheath of latex that had become so necessary in the medical business, yet they moved delicately over Landers' mottled skin.

"Quite a lot of trauma here," he said, but softly, as if he were accustomed to talking to an empty room. Or was he talking to the victim, the dead victim, whom he handled so gently? Without looking at Claire, he asked, "What did this?"

"A shovel, we think."

"Yeah, that explains the large area that is involved. They must have smashed him with the back of the shovel. Maybe we'll be able to tell."

"Smashed him with it? I actually thought he might have fallen on it."

"We'll be able to tell when I examine the meninges." Seeing her puzzled look, he explained, "The brain lining." He bent down again and kept minutely searching down the old man's body. The way he was handling Landers was so gentle and intimate, Claire turned away and studied the room.

The color of the walls hinted at sunlight, which helped lighten up the space. The four windows beamed down sky from above. What Claire really loved about the room, aside from the fact that it had an old oak desk and a beautiful Mission-style bookcase for all the books, was the music that was filling it. She had never heard anything quite like it—a woman's voice soaring in a cathedral.

"I knew him." Dr. Lord turned away from the body but continued to stand between it and Claire. He seemed protective of Landers, as if she were there to do him harm. "He went to my church."

"How long have you known him?"

"Since I moved here, which was about ten years ago. We

served on a couple of committees together. Drank many cups of coffee at the church. He was a good man."

"Yes, I thought so too. I was his next-door neighbor."

Dr. Lord walked toward a cabinet and took out a small saw. "What're you doing here?"

Claire didn't know what he meant by the question. "Here, in Durand?"

"No, here in this room. I've never worked with an audience before. Don't you trust me?"

This might explain why he was acting odd around her, not talking to her, trying to avoid looking at her. Claire smiled and stepped forward. She needed to put him at ease and explain. "It has nothing to do with that. I need to get the information, and I need to make sense of what has happened to Mr. Anderson. When I worked for the police in Minneapolis, we often attended autopsies."

"You city folk." Dr. Lord chuckled. "I don't think you could get Sheriff Talbert to attend an autopsy if you paid him. I didn't know you had worked in Minneapolis. Were you homicide?"

"I worked some homicide cases, yes."

"Is it a secret?"

"No, I just don't talk about it much. I don't think it's generally known around the county. It's hard enough being a woman cop without also being perceived as a know-it-all from the big city."

"Yes, I suppose. I came over here from Rochester. Worked at the Mayo Clinic. I play that down. After too many years of being a specialist, I decided to go back to being a general practitioner. Got tired of seeing people die. I wanted to heal a few people, mend some bones, burn off some warts."

"Me too. I got tired of seeing people die." Claire looked at Landers. His skin had turned to wax.

"You know what the procedure is, then?" Dr. Lord asked.

"Yes, but if you could talk a bit while you do it, I would appreciate it."

"Ask questions too."

"I do have one question."

"Shoot."

"How close can you come to time of death?"

"It's not like in the movies. If we're lucky, within three to six hours. His temperature was eighty when he was brought in. It's been relatively mild out. Body loses heat at about a degree an hour. He came in at about noon. Right there, I'd guess time of death between five and nine last night."

Claire nodded. "The more I've thought about it, that's what I figured too. You see, he was out in his garden. At first I thought he was digging around, but now I think he might have been just puttering, looking at what was coming up. I saw him and talked to him and then went into my house to watch a movie. We started watching it about seven. I think he died right at dusk, just as the sun set, right after we left."

Dr. Lord took a scalpel and made a sweeping cut from Landers' left shoulder down to the middle of his stomach. Then he did the same from the other shoulder. Where the two cuts met, he proceeded down to his pubic bone. The skin pulled back on its own. Claire leaned back against the desk, the world of the body opening up in front of her.

TWO HOURS LATER, the autopsy was over. Claire felt how Landers looked—cold and drained. Wearing a big wool cardigan, Dr. Lord simply looked tired. He covered up Landers Anderson gently, as if he were tucking him in for bed, and they left him in a chilly, dark room. The spring air outside smelled as sweet and clean as an orchard in full bloom. Claire took in deep gulps of it.

"The stink of death comes off of everyone, no matter how good they were during their life," Dr. Lord commented. "You care for a cup of coffee?"

"Sounds great."

He took her to a small café and they got a booth by the window. He ordered coffee and said the pie was good. Claire followed his lead and ordered coffee and lemon meringue pie.

Over the coffee and pie, Dr. Lord told Claire, "Someone hit him on the head with the shovel. It's what we call a coup injury. Fairly readable."

"I was picking that up from what you were saying, but explain it to me." During the autopsy, Dr. Lord had mumbled away to himself, and Claire had leaned against the oak desk and listened. She had also listened to the music that floated through the room. It gave the whole proceedings a rather ritualistic effect. Dr. Lord moved so thoughtfully and meticulously through the body that it became a sort of dance, peeling away the layers of the body and then putting them back together. All that was left on Landers were two incisions—one on the back of the head and the Y-shaped cut across the body—when it was over. Dr. Lord had made some notes.

"You see, the brain's like gelatin, soft but firm, and it's held in a rigid mold, which allows it to keep its shape." He stuck his fork into the pie in front of him and jiggled it. "Kind of like this piece of pie. When the brain is bruised, we can tell by the bruise whether it was caused by a fall or a hit on the head."

"How?"

"If someone falls down backward and hits his head, there is a bruise on the back of the head and a fracture under it in the skull, but the bruise on the brain is on the opposite side. We call that contrecoup. However, if someone is hit, then he has a bruise on the scalp, a break underneath, and a bruise on the brain under that. All the injuries line up. This is what I saw when I examined his brain."

"So someone killed him by hitting him with the shovel?"

"No, not really."

"What do you mean?"

"First he was hit by the shovel, but this did not kill him. Then he died from a heart attack. The blow from the shovel was not the cause of death."

Claire thought about this for a moment. She took a sip of coffee before she spoke. "If someone dies during an assault, even if the death is not a direct result of the assault, it can be considered first-degree murder. Landers was murdered."

Dr. Lord shook his head in a weary, what-is-this-world-coming-to sort of way.

Claire asked the question she always asked anyone who knew the murder victim. "You have any idea who would want to kill him?"

Dr. Lord leaned his head back and squeezed his eyes tight shut. Then he slowly lowered his head and looked at her. "Not anymore. She's been dead about five years."

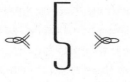

ich's shoulders ached. He had been lugging feed for the pheasants for an hour. After checking a stump over for bird shit, he sat down on it and watched them go at their food. Little chicks. That's what baby pheasants were called. He thought they looked gorgeous. Small puffs of feathers, huge heads. Funny critters, but not stupid. Not like turkeys. Now, there's a stupid bird. His dad had raised them.

He got up and strolled toward the house. In town today everyone had been talking about the fact that Landers Anderson had died. Some were saying it was under peculiar circumstances, although Rich wondered why they thought that. Landers was an old man. An unhealthy old man. Dying from heart disease. Slowly, over the last ten years, the disease had circumscribed his life. You never saw Landers walk down to get his mail anymore. He drove his car the three blocks.

Rich stopped at the pump and washed his hands. His mom had taught him well—"Don't go bringing that bird dirt into the house with you." He walked into his house the back way and shed his shoes at the door. On the other side, a pair of slippers waited for his feet. He had made them himself from a kit he bought through a magazine. He liked to work with his hands. He had his mom's old Singer sewing machine set up in his spare bedroom. He could patch a pair of jeans as well as any woman he knew, better than most.

Just as he was about to stick his head into the fridge and see what looked good for dinner, he heard the pheasants raising a din out in the yard. Something must be spooking them. Or maybe someone. He had found a new baseball bat in the woods behind his coop. Now, maybe it was just a kid cutting through the woods, but his place wasn't on the way to anywhere.

He had thought of calling that new cop, the woman, Claire Watkins. Asking her what she thought he should do about the person who was leaving the footprints. He liked the idea of a woman deputy. He had heard some men at the bar complain about her, or rather any woman taking on a man's job, as they put it. Rich had started laughing at them. They asked him why he was laughing. He explained his mom was the person who had taken care of law and order in his house, why he thought women were highly qualified for that kind of work. When he thought of Claire, he could almost feel her hair in his hands. That long, thick, black hair. She would be a handful.

The pheasants were still screeching. Why would someone come sneaking around his property? Steal a couple pheasant? Hell, they wouldn't be ready to eat for months yet. Months and months. Not till September.

He walked out in the backyard but didn't see anything right away. Then he heard a sound, an almost familiar sound. Like a golf club hitting a golf ball. A thwacking sound. Or maybe a stick hitting a small skull. He yelled and went running toward the sound.

He hadn't gone far when he saw it. A mangled, bloody bundle of fuzzy feathers smashed near the side of the barn. So little left of it, he couldn't tell what had happened. He heard someone thrashing through his woods but didn't bother to give chase. He scooped up the broken body of the bird and wrapped it in a newspaper. He'd dispose of it later. This was the third body of a chick he had found. The other two hadn't been so mangled; they had just looked like someone had held them too tight and smothered them.

WHEN BRIDGET SAW Meg's eyes as she got off the school bus, she was glad she had raised a fuss at work and was there to meet her niece. Meg had a way of sucking in her whole face when she was upset until her eyes stood out in it, like one of those awful pictures of waifs standing in the rain with huge eyes, holding puppy dogs with huge eyes.

Bridget threw her good arm around Meg's neck. "Didn't have to work, so I decided I'd come and bug you." Her doctor had said her arm was sprained and to use it sparingly.

"Where's Mom?"

Of course, that would be the first question. Never far from Meg's mind. The first few months after her father's death, she couldn't leave her mom's side, wouldn't go to school. Claire hadn't forced her. Bridget didn't know if that had been a good idea, but Claire wouldn't budge on it. She was clear that Meg would decide when she could handle going back to school. "She'll get bored, then she'll go back." But Bridget wondered if Claire hadn't wanted her home too. Didn't trust letting her out of her sight.

"She's catching up on some work."

"She wasn't supposed to work today."

"Well, that changed."

"Because of Mr. Anderson, right?"

"I think so."

"She's okay?"

"Just talked to her. She's fine. She's on her way home. Said to have supper ready."

Meg stepped back and looked at Bridget, crinkling up her nose. "What happened to your arm?"

"It's about time you noticed. Slugged someone."

"Did not." Meg scampered up the road in front of her.

"Did tot." It was their joke, the game they played that made them both laugh.

"Who?"

"That cranky pharmacist who works with me."

"Mr. Piss-pot."

Bridget stopped in the middle of the road and wagged her finger at Meg. "You watch your language, young lady. What would your mom say?"

Meg tossed her hair and said, "She'd say, 'You sound like your aunt Bridget.' "

BRIDGET STARED AT the items on the counter in front of her. She knew you could make macaroni and cheese out of real cheese, but she had never done it. She always made it from a box. Meg had requested the dish, and Bridget thought it sounded as easy as anything. The only cheese was parmesan, but that should be okay. Cheese was cheese.

Bridget had spent eight years getting through pharmacy school: four years pre-pharm, four years for her Pharm.D. She knew how to mix sodium metholate and xeron to get caldium, but she didn't know how to cook. At home, Chuck would grill some slab of meat and she would stick potatoes in the oven, and they'd call it a meal. They went out to eat a lot and ordered in pizza. Now that they were settling down, maybe she should learn how to cook.

She put water on to boil. It didn't help any that she had only one good hand to work with. Meg was upstairs doing her home-work. She was such a good kid. If it were guaranteed that she would get a child just like Meg, she would agree to Chuck's request and get pregnant. When the water boiled, she dumped in a box of macaroni. The water stopped boiling, so she turned the heat up higher.

Bridget figured Chuck wanted to try to have a baby for two reasons: one, he didn't want to have to deal with contra-ception anymore, and two, he'd have someone to play with. One of the problems with Chuck was, he didn't want to grow up. Right now, she knew he was over at his brother's, working on some old car. The two of them would drink beer and listen to country music, and if she was lucky he'd come home by midnight.

Some kind of chemical reaction seemed to be going on in the pan. White foam poured over the edge and down into the flames. Maybe she had discovered fusion. Bridget dumped the pasta in the sink, and the drainer kept any of it from disappearing. Then, with her hands, she scooped the pasta into a bowl. She put some butter in the bowl, a bit of milk, and poured a bunch of grated parmesan cheese on top. Looked pretty good. She stuck it in the oven at 350 degrees.

Maybe it could all work out. She would get pregnant easily. She would learn how to cook. Chuck would go to Lamaze classes with her. He would build the baby a crib. He would buy her ice cream. The baby would enter their life gently, slipping into a spot that had always been waiting for it. Labor wouldn't hurt. She decided as long as she was going to dream, she might as well go all the way. They would be a happy family. She would be able to make macaroni and cheese from scratch.

SITTING IN HIS office, Stewy Swanson had explained to Claire that there hadn't been a homicide in Pepin County for over twenty years. In his deep voice, he said it as if her coming to Pepin County had something to do with the fact that there had been a homicide. She had just told him the news of Landers' death, stopping by after the autopsy.

Chief Deputy Sheriff Steward Swanson was the second in command. Because sheriff was an elected position, Sheriff Talbert stayed out of all the cases. Didn't want anything costing him a vote if it didn't have to. Claire had been surprised to find out that the sheriff's job was mainly administrative. Sheriff Talbert had appointed the chief deputy eleven years ago, and Swanson saw that things ran smoothly.

Now, Stewy Swanson was nearing retirement. He had been a policeman for forty years. Joined right out of the army, having fought in Korea. Claire didn't mind working under him, but there was little camaraderie between them. Chief Swanson was about forty pounds overweight, and too much of that fat hung around his neck and face for him to be pleasant to look at. Because his face was so broad, his blue eyes looked like small polka dots. But he was a fair man and slow to anger—both excellent qualities in someone who had to command a sheriff's department of eleven men and, now, one woman.

Swanson leaned back in his chair and appraised her. He folded his arms behind his head and put his head in the cup of his hands. His raised elbows looked like a set of flabby, fleshy wings. "Can you run with this?"

"Yes, sir, I'm sure I can."

"I am too. Think we're going to need help from the crime lab in Eau Claire?"

"I'm going to talk to them. I've got the crime scene secured. Makes it easier that it's right across the street from me. I can keep an eye on it."

Swanson flapped his wings. "Clobbered with a shovel, if that don't beat all."

CLAIRE ARRIVED HOME just as the macaroni and cheese was done. It still surprised Bridget to see Claire in her tan uniform; she hadn't worn one her last few years on the Minneapolis police force, since she was a detective. The outfit didn't enhance Claire's beauty, but she didn't have to worry about that. Even in the ill-fitting suit, her long, slender figure showed through. Bridget scanned her face for wear and tear, but Claire looked almost happy.

"How's it going?" she asked as she walked into the kitchen. "Something smells good."

"Dinner is just about ready. Meg's upstairs, doing her homework. How'd your day go?"

Claire sat down on a chair at the table. She opened the top buttons on her polyester uniform and pulled her hair out of the ponytail. "I can't believe Landers is dead. Not just that—it's a homicide."

So that was it. Claire was back in the business she loved—solving crimes. There was little of that to do in a small county like Pepin. "Someone killed him?"

"Appears so."

"Any ideas who?"

"Yesterday I would have said that everyone loved Landers. But I've learned a few things today."

"Like what?"

"You know, he always spoke so lovingly of his wife. He mentioned her often, Eva was her name. But I guess in their last years together, they didn't get along so good. The doctor who told me this today said she also had a stroke, which can change personalities. But he said there was something else going on. She was absolutely dependent on Landers, and yet she would hardly talk to him. He waited on her hand and foot, and she ignored him or yelled at him."

Bridget pulled the hot dish out of the oven. The topping looked a bit burned, but that might make it taste better. The mixture bubbled in the casserole. She threw down a hot pad and set it on the table. "That can be fairly typical stroke behavior."

"I know, but the doctor said that she was already acting like this before she had the stroke. In fact, he said he thought she was so angry about something that it might actually have brought the stroke on."

"Wow. What could have happened? Did he have any idea?"

"All he said was that one day he was over and Landers left the room. He was alone with Eva. He asked her something about Landers' garden, and she snapped, 'He should stick to putting his seed there.' "

"So he might have been messing around. The racy geriatric set. How do you get away with doing that in a small town?"

"I don't know. Plus, I don't know if the information on his relationship with his wife is of much help. She's been dead for five years."

Meg came barreling down the stairs and grabbed her mother around the waist. "Hi, Mom."

"Hi, sweets. How did school go?"

"Fine. I tried not to think about Mr. Anderson too much. I didn't tell anyone."

"Honey, that's fine. But you can tell people if you want to. It's not a secret."

"I don't like to talk about that stuff. Nobody understands."

Claire gave her a big hug. "I know what you mean. Sometimes it can feel like that."

Meg lifted away from her mother and looked at the table. "What's that?" she asked, disgust deepening her voice.

Bridget leaned against the sink. The macaroni and cheese did look a little weird. For one thing, the color was wrong. The dish should have been yellowy orange, but it was more white than anything. "Dinner," Bridget said hopefully.

"Fancy hot dish," Claire said encouragingly.

"Looks like you forgot something. Maybe you should have stirred it a little more," Meg said.

They all sat down and looked at it. Bridget dug into it and discovered that the dish had stratified. The top was hard and crusty with the burned parmesan, then there was a layer of dry noodles, then there was a soupy bottom of separated milk. She put some on her plate and stared at it. No one said anything for a moment. Then Bridget sighed. "I don't think it's edible."

"You might be right," Claire agreed.

"There's always peanut butter," Meg mentioned.

Bridget picked up a piece of the pasta and put it in her mouth. Tasteless and tough. "I don't think I'm ready to be a mom."

"CLARK DENFORTH." The man getting out of the car held out his hand to her. As they shook hands, Claire introduced herself. She pointed out her house right across the street. Meg waved to her from the window. Bridget was staying on until Claire got back.

The young blond man snapped with excitement. His hair

stood up with some kind of gel in it. His cheeks shone, speckled with freckles. Claire would have guessed his age to be twenty-four, probably just out of college. Maybe had done a tour at Quantico. That could be good. He'd know the latest methods for collecting evidence at a crime scene.

"What've we got here?" he asked, pulling a briefcase out of his car.

She took him to the gate and motioned him to stop. "Mr. Anderson was standing next to his garden bed. As near as we can figure, he got hit in the head with a shovel and dropped."

"Have you kept people out of here?"

"We've tried."

He spent the next two hours taking prints off the small universe of Landers: the white gate leading into the garden, the door handle, the kitchen counter, medicine cabinet, the bottles of pills that stood next to the sink—although Claire had told him they had no reason to believe the perp had gone into the house—and, of course, the shovel. The house and garden were dusted with the fine powder that shows prints. It looked as if someone had taken a bath and gone crazy with the talcum powder.

When Denforth had finished with the shovel, Claire took it from him. The shovel looked its age, dirt crusted on its spade, the handle grimy with the sweat of years. She thought it was Landers' shovel, but that was hard to tell; she didn't know his garden tools that well.

"How do you think the assailant got here?" Denforth asked her.

"Could have walked up from the highway. Parked by the Fort, it's the bar in town. Tomorrow I'll ask around." Claire planned on talking to everyone in town tomorrow. Find out where everyone was at seven o'clock. It should be possible with a town this size. Someone must know something or have seen something.

"You gonna take the shovel?" she asked.

He nodded. "Murder weapon. We'll run a few more tests on it in the lab. Be sure we don't miss anything."

Claire looked at the shovel she held in her gloved hands. What she really wanted to do with it was hoist it up like a bat and let fly with it, but she knew she shouldn't. What if some speck of hair or fiber came flying off it with the velocity of her swing? So she only lifted it in her hands and felt its weight. It didn't weigh much more than her broom. Anyone could have conked Landers over the head with it. A small woman, a big man. Possibly even a child.

Night settled around them. April in Wisconsin was a tease and therefore cruel, Claire thought, hinting of warm, sunny days and then delivering rain and wet wind. But this day had stayed warm. She wrapped her arms around herself as Clark put the shovel in a bag and climbed into his car. Claire watched him leave and gave him a wave. Landers' house, empty of any life, they left dark.

Denforth's car lights flickered around the corner and disappeared. The shovel was going to Eau Claire with him. He'd call her, he said, if they found anything at all. The shovel, that old implement of so much good, had been used in the end for destruction. Why a shovel? Claire kept asking herself.

BRIDGET LEFT SHORTLY after Claire came home. She had done the dishes and put Meg to bed. The remains of the hot dish were nowhere to be seen; Claire assumed that Bridget had thrown the leftovers away. She said her arm was hurting and she just wanted to go home. Claire thanked her, and they hugged the swift hug of sisters who love each other but who rarely talk about it.

Claire went up to check on Meg and found her still awake in bed. "Mom," her little sleepy voice rose up from the covers.

"Yes, sweetie."

"Do you think that the red-haired man came and killed Landers?"

Claire froze. What was Meg telling her? "Red-haired man?"

"The same guy who killed Dad."

Claire dropped down on her knees next to the bed. "Meggy, did you see him?"

"Yes. I'm sorry I didn't tell you before, but I was too scared."

"I know it's not him, so don't you worry."

Claire left her to sleep but sat and worried in the gloaming of the falling night. She stared out at the remnant of rose color left in the west, a drift of clouds adding a purple accent. She now had another piece of the murder of her husband. A red-haired man; that might help a lot. What a queer bird she was. She missed her old life, the buzz of the homicide department, the tearing around at the beginning of a case, the intensity of telling the next of kin.

Claire had left the Minneapolis Police Department willingly. At the time, she thought she never wanted to see another dead body in her life. Her husband's rose up in front of her eyes at the least provocation. But that was nearly a year ago. She was getting tired of sitting in a jail half her shifts and then driving around the blufflands of Pepin County, catching speeders and drunk drivers, for the other half. The only thing she liked better about her job now was the beauty of the country she cruised through.

Originally, she had gone into police work for a reason. She needed to be doing something about the injustices she saw in the world. She had a mind that needed to stretch out and puzzle things back together again. She didn't think that the structure of the social work system helped people. And her uncle, who had been dead for twenty years, had been a cop. A good cop. The best. He had died of cirrhosis of the liver and lung cancer at the age of fifty. She called it dying in the line of duty.

Her heart dropped when she thought of the man who had died. She would miss Landers for a long time. She had known that he wouldn't live forever, but somehow she thought he would stick around long enough to see her really settled, with a lovely garden of her own. And she was sure he would have, if someone hadn't slammed him on the head. She would find that someone.

Organizing the case in her mind, she decided the first person she would talk to tomorrow would be Fred Anderson, Landers' only surviving kin, younger than Landers by ten years. She felt like going over to Darla and Fred's right away tonight, but she knew it would not be the thing to do. She needed to calm down, figure out how to approach him. Because, as it stood now, she was looking at Fred to be the prime suspect in this case. She also wanted to check into the man who had offered to buy his land.

As she walked across the room to turn on the light, the phone rang. She picked it up and heard a male voice, which she vaguely recognized, asking for her. She paused for a moment before she answered, searching for the voice.

"This is she," Claire said.

"I'm calling to report a killing."

Her skin froze. "Another one?"

"It's not that serious, but I wanted you to know."

"Not serious?"

"I'm sorry. I shouldn't have started out that way."

"What?" she asked, still wondering at the voice. "Who is this?"

"Sorry, this is Rich Haggard. Someone has been messing around with my pheasants. One of them got killed. I found it out near the barn."

"A pheasant?"

"Well, a chick really. Barely two weeks old. Sorry sight on the side of the barn. This is the third time this has happened."

"How did they do it?"

"I'm not really sure. Maybe they even picked the chick up in their hand and threw it, although I thought I heard a striking sound."

"How awful," Claire murmured.

"It is, and I just want it to be on record."

"I'll stop by in the morning to make a report."

"Can if you like. But I really called to ask you, what's the legality of me shooting someone on my property, someone who's killing my birds?"

❊ 6 ❊

F red Anderson arrived early in the morning. His car rolled up with the lights off, and he didn't make any noise slamming the door. Maybe he was just being considerate. Slate clouds covered the sky, but a hint of rose tinged them in the east.

Claire saw Fred from the window of Meg's bedroom. Meg lay sleeping, sprawled across the bed as if she were in full flight. Claire hated to wake her up, but it was time for Meg to get ready for school and time for her to stop Fred before he went any further.

She tousled Meg's hair, said calmly, "Get up, noodlehead. Go wash the sleepies out of your eyes," and left the room. Meg would dawdle around upstairs, so Claire headed over to stop Fred. Claire had her uniform on but only one cup of coffee in her when she ran across the street to catch him. His key rattled in his hand, and he was ready to stick it in the front door.

"Mr. Anderson, stop," she hollered at him.

He turned and smiled at her—the Pillsbury Doughboy incarnate. Puffy cheeks soft as pillows, arms that sprang out from his side, and she bet if she poked him in the stomach, he would giggle.

Claire stood down at the bottom of the steps. She wanted him to come away from the door.

"I need to get a few things," Fred said and turned back to the door.

Claire did not want to have to climb up the steps and physically stop him from going in the house. "You can't go in there, Mr. Anderson."

"I have a key." He showed her the key.

"I know you do. But no one is allowed in your brother's house yet."

"I'm his brother. I have a right. There are things inside I need to get." Fred had started to whine, and he turned the key in the lock.

Claire felt an odd kind of anger run through her. This dopey old man wasn't listening to her. She found that she wanted to rap him on the head as if she were his schoolteacher. She ran up the steps and grabbed him under the arm as the door swung open. She threw him off balance but didn't hurt him. However, for a moment, there was a hunted look in his eyes.

The two of them stood in front of the door to the living room. The house already smelled musty. How could that happen so fast? Landers' desk sat in one corner of the living room, and Fred's eyes flew to it. Claire noted that and then reached out and pulled the door shut. Fred jumped. Claire locked the door, handed him back the key, and then, continuing to hold his arm, firmly escorted him down the steps. The muscle of his arm had the soft consistency of bread. Fred wasn't smiling anymore.

Claire didn't want to talk to him right now. She had to get Meg off to school, and she still felt too angry at him. "Why don't you go down to the Fort and get a cup of coffee, and I'll join you in a few minutes."

Fred rubbed his arm as if Claire's grip had hurt him. He looked back at the house. "Darla wanted me to get a few things."

"She'll understand, I'm sure."

"We need to talk to a lawyer. My brother just died. We have to take care of things—like the funeral and such."

"I'm more than aware of that. We'll take care of it over coffee. I'll have time to sit and talk then."

Fred's face had pulled in, lines creasing his cheeks. Worry passed over his face like a cloud, then it cleared. "Cup of coffee sounds good."

THE FORT ST. Antoine Café was the town center: a bar, grocery store, video store, pool hall, dance hall, and restaurant rolled into one. Claire nodded at Wally, the owner, and ordered a cup of coffee before joining Fred, sitting by himself at the window. He hadn't joined the group of older men sitting at the end of the bar. They gathered there every day to talk over the weather and happenings of the world. A nice group of men, including the mayor, Lester Krenz, and board member Sven Hulmer, but Fred didn't fit in. He had come to Fort St. Antoine many years ago but had never become a part of the social workings of the town.

Claire was glad he was alone; she didn't want everyone listening to what she was going to ask him. News spread like fire through this town without her dumping kerosene on it. She sat with her back toward the gathering of men and said hello again to Fred.

"How did my brother die?" Fred asked.

"He had a heart attack."

"That's what I figured. That's what I told Darla. She got all worked up about seeing him in the garden with the shovel lying next to him."

"What was she worked up about?" Claire added cream and sugar to the coffee that had been set in front of her. She had skimped on her breakfast and needed the extra calories.

"You gotta understand Darla. She's very sensitive to all sorts of things. Always has been. She gets feelings about things, and I've come to learn to listen to her feelings. She said when she saw Landers there on the ground, she had a bad feeling. I think she might be a little psychic. I mean if there is such a thing. If there is such a thing as being a psychic, then my Darla is one. But I don't believe in that stuff much, myself."

"Was she more specific about what her bad feeling was?"

"She thought that Landers had come to a bad end, that some-one had killed him. I told her there was no way, but she said his body lying there didn't look natural."

"Well, your wife was right, Mr. Anderson. Landers was, in effect, killed. He did have a heart attack, but it was after someone hit him with the shovel."

"I'm his closest of kin, you know."

Claire took a quick sip of coffee to cover her reaction to his statement. This is how he responded to hearing the news that his brother had been killed? "I had assumed as much. Landers never had any children, did he?"

Fred lurched toward his coffee and took a big gulp. "Nope. His wife was always a little sickly. She couldn't have kids."

"That's what he told me."

"So that means that I own his house and land now. When will I be able to go into his house?"

Claire sat back in her chair. Fred had just learned that his brother had been killed, and he wasn't asking her any of the right questions. He didn't seem to be wondering who had done it.

"Fred, where were you Monday night between seven and eight?"

"On my way to a pinochle game in Plum City."

"Were you alone?"

"Sure. Darla stayed home. She doesn't like to play pinochle."

"What time did you leave the house?"

"About six-thirty."

"Can you give me the names of the men you play pinochle with?"

Fred settled his eyes on her. "Why?"

"That's when Landers was killed. You didn't happen to drive by his house, did you?"

"No, it's not on the way to Plum City."

"You didn't happen to see anybody parked on the highway on your way out of town? A strange car? A strange person?"

"Don't remember that I did."

"Do you know anyone who would want to kill your brother?"

Fred drank another sip of coffee. He puffed out his cheeks and then slowly let the air out. "You think you know my brother. I know you and him got to be friends. But you don't really know him that well. My brother could be very selfish. He was like that all his life. He never wanted to share with anyone. I wouldn't be surprised if there aren't quite a few people who wouldn't have minded giving him a good chop."

"I'd like those names too. Along with your pinochle buddies'."

"Well, you might have to ask around, because my brother and I didn't stay in touch for nearly twenty years. If I were you, I'd start with his partner in business, Leo Stromboli."

"I'll check into it." She handed him a pen and a piece of paper to write down all the names. "Also, your brother had had a call from a man, offering to buy his house. Do you know anything about that?"

Fred fussed. "I told him I'd take care of it."

"You told who?"

"Oh, Ted Brown. He's working with Landowners of America."

"On some sort of development?"

"Yes, and I'm going to be in on the deal this time."

"What's the deal?"

"Come to the town board meeting if you want to hear more about it."

Claire stood up. "I'll do that."

Fred thought of one more thing. "So when can we get his body?"

AS FAR AS Bridget was concerned, everyone was sick.

She counted out sixty tablets of 10-milligram amitriptyline for Mr. Swanberg. He had had shingles and looked like he was still in a lot of pain.

"Felt like my skin was burning. Felt like little electric shocks all over my back. Never felt anything like it," the old man told her, looking up at her from his hunched-over height of under five and a half feet.

She told him to let her know how he was doing in two weeks. It would take the medication that long to take full effect. He wagged his head, and his sky-blue eyes blinked twice. "You're a swell-looking gal," he said.

She laughed and thanked him. He turned away and walked out of the pharmacy with a bit more bounce than he had come in with. Bridget hoped the medication helped him. It was about the only chance he had of relief from that type of pain.

She had filled all the prescriptions that had been called in. There was usually a rush right when she got in, and then it slowed down. Now, all day long, people would be stopping by to pick them up. Her sore arm had kept her up last night, but it wasn't the only reason she had gotten little sleep.

She looked over all the bottles and boxes of pills she had available and wondered which one she should take. She had never done that, slipped a pill into her own hand and tried it. She knew what all of them could do; at least she had studied and read about them. But she knew of none that could relieve the heartache that she was feeling.

Chuck hadn't come home last night. She had called his brother this morning and asked if he was there, and she could tell by the long pause that whatever came out of Ted's mouth, it would be a lie. "He crashed on the couch. I think he left to get something to eat."

She wanted to believe it. Maybe it was true. But Chuck had never stayed out all night long before. He would stay out late, but in the middle of the night, she would feel him slide into bed next to her, slip a hand around her waist, and kiss her on the back of the neck.

She had met Chuck during her third year of pharmacy school. Her car had broken down on the freeway, smoke pouring off the engine, and she had been forced to pull over. Chuck had pulled right in behind her. He had hair that any woman would die for—strawberry blond and down to his shoulders. Cutoff jeans and a torn sweatshirt. He had opened up the hood of her car and had it fixed, and the promise of a date that night, before she even had a chance to look at the engine.

He wasn't her type. He was open and sweet where she tended to like them dark and brooding. He was good with his hands.

Maybe that had been her downfall. He hadn't read a book in years; she couldn't go to sleep if she didn't read for at least a half an hour. He had barely graduated from high school. She was getting a doctorate of pharmacy. He was five years younger than she—she was thirty, and he was twenty-five. They were married within the year.

His family was from Wabasha, twenty-two miles south of Fort St. Antoine, and they moved down there when she was done with school. She got a job at the pharmacy in town, and he started working for the garage. They bought a house, nothing special, a sixties rambler, but she liked it. They could see the Mississippi River from their deck. Since they were on the outskirts of town, she could keep a horse. It had been her lifelong dream. So she bought Jester. Sometimes Chuck teased that she loved Jester more than anyone else in her life. It wasn't true, but it was awfully close. When she rode him, they felt like one body. Chuck was afraid of the horse, wouldn't go near him unless Bridget was around. He refused to ride.

In the last year, their life together had pulled apart. Most mornings, she got up early and went riding, then went to work and came home after dark. Chuck went to work at the garage, came home, and went over to his brother's to work on some old car. Bridget thought what they did to the old cars was rather horrible, but she never told Chuck. He was so proud of them. But they chopped them, they cut them down so that their windows were slits, and the roofs touched your head. They exaggerated the lines of the cars until they were caricatures of their former selves.

After five years together, their relationship had certainly relaxed into an easy contentment, bordering on boredom. Bridget and Chuck made a point of going out to eat every Friday night, most often a fish fry and a few beers. Once in a while Bridget could persuade Chuck to see a movie. Lately, he had been on this kid kick. He wanted her to get pregnant. She didn't want to have a child. She liked her life the way it was—the two of them together, her job, her horse, and her sister. If she was pregnant, the doctor would probably make her quit riding for a while.

A woman came in to pick up a prescription for her birth control pills. She was dragging a two-year-old snot-nosed boy with her. He had long eyelashes outlining his deep brown eyes. He looked up at Bridget and smiled.

Bridget pulled out a sucker and gave it to the boy. The woman took it away from him. Handing it back to Bridget, she said, "I don't believe in giving my children sugar. Did it ever occur to you to ask?"

Bridget handed her the bag containing the birth control pills, glad the woman would be having no more children for a while. "Sugar is a simple carbohydrate that would do him little harm."

"Do you have kids?"

"Yes, I happen to have three healthy children."

The woman snorted and left.

"Three healthy children, huh?"

Bridget saw Chuck leaning against the shelf that contained the antihistamines. He was laughing at her. He looked tired but happy. She smiled, and as he walked up to the counter, she wondered what story he would tell her. She hoped it was a good one, because she wanted to believe it.

CLAIRE HAD NEVER been to Rich Haggard's farm before. The one time she had bought pheasant from him had been in town. Two weekends before Christmas all the shops in town were decorated with lights, the owners handed out cookies and cider, and Rich had set up a small stand on Main Street and sold his pheasants.

His farm was right on the edge of town. If she walked out her front door and crossed a couple acres of Landers property, she would come to the edge of Rich's land. However, she drove. It was possible to catch a glimpse of the house from the road. It was not dissimilar to most of the housing stock along the river—a large clapboard farmhouse with a huge porch from which, she guessed, you could see the lake. But Rich had painted it a dark green, not a normal midwestern hue—most of the houses in the area were white, a few were yellow, and every once in a while you'd see a light blue. In the summer, the color made it disappear into the trees, which was probably Rich's intent. He seemed a very private man.

The driveway curved up from the road, and the house sat facing the lake. Claire parked next to Rich's pickup truck and stepped out of her squad car. The barn, tucked into the woods, was beautiful. She loved old barns, and it did her heart good to see this one—so big and so old—looking in such good shape. It was red, but a soft, almost translucent red that let the wood show through.

Just as she was staring at it, Rich pushed open the barn door and came out carrying a baby pheasant in his hands. He was wearing jeans, an old T-shirt that read *John Deere*, and work boots. His hair fell in his face as he held the bird out to her.

"Ever hold a chick?" he asked.

"No, my parents would never buy us those cute little chickens dyed all different colors at Easter." She took the baby bird from him.

"Smart parents."

"Why, it's just fuzz and bones."

"Hopefully that'll change in a few months."

She wondered at the feeling of it in her hands. Small and full of life. Meg had been bugging her to get another pet. It was hard to think of getting a dog, because she was gone so much of the day. It would be nice to watch something grow up. "Do they make good pets?"

He laughed. "Not particularly. Do you need a pet?"

"Oh, we don't have one. I don't know if that means we need one."

"You want to come in for a cup of coffee while I give you the specifics on the murder scene?"

"Sure." She watched him as he ran back to the barn and put the chick inside.

"You keep the birds in the barn?"

"Not usually, but that one needed a little looking after."

She followed him up the stairs and into the house. At the back door, he slid out of his boots and put slippers on. "You don't need to take your shoes off. I assume you haven't been walking in bird shit," he said as she looked at her shoes. "Have a seat. I'll brew up a fresh pot."

Claire pulled out an old wooden chair next to a round oak table. She was struck by how simple his house seemed to be. Not a lot of furniture, or not much she could see from where she was sitting. Simple and clean. *Spare* was the word she was looking for. "I like your house," she told him.

He looked up from putting the coffee on the stove. "Thanks. I've been here for about ten years. Place was a mess when I moved in. But it's just about to where I want it to be now. I inherited from my uncle. He was an old recluse. When I moved in, that table"—he pointed to the one Claire was sitting at—"was covered about a foot high with old cans and garbage. To eat, he'd simply open up an old cereal box and use that relatively clean surface to eat off of for a while. Weird old coot. My folks would bring him Thanksgiving dinner, but they couldn't bear to stay and watch him eat it."

"So tell me what happened to your bird."

"Near as I can figure, someone picked up one of my pheasant and chucked it at the barn. I've found a couple more dead chicks. I'd seen someone else's footprint in my yard a week or so ago."

"Any idea why anybody would want to do something like that?"

"Yeah." He set out two coffee mugs, thick pottery blue, a bowl of sugar, and a pitcher of milk. "Someone wants to buy my land. I don't want to sell. They're trying to let me know I should reconsider."

"Who?"

"Couple of people who are part of that Landowners group."

"Why do they want your land?"

"It's right next to a bunch of acreage that they want to develop. Mrs. Langston has offered me a good price for my property. But I have no intention of selling."

"So you think they're trying to scare you?"

The coffee burbled up in the pot, and Rich pulled it off the stove. He poured her cup full first, then his. "That's the only thing that makes sense to me. I've heard they're going to be at our town board meeting. It will be interesting to hear what they have planned to do with their land."

"How far does your land go back?"

"I've got about ten acres."

"It comes right up to Landers' land at the far end, doesn't it?"

"Yes, his chunk runs right along the top of mine."

Claire tasted the coffee. Dark and rich, as unusual as the color of his house in this land of insipid coffee. "Mmmm. This coffee is great. Maybe I should show up at the town board meeting."

"Sure. Good way to find out what's going on in town."

Claire hesitated. She wasn't sure quite what she was thinking, and she certainly didn't know Rich well enough to tell him if she did know. "I'd like to check this group out. Any kind of group like that in the county can mean trouble. Or maybe not. That's what I'd like to see."

Rich held silent for a moment. When he spoke, his voice was even but interested. "Rumor is that Landers was killed."

"Rumor's right."

"That's unusual."

"Do you know anyone who would want to kill Landers?" she asked him.

"Not a soul."

AFTER GOING IN to the sheriff's office to do some paper-work, Claire drove back from Durand through Plum City, the scenic route. Faster to come down 25 to 35, but prettier to drive through the rolling hills of the bluffland. Farms dotted the landscape with big red barns like grazing animals tucked under trees. Green was starting to show through the winter grays: patches of grass, hints of leaves, wheat speckling the fields. She never noticed spring coming on this surely and slowly in the city.

She had stopped off in Plum City and talked to one of the men with whom Fred played pinochle—Thor Larsen. She found him sitting at his kitchen table, watching a small television set. He never turned it off while she was there. It must serve as his constant companion. He had told her that Fred had been late; he hadn't gotten to the game until a quarter after seven. They always started promptly at seven. He had missed the first hand.

Claire turned on County Road SS and then back on JJ. There was no direct route from Fort St. Antoine to Plum City, but she didn't mind. It gave her mind room to think.

She had asked Thor how Fred had seemed when he made it to the game.

"He's not a very good pinochle player," Thor had told her.

"Did he seem distracted?" As soon as the words were out of her mouth, she had wanted to pull them back. She had no reason to lead the man on. She wanted to find out the truth.

"Fred always seemed distracted. That was normal for him. No, the other night he appeared cheerful. When I first noticed his cheeriness, I assumed he had a good hand, but he didn't. He was like that all night. You know the old saying, Like the cat who swallowed the canary?"

"Yes."

"Fred looked like the cat."

The road switched back, and she saw the lake. It was always a surprise, hidden down in the trees, only glimpsed for a moment. But whenever she saw the lake, she felt how it was the heart of this area, the reason that all these small towns existed. And land along the lake was getting very valuable. This was an important piece of this case, she was sure.

Fred was late, Fred looked like a cat, Fred didn't ask who had killed his brother. Maybe he didn't ask because he knew. Every time Claire tried to imagine Fred as the killer, she saw him flubbing it. It would be convenient if Fred was the one, but she feared the road she would need to travel to find the murderer was as curving and convoluted as the one she was on.

7

He appeared bigger to her than she remembered. Bruce Jacobs sat at the bar, looking, with his big shoulders, as if he played football for a living. Her old partner. God, it was good to see him. She wouldn't call him handsome, but he had wonderful smiling eyes.

She came up behind him and pulled his ear. A running joke between them, it came from the movies in which Humphrey Bogart played Sam Spade and tugged at his ear when he was thinking. When Claire and Bruce worked together, they used it to signify they were onto something.

"I don't have to guess. I know only one person in the world who would dare do that to me." He turned and threw an arm around her shoulder. He smelled of Old Spice and cigarettes, with maybe a Scotch thrown in. She liked the smell. It reminded her of work and cases that went on for days, hitting a bar with Bruce on the way home to unwind.

Bruce held her by the shoulders and looked her over. "Hair's longer. Smile looks good. Boy, even put a dress on. What's the occasion?"

"Dinner with my best bud."

"Care for a drink?"

"Sounds good."

"Johnny Walker, okay?"

"I think I'll stick with a beer. Miller's fine."

"Let's get a booth."

Claire hadn't seen Bruce in a couple months. Over the winter, she hadn't wanted to travel up to the city as much. He had called and asked if he could come down, but she hadn't felt ready to see him. He had been such a mainstay when her husband had died. He had taken care of everything. But this winter, she had wanted to get grounded in herself. Seeing Bruce reminded her of too many things she wanted to forget. Actually, *forget* was too strong a word. She wanted her former life to move into the past.

"How's Meg?" Bruce asked.

"She's great. Staying with some friends tonight. She's got a best friend, and he's a boy."

"So she's got a boyfriend."

"No, she's too young for that. She asked me the other night if Derrick—that's the kid's name—could stay over. I had to tell her no, and she was a little upset with me. Oh, she said to say hi."

The waitress brought Claire's beer. Claire lifted it to Bruce, and he raised his Scotch.

"What are we toasting?"

"To murder cases," she said, and they clicked glasses.

"Don't tell me." He stared.

But she did. She went over all she knew so far about Landers Anderson's death. She told Bruce who he was, how much she had liked him, what she had found out about his life.

"Fred seems to be your man."

"I know. He's a real possibility. But I don't want to put all my eggs on him, so to speak, and ignore who else might have a reason to do away with that sweet old man. I do think something was going on between him and Landers. If he killed Landers, why wouldn't he act more like he didn't? I haven't confronted him about being late to the pinochle game. I'm going to see him tomorrow."

"Have you talked to the old business partner?"

"Just on the phone. I'm meeting with him late afternoon tomorrow. He lives in a small town downriver."

"You live in a small town downriver."

"Farther down." Claire reached across the booth and touched Bruce's hand. "Wish you were working this one with me. Miss talking to you."

"I could take a few days off. Come down and give you a hand."

Claire pulled her hand back and reminded herself not to ask Bruce for help. He was all too ready to give it. "Don't think it would ride with my boss. After all, you are from Minnesota."

"So are you, originally."

Changing the subject, Claire asked him how his daughter Janet was doing. When Claire and Bruce had been partnered up, he was just recently divorced, playing wild and loose with the women, but trying very hard to learn how to be a good father.

"She's doing good. She does have a boyfriend. Her mom is letting her date. Don't you think she's too young to date at fifteen?"

"It's too young for Meg to date."

"Speaking of a date, Claire—"

Their blond, bouncy waitress waltzed up, order pad at the ready. "What can I get for you two tonight?"

They both ordered burgers; Bruce ordered fries and onion rings, winking at Claire and saying, "I'll expect you'll help me eat these two orders." He knew her too well.

When the waitress left, he began again. "Claire, I'd like to—" His beeper, clipped to his belt, went off. "Damn," he said, "I'd better check in."

When he had gone, Claire sighed and sank down into the booth. She couldn't just put him off this time. She would have to be straight with him.

When Bruce got back to the booth, he said, "I can only stay long enough to eat. We've been watching these guys for nearly a month. They're pulling a beauty of a con. We're going to have to move on them tonight. You understand."

"Absolutely." Claire picked at the tabletop. "But before you go, you haven't, by any chance, found out anything more about who killed Steve, have you?"

Bruce looked at her as if he hadn't understood what she had asked, and then he started to shake his head. Finally he asked, "Do you mean Steve, your husband? What are you expecting me to hear? You know we went over that with a fine-toothed comb when it happened. All leads led nowhere. I didn't sleep for weeks. What do you think we might hear at this late date? Even though you and I have a suspicion it was that drug gang led by Hawk, we got nothing, babe."

Claire watched him as he said all this. He had said it all before. But something was wrong. He wasn't looking at her. He always looked at her when he talked to her. He was staring at his paper place mat.

She tugged the place mat away from him and crumpled it in her hand. "What's the matter?"

"What?"

"Why aren't you looking at me?"

Bruce fixed his big brown eyes straight on her. "You want to know what's the matter? I haven't had a conversation with you in over a year in which you didn't bring up Steve and what happened to him. Maybe it was a hit-and-run. As simple as that. You gotta stop thinking about it, Claire. It's going to make you crazy."

He was right. He knew what he was talking about. After her husband was killed, she went ballistic. Showed up at the office, used everything she could think of to track the man down who had killed him, called in all her informants, stayed up for days tracking down tire prints. Bruce had found her when she fell asleep in the women officers' lounge and brought her home. He sedated her and put her to bed. While she slept for two days straight, he managed to get a leave of absence for her. Probably saved her life. Certainly covered her ass at work.

Some people in the department had felt it could be a hit-and-run, plain and simple. But she had never believed that. Steve had been standing by the mailbox. The angle of the wheels showed that the truck had been aimed at him, instead of heading down the road. The truck didn't hit him on the side; it hit him head-on. And this had all happened right when Bruce and she had been hot on the trail of a new drug gang that had infiltrated North Minneapolis. In three months, there had been seven drive-by shootings, resulting in three deaths. So they didn't shoot her husband. They probably would have if he hadn't stepped out into the road.

The idea that the investigation was dead in the water filled her mouth with acid. Her husband. She couldn't stand the thought of his death never being resolved. She had made her mind up to tell him what Meg had seen. "What if I told you there was a witness?"

Bruce looked at her in surprise. "Don't try that, Claire."

"I'm serious."

"What, did someone just come forward, a neighbor?"

"No."

"Who?"

Claire closed her eyes. Did she really want to put Meg in the middle of this case? Why had she opened her mouth? "Forget it. Forget I said anything."

Bruce stared at her. "It's Meg, isn't it? I thought it was funny at the time that you wouldn't let anyone talk to her. What did she see?"

"You can't tell anyone it's Meg, Bruce. I don't want her involved."

"I don't blame you. You have to decide how you want to handle this."

The waitress came and set down their two plates of food. Neither of them reached for their burgers.

"She said the guy who drove the truck had red hair. That's all she saw. I don't want her interviewed. I don't want anyone to know. Just see if you can do anything with that information."

"A lot to go on. I'll try. I'll run it past Joe and some other guys in the squad who have been working the drug busts. Now, eat your fucking burger."

"Don't swear at me, goddamn you." It had been her one rule with him while they were partners. He could swear all he wanted. Just like all the other cops. She didn't mind the language, used it herself from time to time. But she asked him, told him, not to ever swear at her.

"I wasn't swearing at you, even though I felt like it, even though you deserved it. I was swearing at your fucking burger."

She laughed. She shook her head back and forth and laughed. "You're right." She picked up her burger. "I'm eating." She shoved it into her mouth and took a big bite.

They ate their food. Bruce told her about Janet's new friend, called him a "nerd" but said it with respect in his voice. She told him about Bridget's macaroni and cheese. They laughed together.

When he pushed back his plate, Bruce said, "I'm outta here. But, Claire, I'd like to see you again."

"Sure. Give me a call. This has been nice."

This time he reached across the table and took her hand. "No, I mean really see you. Not just for a burger and old times' sake. I want to go out with you, take you to a nice place for dinner. Go to a movie. Hear some jazz. I think about you all the time."

She thought about him a lot, too. He was a great guy, her best friend, smart, nice-looking. As her mom would have said, he was a real peach of a guy. For so long, she'd been telling him she wasn't ready yet. She couldn't bring herself to tell him that she felt guilty every time she looked at him. She saw her husband's death as her own fault, and somehow Bruce was all mixed up in that. She had been avoiding him because she was afraid that if she saw him, even as a friend, she would want more.

"Maybe." She patted his hand.

He pulled his hand away. "Maybe? What's with this maybe stuff? That doesn't sound like the Claire I know and love."

Bruce tried to make it a joke, but Claire could tell that he was speaking from the heart. "No. That's the problem. I'm not myself. There's hardly anybody I like better than you in the world." Claire took a deep breath. "Give me a little more time."

"I feel like I've been waiting a long time."

"It's not even been a year since Steve died. I'm still in mourning."

He stood up fast. People turned to look at him. He started to leave and then walked back to her. He leaned in so close she could see light reflected in his eyes. "I'm sorry Steve died. He was a good guy. I know what his death did to you. Probably better than anyone else. But I'm alive, and I'm tired of waiting."

. . .

BRUCE JACOBS DROVE away in his car, going eighty on Highway 61 out of Red Wing. Didn't matter. He was a cop. On the way to a job. If he wanted, he could slap on his siren and then really wail. He felt like wailing. He was so angry at Claire, he could have slugged her. She looked better than ever. He could tell she was coming back to life again. It showed in her face. It showed on her body. She was curving out again, putting on the pounds she had lost a year ago. She looked great.

Bruce had worked with Claire for three years. The first year, he was nuts because he was getting divorced, running around with as many women as he could find. And women loved him. Claire thought it was funny. The second year, he settled down. Only dated a couple women, put most of his energy into work. Spent a lot of time with Claire.

By the beginning of their third year together, he was hooked. He knew he was in love with Claire the day that she went into an apartment after someone and he felt his heart leap out of his throat. What would he do if she got shot? He couldn't stand it.

The big problem was, she was happily married. Her husband, Steven, was a nice guy. They had a lovely daughter. They had Bruce over for dinner from time to time. Steven and he had even gone fishing a couple of times. They both liked cigars and didn't care if they caught anything. But that was before he had fallen in love with Claire. That last year, he couldn't go over anymore. It killed him to see them so happy together. He begged off a couple of times.

He had studied Claire hard. He knew her. He knew what she liked. He started dressing more to her taste. He read books she mentioned. If she liked a TV show, he watched it, even if it was *Seinfeld* and he didn't get half the jokes. He was going out with a woman at the time, but Susy meant nothing to him. He made it very clear to Susy that he was only interested in an affair, nothing serious. When he started to think he didn't have a chance with Claire was when he first looked into getting transferred to the Bureau. But her husband's death changed everything—or so he had thought.

Claire had lost it completely. She was unbelievable. She left her daughter with a relative and came into the office the next morning like nothing had happened. No one expected to see her. She scared them. She was working on the case, she told everyone. She started making calls and bringing in street people. Then, for a few hours, she disappeared. And that really scared him. He thought she had gone after someone. When he finally walked into the women's lounge and found her there, he was so relieved, he picked her up. She tried to slug him. He held her in his arms and carried her to his car.

Somehow, he got her home. He made her take a couple Valium with a glass of wine, and she fell asleep in mid-rant. He carried her into his bedroom and put her to bed. He took her clothes off down to her underwear and then covered her up in his blankets. She was the most beautiful thing he'd ever seen. He wanted her so bad, his bones ached.

Two weeks later, she slept with him. Maybe he had taken advantage of her. He hated to think that's why it had happened. She'd had a lot to drink and was crying. He had consoled her. They ended up in his bed, together.

The next day, she left before he woke up. A note said, "Sorry about last night. I was pretty out of it. It won't happen again." And it hadn't. He had tried everything, but she shied away from him. She let him help her, especially if he offered to work on finding the killer, but she wouldn't be alone with him. She said it had been a mistake.

Bruce watched the lights of the cars buzz by him. He almost wished some highway patrol guy would pull him over, so he could scream at him. What was he going to do about Claire?

Only one hundred and eighty-four people now lived in Fort St. Antoine. Claire wondered how many of them would be at the meeting tonight. The word had gone out that a controversial housing development backed by the Landowners of America was coming up for discussion, and the meeting was a public hearing to help the board gauge public feeling on this issue. She had been to only a couple of meetings before. They had been quiet; simple things had been decided, like what company to use to clean the latrines in the park, and where No Parking signs should be posted to keep tourists' cars off lawns.

Claire reached the bottom of the hill and started down Main Street. Main Street was two blocks long and hosted four antique shops, one bookstore, an ice cream parlor, a craft shop, a bar, a hardware store, and a bakery. The merchants lived off the tourists who came down from the Twin Cities.

Most nights, the town died. A few cars would be parked in front of the Fort, the only bar in town, but all the shops closed at five. Tonight, however, there were cars parked on both sides of the street in front of the old bank, now used as the town hall.

Claire recognized some vehicles: Lester's blue Ford pickup, Norma's Volkswagen bug, and Rich's truck. Then she remembered that he was a board member.

As a deputy in a small town, she had to pay attention to cars and trucks to determine if whoever was parked in a driveway should be there. A strange car could mean trouble, although there wasn't much trouble along the river. Mailbox bashing might be the highlight of a month.

The streetlights buzzed, and she hugged her leather jacket around her. The radio said it would only drop down to forty degrees tonight. The land was slowly pulling out of winter. At this rate, they might be able to plant tender annuals by mid-May. It could be such a gamble in Wisconsin. Landers had told her how last year he had put in his basil on May 15, and on the twentieth they had a frost. "Tipped the ends black on all my plants. I swear those basil plants freeze at about thirty-four degrees. I had to pull them all up and replant at the end of May."

Claire nodded at people as she walked in the town hall door. She slid into a folding chair that was up against the wall. Twenty people crowded the room, many of them staring at her as she sat. She heard a few whispers, knew people were explaining who she was. A woman deputy was still an anomaly down here, but people were getting used to her. The small room was nearly full. The five board members sat around a long Formica table.

The mayor, Lester Krenz, cleared his throat, then plucked at his neck, but no one took much notice. His hair stood up on his head like a rooster's comb, and his glasses gave his eyes a wide look. Not an imposing man, Lester had been elected mayor last term, she had heard, because no one else had run. Lester had lived there all his life, and many people figured that qualified him to be mayor.

The board members were all men. She had a feeling the real mover in the group was Stuart Lewis. He ran the bakery in town and made the best éclairs she had ever tasted. He was looking around the room now, his papers all in a neat pile in front of him. When he saw Claire, he smiled, and she winked at him.

Lou Johnson, at twenty-five, was the youngest board member, and Sven Hulmer was the oldest at near eighty. They sat next to each other on the far side of the table with their chairs pulled back far enough so their bellies had enough room to breathe. Round, light-haired men, they were kind and gentle, just didn't want things to change much.

Then there was Rich Haggard. Claire took the time to look him over. Mid-forties, bone-thin. Claire loved seeing the pheasants when she drove by his place—sleek, exotic birds that didn't seem like they belonged in this part of the country. She knew they had been brought over from China, and to her they still retained an Asian allure. She and Meg had roasted one of his pheasants for Christmas. She had never noticed before, but looking at him now in the glare of the fluorescent light, his dark hair slicked back, his red flannel shirt tucked into jeans, Rich reminded her of a pheasant—handsome and easily spooked.

Stuart tapped the table with his hand and said to Lester, "Let's open up this meeting." At the sound of his voice, people paid attention. Lester leaned forward and said, "I hereby start this meeting. Glad so many people could make it down tonight. We got a building permit we'd like to discuss here. Stuart, you ready to present this thing?"

Claire remembered that Stuart had taken on the post of building inspector, so it was his job to issue building permits. Stuart stood up and smoothed the front of his plaid shirt. He looked freshly shaven, his crisp brown hair combed down. Some mornings, after hours of baking, he could look like a wild man, his hair spiking out in all directions. Tonight, Claire thought he looked like anyone's innocent younger brother. She also thought he had done it on purpose. Stuart liked to win at whatever game he played.

"Let me begin by saying that the town of Fort St. Antoine established its comprehensive zoning ordinance about ten years ago, setting up four zoning areas: residential, business, light industrial, and agricultural. In the residential, it was decided that a maximum of two dwelling units on a lot would be allowed. Mr. Brown, representing the Lake View townhouse development, is suggesting that we grant his organization a variance to put four townhouses on each lot."

Two chairs down, a man stood up. His brown hair was greased back into a ducktail, and his large body bulged out at the hips under a sweatshirt that read "Vikings." He was off to a poor start, Claire decided, if he didn't know the allegiance of most of the residents to the Packers. Everyone turned to look at him as he stood swaying back and forth. "I object."

Stuart, who had been watching him, didn't say anything for a moment, but let Brown's words hang in the air. Then he said quietly, still sitting, "There's nothing to object to."

"We have come to the board in good faith."

"We've no doubt of that, sir."

"I've talked to my lawyer—"

"Let me finish my presentation of the conditional use of your property," Stuart continued. When Mr. Brown sank into his folding chair, Stuart explained the conditional use procedure and why it was important to understand that in granting his request, they might well be setting precedent.

The mayor plucked again at his throat. Claire expected a low note to emit from his half-opened mouth. Instead he said, "Explain."

"What we do here tonight could establish what can be done in the future. You might think it's all right for this one development to take four lots and put four townhouses on each one, but would you want all of the lots in town to be like that? Once we allow this kind of development to come in, it will be very hard to keep anyone else out."

Fred Anderson stood up. Fred pointed a finger the size of a sausage at Stuart. "What about your bakery? You put that in an old house—shouldn't that be residential?"

"We're not here to discuss my bakery. Besides, the house is located in the business district, so I am in compliance."

Brown pushed up the sleeves of his sweatshirt, and Claire sensed he would pull no punches. "I won't let you people keep me from doing what I want with my property. I'm ready to sue to get the variance for this development, and I have the backing of the Landowners of America. I paid top dollar for that land, all with lake views, and if I don't develop it, there is no way I'll get my money back. We have a constitutional right to do what we want with our own land. No rules, like this so-called ordinance, can stop me." He took a deep breath and ended with, "I will sue each and every one of you board members."

At the second mention of the word "sue," Lou and Sven hunched down in their chairs. Lester rubbed his knuckles.

Rich put both hands on the table and leaned forward, saying, "I must point out to you that the constitution is a set of rules, designed so that people can live together, as is the town ordinance. It's important to know your neighbor can't build a high-rise right in front of your house and vice versa."

This time, Brown exploded from his chair. "What about foul-smelling pheasants? Anything in the ordinances against them?"

Rich rolled his eyes back in his head and looked at Stuart.

Just as Stuart was about to speak, an older, heavily made-up woman with brittle blond hair sitting next to Brown yelled out, "What about us farmers? Don't we have a right to make some money off our land? It's our investment. How can I sell my property when I retire, if you won't let anybody develop it?"

Stuart spoke up. "Mrs. Langston, please, this has nothing to do with—"

Brown bent over and, in a thin voice, imitated Stuart. "Mr. Mayor, please, this has nothing to do with this fairy here. Why aren't you running the meeting?"

A shock wave of silence hit the room. Claire couldn't believe what she had heard. Had this fat man really called the building inspector a fairy? Stuart looked as if he'd been slapped, flames of red on his cheeks. Had the mayor even heard? Everyone was waiting for Lester to do something, but he was staring straight ahead. Then Claire did hear something. The mayor was humming "Waltzing Matilda" under his breath.

Rich slapped his hand flat down on the table. "There is a proper way to go about this, and you are out of order."

Brown rocked up on his toes and roared, "There is no fucking order in this crazy town. I want a decision made tonight on my building permit. You have my plans. I've checked with the Wisconsin housing code. They're in complete compliance. You have no right to deny me a permit. Every day you put me off is costing me money. I'd like to get going on the first set of townhouses this spring."

Tapping a set of plans, Stuart said, "I just received these plans yesterday. By law, whether you are granted the conditional use or not, we have thirty days to go over them. I, too, will need to run them past our lawyer. I would appreciate it, Mr. Brown, if you would refrain from using the word *sue* until you have cause to." Stuart stared him down. "Now, I think we need to hear from the other people in this town about how they feel on this issue."

Claire didn't raise her hand. She didn't know how she felt. She hadn't studied the issue of rural development enough to know what kind of threat or opportunity this townhouse development would pose. She listened as her neighbors talked about why they lived in Fort St. Antoine, how they saw it as a place to raise families and crops of beets and flowers and even, yes, even pheasants. They weren't comfortable with allowing this increase in the density of housing.

Brown glared from his seat. Fred Anderson spoke up again and said something nonsensical about "progress being like a steamroller that will flatten all the one-family houses." Everyone looked puzzled, but Mrs. Langston gave him a "Hear, hear."

After several other people had had their say, Stuart announced that the board would make a decision on it at the next meeting. He then excused everyone and told them the board would now get on to the regular business of the meeting.

CLAIRE STEPPED OUT of the town hall door behind a husky blond man. She guessed he was about thirty years old. His hair bristled out from his head in a crew cut. He looked back at the meeting and spit out the word "Fascists."

His use of the word shook Claire. She stopped on the bottom step, which brought her to his eye level, and asked, "Who are you talking about? The Landowners of America?"

"No, it's town boards like this that are ruining the country."

"This isn't the Wild West," Claire told him, trying to keep her voice calm. "We ran out of frontier land in 1890. We need laws to live together. If you don't like what the board decides, why don't you run for office?"

"Can't. I don't live down here. Just own property. It's been in the family for many years, and now they're telling us we have to rip the new deck off our house. Fucking pigs."

Claire knew she was not on this man's side and decided there was not much to be gained by talking to him. Then she saw Mr. Brown step out of the building and went over to talk to him.

She introduced herself, but didn't mention that she worked for the sheriff's office. "I heard you're interested in buying some land."

He smiled at her. "Land's a great commodity. Always interested. You have some land for sale down here?"

"Well, my neighbor, Landers Anderson, had a gentleman call him about buying his property. Offered some good money. I wondered if that was you?"

Brown shifted onto the front of his toes and rocked forward. His face shut down, and then he said, "Might've been me. He certainly has a nice piece of property."

"I live across the street from him. Could I take your number?" He handed her a card, and she thanked him. She would do some checking on Mr. Brown. She walked around him and started up the hill. Appalled at the anger expressed at the meeting, she felt the sense of security she had acquired in this town being undermined. What would people do to acquire land? Kill someone?

No moon, just a shroud of stars in the sky. Not many people from her former life even knew where she lived. She had changed her last name back to her maiden name, Watkins, and left no forwarding address.

She knew she had to go get Meg from Ramah's, but she sat down in the grass in front of her house to calm down. Things set her off, like the meeting tonight. She could feel the anger in the room, and it brought it out in herself. Her anger scared her sometimes. It made her mind shut down. She felt scared now. The dew soaked into her pants, but she pulled in her knees and huddled in a ball. She looked up at the sky, but the stars seemed to have moved farther away.

9

Darla and Fred Anderson lived in the newest house in Fort St. Antoine. They were right on the outskirts of the small village, and the first thing you saw when you drove up to their house was their three-car garage. Wooden butterflies stuck off the side of the garage. Claire stared at them and decided they were brightly painted monarch butterflies with the wingspan of a hawk. The orange of the butterflies' wings matched the orange of the front door.

Claire knocked on the door and waited. She could hear some noise inside. Maybe they were watching TV. She hadn't called ahead, because she wanted the modicum of surprise an unexpected visit would lend her and because one didn't need to in a small town. She knocked again. She heard a clanging and banging as someone approached the door. The noise stopped, then the door swung open.

"I'm mopping the floor," Darla said. Her white-blond hair was tied back in a pink bandanna. She was pushing a bucket and carrying a mop. Wearing little makeup, she looked like a charwoman, old and tired. The only accessory that was missing from her outfit was a cigarette dangling from the lower lip. But she mustered up a crooked smile and said, "Didn't expect any company."

Claire didn't quite consider herself company. After all, she was in uniform and had come out on official business, but if it made Darla feel better to think of her as company, so be it. "Sorry to catch you in the middle of cleaning. May I come in?"

"Of course you may. Let me finish up this floor, and I'll be right with you. Sit down on the sofa there. Oh, don't mind those hats. Push them to the side."

Claire didn't see any hats. All she could see were beer cans, so she picked them up and put them on the coffee table. Then she saw what Darla was talking about. Someone was making hats out of the beer cans, cutting them up and using yarn to stitch them back together. Talk about recycling. Claire wondered who had consumed all the liquid contents of the cans—Darla or Fred?

Darla came back out into the living room, fluffing her hair up as she walked. "I don't even have any lipstick on. What can I do for you, Claire? My manners. Would you like a cup of coffee? I'm going to have one."

"Sure, that'd be nice." Claire never said no to a cup of coffee. "Is Fred around?"

"Yes, the poor guy is still sleeping." Darla stopped in the doorway to the kitchen. "I think his brother's death has really upset him. He didn't sleep at all well last night."

Claire sat by herself in the living room and looked around. Lovely old antiques surfaced around the room, surrounded by gewgaws and cheap furniture. What she wouldn't give for that old dresser with spoon carving on the front! Since moving to the country, she was slowly acquiring some older pieces, but they were expensive.

Darla came back in, carrying a tray. Two porcelain cups

rimmed with gold sat on matching saucers. A plate with Oreo cookies on it accompanied the coffee. Darla poured them each a cup and sat down.

Claire made an appreciative noise as she sipped her coffee and then surprised herself by reaching for an Oreo. She didn't usually buy them, but they looked rather good. "I'm afraid I'm going to have to ask you some questions about the night that Landers died."

"I wondered if that's what brought you over here. I really don't have much to tell. You were there when I found out that Landers had died."

"What did you do the night before?" Claire pulled out a small notebook but didn't draw attention to it by writing anything down yet.

"Why, I was here. Sitting in front of the TV set, making my hats. I'm trying to get a whole bunch of them ready for the Ladies' Bazaar at church. People really like them. I sold quite a few last year. Everyone seems to want their favorite beer, so I try to have an assortment. You know—Miller, Budweiser, Leinenkugel."

"What time did Fred leave to go to his pinochle game?"

Darla started to stiffen. She patted her hair before answering. "Same as always. Right about six-thirty. He's not a fast driver, and that road to Plum City is winding."

It took only twenty minutes to drive to Plum City, and that was staying slightly under the speed limit. Claire had clocked herself when she came back from there. Fred was late getting to the game. So where had Fred been? Had he stopped on his way?

"Did you talk to anyone that night?"

Darla laughed. "Do you mean, is there anyone who can give me an alibi for my whereabouts? Jeez, I don't think so. Nobody called as far as I can remember. Are you going to write this down?"

"If I need to. It's routine to check these things out."

"Check what things out?" Darla fluffed at her hair with anger. "What are you doing here, anyway? I thought this might be a sympathy visit. Can you seriously be asking me these questions? You live here not even a year. You're nothing but an outsider. Fred didn't kill Landers. Fred couldn't wring a chicken's neck." After the words came out of her mouth, Darla looked horrified at what she had said.

At that moment they both heard a noise in the hallway, and then Fred appeared. "What'd you want, Darla?" He looked like he had been through a wringer, literally. His sparse fine white hair was screwed up on top of his head, and his pajamas were wound around his body. Claire was surprised he could even walk in them. His eyes had a red gleam to them—too little sleep, or too much drink.

"Whyn't you go get a bathrobe on, Fred? Claire's here, and she thinks she needs to ask you some questions. I'll get you a cup of coffee."

Fred backed up and went into his room, and Darla returned to the kitchen to get him coffee. Once again, Claire was left alone in the living room. This time, her eyes found the pictures lining the mantel. One was a wedding picture of Fred and Darla. She must have been around thirty. He looked to be a teenager, but he must have been in his twenties; Claire knew he was at least five years younger than Darla. Darla looked clear-eyed and handsome. She was more filled out than she was now, and the extra weight looked good on her. She wasn't wearing a wedding dress, just a nice suit. Fred wasn't looking straight ahead. It seemed like someone or something was distracting him. His gaze went off the side of the picture. He had on a suit also, and the sleeves were too short. He looked as gangly and awkward as ever.

Right next to their wedding picture was a photograph of a young man, circa 1975. He had slightly long hair in the style of the Beatles. Claire was shocked at the family resemblance—he looked so much like an Anderson, she would have thought he was Landers' and Fred's brother, rather than their nephew and son. She had known that Darla and Fred had a son, but had never met him. She wondered where he lived.

Fred flopped into the room. He wore slippers with the backs pushed down onto the soles. He had a blue terrycloth robe belted around him, and his hair had been slicked down with water. "What time is it?"

"Nearly ten."

"What do you want?" he asked, not very pleasantly.

Darla came bustling in with more coffee. Claire noticed that Fred received it in a sturdy pottery mug, probably the mug he always drank out of. "Claire's just checking on our whereabouts when Landers was killed," Darla said with a sneer.

"I already told you that I went to pinochle."

"Yes, you did, and I did talk to one of the men you play with, Thor." Claire pulled out her notebook to quote him. "He said you were there, but you came late. He said you never come late. What happened to you?"

Fred stared deep into his coffee cup, then he looked at Darla with pleading in his eyes. But Darla wasn't looking at him. She had picked up one of her hats and was fussing with it. Finally Fred said, "I must have stopped for gas."

"Oh, you stopped for gas? Where?"

"Well, I must have stopped at that gas station in Plum City."

"But it's on the other side of town from where you came from."

"Yes, but it's the only one there is."

"So you stopped there before you went to pinochle?"

"I think so." Fred set his coffee mug down hard. "You know, I didn't know I was going to have to remember this."

Claire jotted something down in her notebook. Then she said, "This is only two nights ago. It shouldn't be that hard to remember."

Darla reached over and snatched the top page out of Claire's notebook. She tore it up. "What we say shouldn't be that hard for you to remember either." She spoke calmly and smiled. She handed the shredded page back to Claire. Claire noticed that Darla's pupils were quite large, turning the eyes into dark holes in her head.

Claire decided she had as much information from these two as she would get right now. Shoving the torn page into her pocket, she stood up and thanked Darla for the coffee. Then she turned to Fred. "In answer to your question from yesterday, you should probably be getting Landers' body back in the next day or two. Have you talked to the coroner?"

"No."

"Well, he'll call you, and you should just tell him what funeral home you want him taken to."

"Who's going to pay for it?"

"Pay for what?"

"The autopsy."

"The state pays for the autopsy."

"Okay, then, that's fine."

Claire walked toward the door and then turned again as she remembered one more question. "Where's your son these days?"

Darla dropped the hat she was working on and raised her eyes as if Claire had uttered something blasphemous. Fred stared down at the floor. Neither of them said anything for a moment, then Darla asked, "Why do you want to know about him? He's not involved in this."

"I'm sorry. I didn't mean to sound so abrupt. I was just admiring your pictures and wondered where he was."

"We don't see him too often." Darla explained.

Fred said bluntly, "We don't see him at all."

BRIDGET HAD THE whole afternoon off. It was her favorite day of the week. Chuck had explained that he'd been at his brother's and she had believed him. She needed to believe him. She was puttering around the house, cleaning and straightening, with no one asking her what she was doing. She loved the quiet. Then she'd go for a long afternoon ride. That's what she usually did. However, today she was feeling rather sleepy.

First, she had to eat lunch. A roast beef sandwich sat on her plate. A smell wafted up from it like steam rising. Bridget lifted it up and sniffed it. It smelled funny. She took a bite and chewed. The whole sandwich tasted slightly off. The mustard was bitter. She made herself take another bite. She knew the meat was good. She had just bought it yesterday. After the third bite, she wrapped it in tinfoil and put it in the refrigerator. Maybe Chuck would eat it.

She was going to make herself go riding. Her arm, wrapped in an Ace bandage, felt much better. If she didn't ride today, it would be two more days before she could ride again. Such a pleasant time of day, the sun warming the fields. But she felt so tired. She had on her riding clothes, so she walked out to the barn.

Jester was waiting in his stall. She knew he didn't know what day it was, but she could swear by the look on his face that he was ready for a ride. She dug in the oat bag with her hands and brought him a scoop full of oats. She loved feeling him snuffle through her fingers for the feed. His velvet-soft muzzle clumped down on the oats, and his back teeth ground them down. He had a good appetite. Jester was all ready to go, but she wasn't. She felt exhausted.

If only what she was feeling was caused by the changing seasons, and she was experiencing spring fever. In Minnesota, it could hit like a disease. The symptoms were often a kind of enervation. After the long winter, spring could feel like too much of a good thing. Bridget fed Jester another handful of oats and then sank down in a pile of hay.

The roof of the barn swam above her, nests of swallows tucked into the beams. If she closed her eyes, she knew she would sleep. She kept them open and stared about her. Forms moved in and out of her vision.

She knew what was wrong with her. An alien had invaded her body. It wasn't making any major changes yet, but it would soon be apparent. The world she existed in was not her own anymore. Every little detail was skewed. Nothing looked like itself or tasted right or smelled good. Slowly, this new life would begin to devour her from within. It would feed off her until she was hardly able to move. And then, when she was wasted to nothing, it would come shooting out of her body, demanding even more from her.

Bridget knew there was only one thing to do. She knew she had to take a test. But she was afraid of the results, afraid the piece of paper would turn blue or pink or a stripe would appear, and her fear would be confirmed. She was afraid she was pregnant.

10

After the school bus dropped her off at the corner, Meg walked up the hill to Ramah's house. Ramah watched her until her mom came home from work. The hill changed from day to day. Some days it was very steep, and some days it wasn't hard to climb at all. Or else her legs were stronger and then weaker again. Today, it was medium. Climbing the hill felt like work, but she did it confidently.

It had been fun having Bridget at their house the other night. Nice to have someone for Mom to talk to. Meg liked sitting upstairs in her room and hearing the two women laugh downstairs. Their laughter sounded like birds' wings to her, rising in the air. She remembered when her mom and dad would laugh downstairs when she was already tucked into bed. It made her feel so comfortable, like nothing could go wrong.

She reached the top of the hill and looked into the woods to see if any of the flowers were peeking up from the dead leaves yet. She didn't see any, and she knew she shouldn't dillydally. Ramah was a nice old lady, but she was a fussbudget. She worried about Meg if she was even a minute or two late.

Often she'd been standing outside her door, watching for her. Meg had to walk by Landers' house, and she kept herself from looking at the place where she had found him. Never again would she cut through his yard. When a bad thing like that happens in a spot, you never go there again.

That's what she had learned when her dad died.

It had been a completely normal day. Her mom was in the kitchen, cooking beef stew. She was watching TV in the living room. She heard her dad's car door slam. She ran to the window to see him come up the walk, but when she looked out, he wasn't there. He was walking out into the street. He looked mad. He was waving his arm at a truck. It was coming toward him. Meg thought he wanted to talk to the man in the truck, so he was trying to get him to stop. But instead of stopping, he went faster. The truck—it was black, she remembered, or maybe she had turned it black in her mind—came right at him. Meg grabbed the curtain in front of the window. The truck hit him, and he went flying over the top of the cab. He slid right up on it and then over and through the air until he hit the ground.

Then Meg ran outside. She shouldn't have done that. It was wrong. Her mother would be mad. She ran back into the house and hid in the curtains.

MEG WAS CLOSE to Ramah's house now. Ramah was standing outside, shaking out a rug. Ramah was old, twice as old as her mom. She had white, fluffy hair, and her hands shook when she tried to pour a glass of milk, but she was pretty strong. They played cards together; Ramah had taught her Five Hundred. She waved at Meg, and Meg waved back. Ramah would have a treat ready for her, often fresh-baked oatmeal cookies. But Meg's favorite treat was graham crackers with butter spread on them. She loved the way they tasted with a big glass of cold milk. They just went together.

Once Ramah had asked her about her father's death, what had happened to him. But Meg told her what her mom told her to tell anyone who asked. That she didn't know anything. She hadn't seen anything. She really didn't remember what had happened. She was so glad that she had finally told her mother. The secret had been tearing a hole inside of her, and now that was over.

After the ambulance came and took her dad, she and her mom had left the house and had never gone back.

But Meg had never forgotten. She remembered what the man who drove the car looked like. He would be hard to forget. He had red hair, and he wore it down to his shoulders. He looked a little bit like Jesus Christ did in the Bible, except he had red hair.

CLAIRE FOUND LEO Stromboli settled into a big, uphol-stered chair in his living room, a remote control in one hand, a cigarette in the other. A tall man with hooded dark eyes, silver hair greased back and a white shirt on, he sat in a lift chair, he explained to her—a chair that would mechanically lift him up when he wanted to get out of it. He was still living on his own, but his daughter lived just down the street and checked on him all the time. He wasn't a well man, she could tell by looking at him. He sounded like he had emphysema, and he moved like he had arthritis.

Word of Landers' death had already reached him, so she didn't see his reaction to the news. But he told her he would miss him. They had been like brothers, only better, because there was no blood between them.

Leo Stromboli and Landers Anderson had owned a clothing store in Wabasha from 1945 to 1985. Forty years they worked together. "Never a mean word between us," Stromboli told Claire.

"Now, I'm not saying he was an angel. Don't get me wrong. He was a man like all of us." Stromboli took a gasp of a puff on his cigarette. A shaky hand guided it back to the ashtray. "But he was a straight-ahead guy. No one would want to kill him."

"How did you two meet?" Claire asked.

"We go back to the war. Met over in Italy. With a name like Stromboli, and I could hardly order a pizza." His chuckle went deep and then exploded into a cough. After a moment, he regained his breath and took another puff on his cigarette. "Landers was in my squad. We were both of us from Minnesota. Landers lived in Lake City, and I came from Wabasha. So that kind of made us stick together. When the war was over and we had both made it home, we went into business together. Landers ordered the clothes and paid the bills. He was the brains. I was out on the floor, selling, selling, selling. I was a hell of a salesman in my time. Nobody better. We carried good stuff too. Easy to tell the women how good they looked in our hats. See, women used to wear hats back in the old days."

"I vaguely remember that." Claire laughed. "My mom had some great hats. My sister and I would dress up in them."

"Yeah, women had style back then." Leo closed his eyes for a moment as if remembering.

"What, you don't like my outfit?" Claire teased him.

He waved his hands at what she was wearing. "You got a job to do. I understand. But I hope you wear a dress once in a while. A woman with a figure like yours gotta wear a dress."

"So did you know Landers' wife very well?"

"I guess you could say that."

"Oh?" Claire wanted to follow up on his ambivalence.

"Ah, you know how it is. I saw her a lot. She would come and work the sales. But Landers didn't like her to work. What's the matter with a little work? I'd ask him. But no, for his wife, she needs to stay at home. I don't know what she did with herself. They had no kids. She was delicate, Landers would say. 'Cuz she didn't get out enough. That's what I think. I think she suffered from depression. Maybe she had a hard time when she couldn't have any kids, who's to say? But she wasn't a happy person."

"Did they get along?"

"I always thought so. Right toward the end, she got a bit touchy, but hey, wait until you get this age, and see if you can be a Little Miss Pollyana all the time." He looked at the short stub of a cigarette he held in his hand, then decided it was done. He stubbed it out in a well-littered ashtray.

"Someone else told me that too. That the last five years of her life, they didn't get along so well."

Leo shrugged his shoulders. "My wife and I could go at it. Scream at each other. Cuss and have a real row, then it'd be over and she'd ask me what I wanted for dinner. God, I miss that broad. So who's to say what goes on between people?"

"What about Landers' brother? Did you ever know him?"

"Yeah, I met him all right. Knew him better than I wanted to. When he moved back to this area, he wanted a job at the store. Landers said he could have a go at it. Working the floor. Have you met the guy?"

"Yes, I've known him for a while."

"It didn't work out. I had to tell Landers. At first, he didn't want to hear it. But when we caught Fred looking in the ladies' changing room, that was it. Amscray."

"He was peeping?"

"Yeah, we didn't do anything but fire him. I'm not even sure

Landers said anything to him. I wanted to belt the guy, but he was such a wuss, I didn't. Peepers are like that. Real quiet. Often kind of goofy. They're pretty harmless. But yuck, what's the matter with them? Made me wonder about the wife, that Darla. Wasn't she giving him any?"

"Hard to tell."

"I can say this stuff to you, can't I?" Leo leaned forward, watching her face. "I mean, I'm talking to you like you're a cop, not a lady. Is that okay?"

"It's fine. This is very helpful."

"So who gets all his estate? The brother?"

"I'd assume so."

"No will?"

"Not that I know of."

"So in Wisconsin that means it'll all go to the closest of kin. Since he has no children, it'll go to his brother." Leo shook his head. "That surprises me. I just don't think Landers would have liked that."

RED WOKE UP. The phone was drilling a hole in his head. He thought of throwing it at the TV that was droning away in the corner. Stop both of them from making all the fucking noise. He struggled up out of the couch and stood in the middle of the room, feeling it rock around him like a giant ship. He grabbed the phone and grunted into it, "What?"

"This is Hawk."

"Yeah. I figured."

"We got a problem."

"What's new?"

"I just heard from my police sources that the little girl saw you."

"Yeah, so?"

"Yeah, not good."

"Why'd it take so long to find this out?"

"The mother was keeping it a secret. But guess she felt like the cops had dropped the case, so she brought it up. It could mean trouble. I want you to disappear."

"Don't worry about it. I've been keeping my eye on her."

There was silence on the other end of the line, then Hawk said, "You have? You know where she is?"

"Sure. I tracked them down there one day, followed Claire from work. They're in Wisconsin."

"This is bad timing. We got that big deal coming down. I don't want you around here. I want you to leave town."

Red thought for a few moments. The woman on the TV, Martha Something, was showing a man how to make your own doilies out of paper napkins. God, how some people wasted their lives. "I've got a better idea. Let's do something about the little girl."

"Not a good idea. Like sticking your hand in a hornet's nest."

"Hornets don't sting me. I'm magic."

11

The woman Claire saw in the mirror had dark blue eyes, black hair pulled back in a clip, no makeup. She didn't like this image of herself particularly. Too severe, too somber. Claire wiped her hand across the mirror as if to change what she was seeing in the glass. Other than growing her hair out, Claire had done nothing to change or improve her looks in years. She had always been serious, but now she looked worse than that—she looked set in her ways, as if she wouldn't even try anything new.

Wearing her hair pulled back probably didn't help. When she was a kid, she saw movies where the secretary would transform herself by taking off her glasses and letting down her hair and—voilà!—she was the hottest number around. Claire reached back and took the clip out of her hair. She smiled. It did help. Her hair was getting long; it probably needed a trim. It hung down below her shoulders.

What about lipstick? This wasn't a date or anything, but she was going out in public. Her mother wouldn't have been caught dead in public without lipstick. Her mother had always worn a deep red, even to go to the grocery store. Claire pulled a tube out of her top drawer and put on a light film of red, a rosier red than her mother's color, then blotted it. Nice. Color, she needed color, otherwise she could look sallow.

Because of Leo Stromboli's slight criticism of her clothes, she was wearing a dress. One of those flowered dresses with a hip waist. She was even wearing shoes with a slight heel; they were a dark burgundy color. She had bought them for someone's wedding, maybe Bridget's.

One more glance in the mirror. Better and better. One thing was for sure—she didn't look like a cop. Maybe people would forget she was one and talk more easily around her. It was for the same reason that she had asked Rich to drive; she didn't want to pull up to this meeting in the squad car. Rich should be here soon. He had called her this morning and told her about a meeting of the Land-owners of America. He said he was going to check it out and asked if she wanted to go with him and she had said yes immediately. She ran down the stairs to see how Meg and Sissie were doing.

The two girls sat in front of the TV, each with a bowl of popcorn in her lap. Sissie was fourteen, and she and Meg some-times acted like friends. Claire was glad they got along so well together. She didn't ask Sissie to baby-sit when she was going to be out late, but since the meeting would only be a few hours, she should be fine.

"Bed at what time?" Claire asked.

Meg craned her head back and then turned completely around when she saw her mom. "Wow, like, you look gorgeous!"

"What is this, like, *Baywatch* talk?" Claire tweaked Meg's nose.

"You look nice, Claire," Sissie said. "Cool dress."

"I helped her pick it out at—guess where," Meg explained proudly.

Sissie looked puzzled.

"Mall of America!"

Claire and Meg had gone up to the mall for a treat in the middle of the winter, when no end to snow seemed in sight. Claire bought a few things for herself, and even though she hadn't been in favor of the mall when they had built it, she had enjoyed the shopping trip. The air in the mall was humid and warm, thanks to all the trees they had planted. The shrieks of children zooming around on the roller coaster had filled the atrium. Meg had thrown all Claire's pennies into the fountain and made lots of wishes. A good day for both of them.

"Nine at the very latest. Even if you're watching something on TV that's fantastic. Sissie, I shouldn't be home any later than ten. Is that okay?" Weird to be asking your baby-sitter if you could stay out late, but that was the way it was handled these days.

"Yeah. My mom said it was okay."

CLAIRE WALKED OUT of the house as soon as she saw Rich's pickup pull up into the driveway. She didn't want him to come in. The only man Meg had seen her with since her husband's death had been Bruce. Meg knew where she was going and who she was going with, but Claire wanted it to seem very casual. Which it was.

The dress complicated climbing up into the pickup truck. Reaching up for the door frame, she suddenly felt her wrist gripped firmly. The next thing she knew, she was sitting in the cab next to Rich.

"Hi. Thanks."

"Howdy," Rich said. "You look nice."

"Thanks. Don't get much chance to dress up around here." She glanced over at him. He looked all cleaned up. He was wearing a cotton plaid shirt with the sleeves rolled up, jeans, and black cowboy boots. He was clean shaven and his face scrubbed. He even smelled good—a woodsy smell, dark with a hint of spice.

He nodded and backed out of her driveway.

Claire looked around the truck and was surprised by how neat it was. Just like the house. Nothing out of place. An old, worn copy of Twain's *Life on the Mississippi* stuck out of the side pocket.

"I haven't read that." She pointed at the book.

"Oh, the Twain. Yeah, I just picked that up. I read it when I was a kid and was sure that the life of the captain of a riverboat was for me. Closest I've come to it is living on the lake."

"That's pretty close." Claire looked out at the lake as they drove up alongside of it on 35. "You know, I've never been out on the lake. Funny to live so close to it and not have taken a boat out on it."

"Oh, I've got an old canoe. If you want to go canoeing some-time—"

"Is that safe out there with all the motorboats and sailboats and barges?"

"I stick close to the shoreline. I watch out for the other boats, because I know they're not going to be looking for me."

"That'd be fun."

They were silent in the car until Maiden Rock. As they drove through the town, Claire tried to think of something to say. She felt uncomfortable not talking; she didn't know Rich well enough to be silent with him with ease. "Where'd you find it?"

"What? The canoe?"

"No." She laughed. "The book."

"In one of the antique shops."

"You go into the antique shops?"

"Why is that surprising? I find a lot of great old stuff there.

Old tools, saw blades. I've bought a lot of my furniture there. After I fixed up all the pieces that were worth saving of my uncle's."

"Most men don't like them. My husband wouldn't set foot in an antique store."

"So you did have a husband? What happened to him?"

Claire said what she always said to that question. "He died."

Rich reacted the way most people did. They shut up. They figured if she wanted to tell them more, she would. She never said anything more.

AFTER HE HAD asked about her husband, silence hung in the cab of the truck for a few moments. Rich watched the familiar scenery slide by—glistening lake, points of land sticking out into it, bluffs rolling up near to the road and then pulling back. He loved this place.

He heard Claire clear her throat. "So tell me about this Landowners group. How did they get started? What's their purpose? Are they peculiar to Wisconsin?"

"No, they are not only indigenous to Wisconsin. They're sprouting up all over the States. I've been reading up on them. I think they're part of this new right-wing movement we see taking over politics. People afraid of losing their freedom. They're not even sure what they mean by that, but they're going to hang on to it, goddamn it, no matter what it takes. After their own personal freedoms, their property means the most to many of them. After all, land was what brought their ancestors to America. The Landowners of America group formed about five years ago in reaction to some land-use ordinances that were being passed along the St. Croix River to preserve the riverbank. A lot of farmers and old-timers are in the group." He paused. She nodded at him, and he continued.

"They see many of the new people who are moving into this area from the Twin Cities and Rochester and Madison as the problem. These rich folk come in, buy up the land at cheap prices, then lay down a bunch of laws so farmers can't make money on their land, and then the property taxes go sky-high. Many of the old-timers can't afford to pay those taxes, so they can't afford to keep their land. And because of the new laws, they can't sell it for what they think it's worth. They're plenty mad." He needed to stop. He could feel himself getting riled up. He wanted to be levelheaded going into this meeting, and he didn't need to bore Claire to death.

She touched him on the shoulder, a slight touch, letting him know she was still listening. Then she asked, "What do you think of it all? Are you considered an old-timer?"

"My family is from here, so I'm grandfathered in, so to speak. I believe in moderation. I think some of the new laws—the bluff ordinances, the wetland things—sometimes go too far in trying to preserve an unknown. But I believe we need the laws. I think we need to look at the land in a new way. That it is a gift we have for a while, and then we should be willing to pass it on in better shape than we got it."

"Better shape?"

"Means different things to different people. Many farmers believe nothing like a couple silos and a pole barn to spruce up a place. Mow everything in sight. No hedgerows for these folks. Myself, I'm partial to trees. First thing I did when I took over my uncle's farm, I planted five thousand pine trees. I won't live to see them in their prime, but I've been enjoying them every year I've been there." He remembered the weekend they were delivered to his house. It was in early April, frost lifting out of the ground, slightly drizzly day, not a great day to be outside, but excellent tree-planting weather. He had dug holes for hours and then would go back over a row and lay the trees gently on their side. The next pass-through, he would firm the soil around their roots. The rows lined up, and after two days he had his forest planted.

Next to him, he was aware of Claire sighing. Then she said, "I'd like to have a pine tree on my property. I love the way snow sits on their branches in winter."

THEY PULLED UP to the VFW and got out of the car. The hall was an old barn, still painted red but with "VFW" in huge yellow letters over the door. The front of it was lit up with a floodlight, and twenty cars were lined up in front of the building, half of them pickups. Rich remembered his mom and dad bringing him to square dances here in the late sixties. He had hated coming, thought it was sissy, but when his mom got him out on the floor, he had fun. The whirling and twirling of all the intricate steps made him laugh until his sides ached.

When they stepped through the front door and into the hall, they could hear the noise of chairs being pushed back, people talking. Rich recognized Mr. Brown from the village board meeting. He sat on a stool at the front door and welcomed people. Mrs. Langston was talking to Fred and Darla Anderson up near the podium, but when Claire and Rich walked in, she came right over to the door.

"I am sorry," she said insincerely to Rich and Claire, "but this is not a public meeting. Members only." She tilted her head. "I'm sure you understand."

Rich waited a beat, then reached into his pocket and took out his wallet. "I certainly do, Mrs. Langston." He extracted a membership card. "That's why I joined. Claire is my guest. I'm sure that's fine, isn't it?"

Mrs. Langston shriveled. Her chin pulled in, her eyes sunk, her mouth tightened. "Oh, you are a member. When did that happen?"

"When I heard you were coming to the town board meeting. I wanted to get to know your organization a little better." A glance at Claire told him she was trying to keep a straight face through this exchange.

Mrs. Langston turned away without a word.

Rich took Claire's arm and walked her to a folding chair toward the back.

"Wow. Why did you join?"

"I like to know the enemy."

The meeting started out calmly enough. The minutes were read, and news of recent development along the river discussed. Prices that bluffland was attaining were read with good cheer. Defeat of a bluffland ordinance—forbidding building on a certain slope and a certain distance from the edge—in another county in Wisconsin was cheered by all except Rich and Claire.

They had sat toward the back, and Rich felt as if he were watching the proceedings of a religious group. That kind of fervor floated in the room. Off to the side a small fire was burning in the fireplace of the old hall, taking the chill off the cooling night air. Rich watched it burn comfortably. Maybe they'd serve coffee and cookies afterward, and he would feel like a fool for coming.

Mrs. Langston led the meeting and asked different speakers to take the stand. They all preached the same rhetoric. He recognized much of it; he had bought pamphlets from the extreme right, just to see what they were up to. Landowners should be able to do whatever they wanted with their land. Neither the federal nor state and most certainly not local government should restrict their use in any manner. They were against the DNR, strongly against any environmental groups, often against their neighbors' wishes expressed in the local village and township board meetings.

Then Mrs. Langston asked Fred Anderson to get up and speak on the possibility of a large development right on the border of Fort St. Antoine. Rich had always thought Fred was a sorry man—never made much of himself, supported by his brother Landers for much of his life. Fred went to all sorts of meetings, forever trying to fit in someplace. Maybe he had found his niche with the Landowners group.

Fred climbed up on the small stage and put a large map up on a stand. Rich recognized the Fort St. Antoine township, the area that surrounded the village. Fred smiled his awful grin, lips stretched across crooked teeth in a pained way, and looked down at Darla sitting in the front row. She nodded at him, and for a moment, the smile turned warm. Then Fred started to speak. "We've had some experts draw up this map for us. It's the beginning of what could be a big boom time for this whole region. And if you ask me, it's about time. Those who have stood in our way, watch out. For here we are."

He slapped the map with his hand, and it flipped off the stand. When he bent over to pick it up, he knocked the stand over. Darla came running up to help him. She grabbed the map away from him and set it back up.

Rich stared at the map. He had heard talk of this project before, but this was the first time he was privy to the exact layout of their development. The land they were talking about included a huge chunk of Landers' ten acres. At the moment the boundary ran right along the top of Rich's land, but it was obvious what his land would mean to the development—much better access to highway 35, better land with better views. Down here people paid top buck for a view of the lake.

Fred rambled on about everyone pulling together on this. How it would provide jobs for the whole area. Rich thought about how hard it was to find anyone to work already; Stuart often complained that he couldn't find enough people to work in his bakery. He wondered where they were going to find this labor pool to support the infrastructure they had designed: grocery store, nature center, amphitheater, art gallery, day care center. Much of it sounded good, but not even slightly realistic. Fred talked of building homes for five hundred people. That would make this development over three times the size of Fort St. Antoine.

Rich raised his hand. Fred ignored him.

Rich stood up and began speaking. "Have you run these plans past the DNR? Seems to me like a lot of your development takes place on the floodplain. I don't think they'd approve any new building down there. Why, they're trying to buy up property of people who already live in the floodplain."

"We would build it up. Structure it so it wouldn't be that low anymore."

"With what? How? If you dredge the lake, the muck you get off the bottom has got to be put in a toxic waste dump. You can't use that to build up land. It's too loaded with PCBs. How are you going to make this all happen?" Rich heard an edge creep into his voice. He needed to calm down. Talk slowly, make sense. Don't let the anger ruin what he was trying to say to these people.

Fred glared at Rich. "That's none of your business."

Rich let his words hang in the air for a moment before he answered, then spoke slowly and clearly. "Yes, it is my business. I will be as affected by this development as anyone else." Rich paused and looked around the room. All eyes were on him. "I am not against development of this area. It will come in spite of any of us. But I think we need to be very thoughtful about what we allow to happen to our region. We don't want to destroy the very things we love about our river valley." Rich sat down.

Talk went on for a while longer. People were excited about the potential money they could see getting for their land. Fred told anyone who was interested in more information on the development to see him after the meeting.

To end the meeting, Mrs. Langston led them in a rousing chorus "My country 'tis of thee, sweet land of liberty, of thee I sing. . . ." All voices rose on "Let freedom ring."

Then she held up a straw figure that been hidden behind the podium. "Let me introduce you all to one of our favorite people—Mr. DNR Agent. We've built a wonderful fire just for him." She waved the sorry figure in the air and then carried it over to the fire. The straw figure had no face. A DNR hat perched on top of the straw mass. A striped blue T-shirt and a pair of jeans made up his outfit, with mismatched gloves for hands, and old Red Wing boots tied onto his feet. Mrs. Langston tossed him in, to applause, and then said if anyone had an item for the "avenging fire," to bring it forward.

Rich could feel Claire getting agitated next to him. It was pretty ghastly watching someone being burned in effigy. He had heard of such things, but had thought they were relegated to a distant past, when crowds in small towns could lose control. And now it was happening in his territory. Claire rose to her feet, staring at the fire.

Rich stood up next to her and motioned with his head toward the door. She nodded, and they filed out.

Outside, the air smelled like spring, and the stars scattered light across the sky.

"What did you notice?" he asked her once they had climbed into the truck.

"I saw something in the fire."

She was shivering, and he felt the urge to put an arm around her. Instead he turned the truck on so it would heat up. "Yes?"

"The effigy was wearing one of Landers' gardening gloves."

"How can you be sure it was his?"

"I gave the gloves to him."

⚜ 12 ⚜

When Claire heard the doorbell ring at six-thirty in the morning, it scared her. She sat up in bed and thought, I don't want to get that. It can only be bad news. She looked down at her hands and saw them clutching the sheet. Wake up, she told herself. Answer the door. It could be anything.

When she ran down the stairs and saw Bridget on her doorstep, she went into a real panic.

"What?" She flung the door open. "Why are you here?"

"I'm okay, big sister. Calm down."

"Calm down. Did you stay up all night? You're never awake at this time of day."

"I did not manage to sleep much last night."

Claire looked at Bridget. She was wearing a nightgown under her jean jacket. Her blond curly hair was knotted on top of her head. Her eyes looked sore and weepy. But it was the set of her shoulders that got to Claire. Bridget always rushed forward, her shoulders straight and steady. Now they seemed broken into her body. "Come on in, sweetie. What's going on?"

"Chuck didn't come home again."

"Again, what's this again?" She pulled Bridget through the door.

On the rug inside the door, Bridget sank to her knees. "Claire, what am I going to do? He's too important to me. I can't bear the thought of losing him."

"Bridget, stand up. You're coming into the kitchen table to have a cup of tea. And be quiet. Meg is still sleeping." Claire could hear their mother in her voice. When faced with calamity, get mad. Yell at whoever. But, absolutely, make tea. Tea solved it all in their family.

She put the water on and let Bridget compose herself. When she looked over at her sitting at the table, Bridget was smearing tears around her face with the backs of her hands. Claire handed her a paper towel and sat down opposite her.

"Talk."

Bridget looked up at her, and Claire saw the deep pain she was in. It floated like an oil slick on her eyes. She took Claire's hand and said, "How did you do it?"

"What?" Claire asked, even though she thought she knew what Bridget was asking.

"How did you stand it when Steve died?"

"Oh, I don't know."

"If this feels anything like what you went through, I had no idea."

"Tell me what's going on, Bridget Hanora."

That got her. Bridget snuffled another tear or two, wiped her face thoroughly, and got herself in hand. "Two nights ago, he didn't come home. This has never happened before. So I called his brother in the morning, and he claimed Chuck had just left. But I didn't believe him. Then Chuck showed up at work. Said he had one too many, it was too late, he didn't want to call. Fact is, he said he felt pretty stupid about it. Him, I believed. You know him. So he does the same thing last night. Goes over to his brother's. He tells me they're almost done with this new car. He's gotta finish it up. I fall asleep on the couch watching TV. When I wake up, it's after two. He's still not home. I call his brother. This time he can't cover for him. He tells me Chuck left hours ago. I sat up until three. Then I drove down to the all-night diner. Then I came here." She burst into tears again. The teakettle started to wail.

Meg shuffled down the steps and said, "I had a bad dream."

Claire poured the water into the teapot. Then she grabbed Meg, carted her to the table, and held her in her lap, something she hadn't done in a long time. Meg was all arms and legs, like a spider. She smelled sweet and warm from bed. She's growing so, Claire thought.

"What do you think is going on?" Claire asked her.

"I'm afraid he's seeing someone else."

Claire thought of Chuck. She would never forget the first time she met him. He was fishing and had just caught a large trout in a stream near Lake Pepin. He was so excited, he was screaming. His cry was such a pure sound of joy, it brought tears to her eyes. He clapped his hands on her and then realized he had smeared her with fish slime. He had started to try to wipe her off, but they both ended up laughing too hard to do anything about it.

He read like clear water. She couldn't imagine him doing anything to hurt Bridget. He loved her as dearly as he loved his own life. Or did Claire just want to think that?

Claire rocked Meg in her arms, held on to her a little too tight, so she squirmed. "I don't believe Chuck would do that."

RICH GOT UP early the morning after the meeting. The sun was not up yet, but the sky held its rose promise. After checking the bread drawer and finding it empty, he decided he needed a couple scones to help him start out the day. He threw on his clothes, hopped into his pickup truck, and sailed down to the bakery. Stuart wasn't officially open for business this early, but he let Rich come and get some goodies if he needed them.

It was Rich's favorite time to stop by. He would stand in the doorway to the kitchen, eat a scone or two, and watch Stuart whiz around the kitchen, pulling loaves of bread from ovens, weighing rolls, and then twisting them into mounded shapes.

"Well, my Lord, if it isn't Monsier le Faisan." Stuart was in high humor.

"How many cups of coffee have you had?"

"I'm way ahead of you. Help yourself." He pointed at the pot that stewed on the stove and kept the coffee more than warm, bordering on simmering, and growing in strength as the day progressed.

Rich poured himself a cup in the mug Stuart kept on hand for him. They were friends. It surprised Rich. He hadn't known many gay men before Stuart had come to town. He had never seen himself as antigay, more he just wasn't sure what he'd have in common with them. But he got along great with Stuart.

Their friendship had started the day the two of them volunteered to build two new picnic tables for the park. Stuart confessed that he didn't know how to hammer a nail into a board after handing Rich two fresh-baked rolls and a huge cup of coffee. Rich looked at the food in his hand, said, "I guess a fellow can't know how to do everything," and set to work showing him some basic carpentry. Late afternoon, the picnic tables were done, Stuart had only pounded his thumb a couple times, and Rich had laughed as hard as he had working with his grandpa. They went to the Fort and had a couple beers. That was eight years ago. If anyone had asked, Rich would have said that Stuart was his best pal.

Rich said, "You know, I'd have to say you're more in the know down here in town. Am I right?"

Stuart pushed his cap back on his head and wiped his hands with a towel he kept tied to his apron strings. "What do you want to know?"

"Well, do you know Claire Watkins very well?"

"Claire, huh." Stuart nodded and went back to kneading some dough. "That doesn't surprise me a bit."

"What's to be surprised about? I'm just curious about something."

Stuart stopped kneading the dough and slapped it a couple times on the big wooden table. Then he turned to look at Rich. "Yes."

"What's the story on her husband?"

"She doesn't talk about him much."

"I know that."

One final slap of the dough. "She doesn't talk about him at all. But I heard from Ruth, you know Ruth up on the hill, that she heard from a friend of hers in town that her husband was hit by a truck and killed."

"What's so mysterious about that?"

"Well, I don't think that's the whole story. There was something weird about it. He was hit by the car right in front of their house. In broad daylight. Claire was a detective for the Minneapolis Police Department at the time."

"So, maybe not an accident?"

"Maybe. I've never gotten a word out of Claire. When she chooses not to speak, she can remain very silent."

Rich thought of Claire seeing that, running out to find her husband dead in the street. He didn't blame her for not talking. "Yeah, I know. Or change the subject."

"But I approve." Stuart cut the dough into hunks.

"You approve. What does that mean?"

"Claire's certainly your equal." A timer went off, and Stuart pulled a tray out of the oven.

"What are you trying to say?"

"It's a scone you were waiting for, wasn't it?" Stuart handed him an absolutely warm blueberry scone right off the cookie sheet. "I'm just trying to say that it's about time you had a little something sweet with your coffee. All work and no play. And I think Claire's a good choice."

"Well, I'm delighted you think so. I'm still not sure what you think I've chosen her for."

"Right. But let me give you a bit of advice."

Rich took a bite of his scone, actually enjoying himself. "This should be good. The master of relationships is about to give me advice."

"Don't put the make on her."

"What code are you talking this morning?"

"Don't give her the big rush. I'd give her a lot of room to move. She's probably not ready for a relationship, and she certainly thinks she's not ready. So easy does it."

Rich pushed the last bit of scone into his mouth and chewed. When he had swallowed, he smiled at Stuart and said, "Good scone."

"Glad you liked it."

"Different subject. If Landers Anderson was killed by someone, and Claire says he was, who would you suspect of killing him?"

"Besides you?" Stuart said jokingly.

"Why would I kill him?" Rich asked, half serious.

"Same reason as anybody else. For his land."

· · ·

AFTER PUTTING BRIDGET to bed and getting Meg off to school, Claire climbed into her uniform and walked across the street to Landers' house.

As she pushed shut the gate, she slowed down. Green shoots spotted the garden. Tulips and daffodils were popping up. Landers had been waiting for this so hard all winter long. He had marked each plant carefully, and she walked down the garden path and read the names: *Tulipa darwiniana*, *Alcea rosea*, etc. Bending down, she pulled a matting of dead oak leaves off a part of the bed to give the new sprouts a better chance at the sun. This weekend, she would come over and take the mulch off all of the garden. If anyone questioned her, she could claim it was part of her police work, just say she was looking for more evidence.

Claire walked around the house and stepped into the two-car garage. Landers' brand-new car, a Toyota Celica, sat in the middle of the floor. His garden tools and a potting stand were all on the side toward the house. She turned on the overhead light and walked to the potting stand. One leather glove was crammed into a basket. The other one was missing. She put the one into an evidence bag and sealed it.

Then she got into her squad car and drove up to Bay City. The view of the lake in the morning mist—like a Swedish fjord, she imagined, the finger of the lake probing in deep through the limestone bluffs—lifted her spirits. The trees on the bluff sides were silver gray in this eastern light. She felt, as she often did, that this was a magical place, this lake, the land. This was a place where a person could start over again, have a new, happier life; one that included sunset walks, ripening tomatoes, good neighborly gossip. If she could just clear up this murder, she could get back to working on this new life. She thought of Rich, and for a moment a bird fluttered in her chest, a whisper of a hope.

When she arrived at the VFW, she saw with relief that the door was propped open. She wouldn't have to track anyone down to open it up for her. She peered into the gloom and saw a heavy-set older woman sweeping in the far corner of the room.

"Hello!" she hollered.

The woman kept at her work, didn't even look up. Claire walked closer. The woman looked to be in her late sixties, with a broad face, braids set on top of her head. She seemed about as Scandinavian as you could get. "Hi," Claire yelled again.

This time the woman looked up and stared at Claire. "Are you a cop?"

"Yes, ma'am, I am. Claire Watkins." The uniform seemed to raise questions in some people's minds, rather than answer them.

"Helma Lundquist. What can I help you with?"

"I was at a meeting here last night. They had a fire, and I wanted to retrieve something."

"What is it with those people? They're always burning the strangest things in the fireplace. What were they burning?"

"Some kind of straw dummy."

"What a mess. I already cleaned it out."

Claire turned and saw the emptied fireplace. "What did you do with the ashes?"

"They're over there in that bucket. I was going to put them on my compost pile. Ashes are good for it, you know."

"That's what I've been told."

Claire walked over to the bucket and squatted down. She stared at the ashen mess and poked at it with her finger. Was anything left in there? She took out her Swiss Army knife and carefully started sifting through the bucket, emptying out the contents bit by bit onto a piece of newspaper. Few remnants were left in the ashes.

"What're you looking for?" Helma leaned on her broom.

"A piece of a glove."

"With red trim?"

"Yes." Claire stood up. "Do you have it?"

"I pulled it out and threw it in the garbage. Didn't know if it would break down in the compost." She pointed to the metal garbage can.

Claire walked over and immediately saw the bit that remained of the glove, a charred piece of leather and part of the wrist. The red trim still showed on the edge. She pulled another evidence bag out of her pocket and picked it up with the edge of her knife.

"Thanks." She nodded at the woman.

"What're those folks up to?" Helma asked.

"Possibly no good," Claire couldn't resist telling her.

"I don't like them. They always leave this place in such a mess. Like a bunch of teenagers, if you ask me." Helma shook her head and then spit out a judgment as if it were the worst of curses: "They have no manners."

❧ 13 ❧

On the way to the office, Claire got called to a car accident in Frankfort, just southwest of Durand. When she got to the scene, an '83 Dodge Dart was sitting with its nose up a tree. The middle-aged owner, a tall, lanky man name of Stan Jenkins, complained about his back, but other than that seemed to be all right. He had swerved to miss a skunk and lost control of his car. Claire took down all the information and offered to give Jenkins a lift into Arkansaw, a town on the Chippewa River, only a couple miles from Durand.

He climbed into the car, and they started off. After a bit, he leaned over and said, "Since when've they got women on the police force? Hell, I'da joined."

Claire said nothing. She just kept her eyes on the road. But she was not sure of this character.

"So if I asked you out, would you get me for sexual harassment?"

"No, I'd just say no."

"You're not married, are you?"

"Sir, that's none of your business."

"I suppose you know karate or something. One of those martial arts to take care of the tough guys."

"I received the same training as my fellow officers."

Jenkins reached out and touched her arm. "Can I feel your muscle?"

Claire pulled over to the side of the road. They were a mile or so from Frankfort, but she wanted him out of the car. "Get out."

"But you said you'd take me to town."

"I lied."

When Jenkins turned toward her, she moved on him.

For a moment, she flashed back to sixth grade. A small, serious girl, she had gotten into a fight with one of the boys in her class, Scott Tarnowski, when he had taken the book she was reading. She won the fight. In order to do it, she had scratched his face, bit his hand, and pulled his hair. After the fight was over, he stood a fair distance from her and yelled at her, saying that she cheated, that she had fought like a girl.

His criticism of her fighting style had stung, and she asked her mother about it when she got home.

"I don't like you fighting. But let me tell you that boys don't make the rules. You should fight like a girl—use what you're good at." Then she had showed Claire the underarm twist.

Claire grabbed the flesh on the bottom of Jenkins' upper arm and pinched and twisted it as hard as she could. He opened his mouth to speak, but no words came out. Instead his mouth contracted into a grimace that showed his crooked teeth and coated tongue. She should have given him a Breathalyzer test. But now she just wanted him out of her car.

When Claire pushed, he moved. She let go of his arm, and Jenkins scampered out of the car as fast as he could. He ran down into the ditch and up the other side, smack into a barbed-wire fence. She drove off, watching him in the rearview mirror as he tried to extricate himself from the barbs.

CHUCK TRIED TO call Bridget at home one more time, but the answering machine picked up again. He heard Bridget's voice explaining carefully how they weren't there but they'd like to know who called. He slammed the phone down.

Where the hell was that woman? He had been trying her all morning. He thought maybe she had gone riding. He knew she didn't have work. He was starting to get worried. Maybe she had gone to Claire's. She hadn't mentioned they had any plans, but she didn't always tell him everything she did. It was one of the things he liked about her, how independent she was.

Some guys teased him 'cuz his wife made more money than he did. He just laughed in their faces. He'd tell them, "And she's smarter than me too." He and Bridget laughed about their jobs, saying he fixed cars and she fixed people, same diff. He guessed true equality came when it didn't matter who made more money. Why should it be seen as so unusual when the woman did? And for that matter, he guessed that those guys who teased him were just envious. As they should be.

He did wish that she wanted to have a kid. He wanted to teach someone the things he knew. It didn't matter to him if it was a boy or a girl. They would know how to change the oil in their car, they would go fishing with him, they would play catch in the yard, he would poke his head into their bedroom to make sure they were sleeping and probably poke his nose into their business too much for his own good. He just thought having a kid or two would add a lot to his life, to Bridget's and his lives. And he knew the two of them would make a beautiful child—strong and smart and full of good honest energy. He figured the world needed a few more people like that.

He was going to try Bridget again when he saw his boss looking over at him. He had a damn timing belt to put into an Isuzu. Stupid job. Had to practically disassemble the engine to get to the belt. Took five minutes to change the belt and an hour to get to it and an hour to put the whole thing back together again.

He'd try Claire's in a while. He hoped Bridget would call and tell him something insignificant, like where she wanted to go for dinner, since she wasn't much of a cook. He stared at the phone and put a spell on it: "Ring, ring." Then he went back to work on the car.

HE TUCKED HIS hair under a baseball cap and tied it back so none of it showed. Red hair was too distinctive. But his hair was his badge. Women loved it. When they'd come close to him at bars, he could tell they just wanted to touch it. They wanted to touch him. He was like fire, his hair his flames.

But he didn't want anyone in this podunk town to remember him. He had borrowed a friend's old beater pickup truck and rubbed mud on the license plates. Tucked into the shade across from the elementary school, he was waiting for the school buses to load up and head out.

He had done this before. Come down and parked near her school and watched her board the bus. But this time he was going to follow her home and see if he couldn't snatch her.

The bus pulled out, and he followed it. He couldn't be stopping behind the bus as it traveled down 35. The driver would notice him.

He sped around the bus and drove an easy sixty miles an hour down the road. Didn't need no speeding ticket. That's for sure.

Didn't need anything to jeopardize the deal that was just about to happen. Hawk might not like it that he was down here, but it wasn't his head on the line. The little girl had seen him. The woman cop might decide to circulate that information at any moment. She had already fucked up his life big-time.

But this would teach her a permanent lesson. People will do anything for their kids. Especially women. He remembered one tasty number he had coerced into doing all sorts of fun stuff for him. He had merely suggested if she didn't comply, he would go make her ten-year-old daughter, who was sleeping in the next room, do it. She couldn't get to work fast enough. That was one night he would never forget.

He couldn't believe people would choose to live down here. Sleepy beyond words. Nothing going on. Big excitement would be fishing on the lake. Not his style. It made him nervous just sitting in the shade. Pretty hard to be anonymous here. He pulled up to the bus stop and got out a map. He could both hide behind it and pretend he was checking it. In the rearview mirror, he could see the bus was still down the road a ways.

What the hell was he going to do with this kid? He didn't even know where to take her. He actually didn't much fancy little girls, though he knew some guys got off on them. But who knows. Maybe she'd be really cute, have some little titties coming in. He'd have to wait and see. He wasn't even sure he would keep her for long.

A young woman was coming down the hill toward the road. He sneaked a good look at her from behind the map. Man, was she stacked. He'd like a piece of that action. Long blond curly hair. He could go for that. He loved long hair. Long hair so you could get a real good grip on the bitch, and a nice firm butt to pump into. That's what got him revved up. She looked his way, and he ducked behind the map.

After a moment, he dropped the map again. She was much closer. She looked all warm and sleepy. Like she had just rolled out of bed. He'd like to roll her right back in. Too bad he had work to do. Too bad he couldn't be seen here. Maybe some other time. After the deal went down. Who knows, he might just have to get a fishing rod and start trolling in the lake. Catch himself a big one.

The bus pulled up, and it blocked his view so he couldn't see anything. When it pulled away, the little girl was standing right where it had dropped her off. Skinny little thing. Meg Watkins. He knew he didn't have long to nab her. Be a cinch just to hoist her up and lift her into the car.

But he couldn't make a move until that woman left. Maybe she was heading down to the post office. The little girl started to run. Shit, she ran straight into the bitch's arms. Who the hell was this woman? Was she the baby-sitter? He thought the baby-sitter was some old broad that couldn't hardly walk and that she never came down to meet the bus.

He knew it wasn't Claire. He hadn't seen her in a long time, but the last time, she had short black hair. That couldn't have changed. Plus, he had called her office and found out she was still at work, and Durand was a good half-hour drive away from Fort St. Antoine.

Well, that did it. He slammed his hand into the steering wheel. No way he could pull this snatch off. He wasn't prepared to grab two people. It would have to be another day. In the meantime, he'd have to find out who the broad was. Maybe he'd have to pick her up too. At that thought he smiled, his lips like two rubber bands stretched, then smacked back together.

He stretched and watched the two walk back up the hill. They were holding hands and swinging them back and forth.

Meg was chattering away. Even from behind, the long-haired woman looked good. Nice back action. Now, she was more his style. He wouldn't mind spending some time alone with her. Get rid of the girl. That's what he would do if he grabbed the two of them, just get rid of the little girl.

14

The church ceiling soared into dark rafters, with old golden candle-like lamps hanging down on chains. The walls were a soft cream white and the altar cloth a deep rich red. It was a beautiful country church, with all the pews filled to mourn the passing of one of their own. Claire had come alone but nodded to many people who passed her. She had chosen to sit in one of the last pews, close to the door, so if the service proved too hard on her, she could make a quick exit.

She hadn't been to a funeral since her husband had been killed. She hadn't been inside a church since then. But as she looked around the small church, she wondered if this wasn't a place she could come and find some solace. The sun poured in the western windows, and the dust motes danced in the late-evening air. The organist played "Abide with Me," and the music drifted down from the choir loft.

Claire had left Meg in Bridget's care. She knew this funeral would be hard enough on her as it was, without Meg by her side. She imagined it would have also been difficult for Meg, although sometimes her daughter surprised her with her strength.

Meg had handled her father's funeral well. She had been pleasant and talked to everyone and been a model little girl. She had dressed herself and kept her room clean and taken a bath without being told. But she had started biting her nails and sucking on her hair and grinding her teeth at night, all nervous habits that she didn't seem to be able to control. She wouldn't sleep without a light on in her room and didn't want to go outside after dark. Claire bought her a special soft light for her room and tried to avoid anything that would take her out of the house after the sun set.

But the night that she found Meg sitting in the corner of the bathroom, soaking wet from wetting her bed and crying from a bad dream, was the day she decided they had to move. She found the clean old farmhouse down on Lake Pepin, close to Bridget, who Meg loved. She bought it as soon as she saw it and quit her job the next day. She had never returned to work since the leave of absence she was asked to take for mental health; given two months off, she had quit a week before she was to go back. She and Meg moved down to Fort St. Antoine a month later, before their house in town had even sold.

At first the trains passing at night would wake Meg and scare her, but soon Claire could see the country was soothing her daughter. Meg stopped sucking her hair, and her nails grew small crescents of white on their tips.

One night, after they had lived in Fort St. Antoine a month or so, Meg had told her that she was afraid.

"Why are you afraid?"

"I'm afraid that I'm going to forget Dad."

"You might not always remember him as well as you do now, but he will always be with you."

After reassuring her daughter, Claire had gone downstairs and pulled out some old photos of them as a family. A few days later she had one framed and put it up in the house where they could both see it every day. Steve looked so full of himself in the picture, happy to be with his family. Claire wasn't afraid of forgetting Steve; she was afraid she wouldn't remember how human he had been. They had loved each other, but their love wasn't perfect. They had irritated each other, quarreled over stupid things like how to load the dishwasher and the correct way to dress the bed.

She remembered their last fight. He had asked her to pick up milk on her way home, and she had forgotten. He harped about it, saying she probably had to stop off for a drink with Bruce. Lately, her relationship with Bruce had been getting on Steve's nerves. He claimed she spent more time with her partner than with him, her husband. Claire could not deny that; eight hours a day added up. Then he yelled that she seemed to like Bruce better than him. She had stood in the middle of the kitchen, shaking her head.

The next day he was dead.

What Claire was afraid of was that she would make him a saint, and then certainly no one would ever be capable of taking his place.

The organ started another song, and the congregation rose as the pastor came down the aisle. Claire sank into a reverie as the pastor started speaking. It always happened to her. The church she had gone to growing up had had a pastor who droned, and whenever she heard anyone with a similar voice now, she drifted off. She didn't go to sleep, she just went deep into her thoughts.

She started to plan her garden in her mind: the rosebushes she would line up next to the road on a white fence, the lilac bushes she would plant, and the hollyhocks she would put next to the house. And then in herself, she knew that Landers was gone and would not be there to answer her questions, and she felt tears, like a good slow rain, run down her face.

BRIDGET TURNED THE page and looked at the picture. Laura and her sister were staring up at the pig their dad had slaughtered. Bridget found the picture rather grisly, but Meg, who was tucked in next to her in the bed, didn't seem to mind it. Bridget read about how the girls went sledding all day long, and when they arrived home their mother had pig's tail ready for them to eat."

Bridget turned to Meg. "They eat pig's tail?"

Meg explained, "They didn't have much good food when this whole place was nothing but a big forest." Meg waved her hand around. She had told Bridget that *Little House in the Big Woods* was set just a few miles south of Fort St. Antoine when they started reading the book.

"Haven't you ever been to the birthplace of Laura Ingalls Wilder?" Meg had asked, astonished. "Jeez, we go there every year from school. It's kinda cool."

"No. I've never been there." No reason to go, Bridget thought to herself. No kid to take. Bridget shut the book and asked Meg, "Do you like being an only child?"

Meg stretched out in bed and closed her eyes for a moment, thinking. Opening her eyes, she gave her answer, "Usually I like it fine. But I worry about Mom. When I grow up and go away, she'll be all alone. And I think it would be fun to have someone to play horses with."

"How do you play horses?"

"You know, you pretend you're a horse. They pretend they're a horse, and then you go running through the fields. Hard to do all by yourself. Or play secret fort."

"Do you have a secret fort?"

Meg didn't say anything.

"Oh, I see, that's a secret." Bridget poked her gently in the sides, and Meg curled up and giggled. "What would you think about having a cousin?"

"You mean, like a baby?"

"I guess that's the way it would start out."

"I think it would be neat to have a baby. I'd like to learn how to change a diaper. Except for poopy diapers."

"Oh, this baby would never have poopy diapers."

Meg sat bolt-straight up in the bed and stared at Bridget. "Are you going to have a baby?"

"I don't know."

Bridget turned her head as they heard a car pull up in the driveway. "Who's that?"

Meg shook her head. "It's too early for Mom, isn't it?" She hopped out of bed.

"Get back here," Bridget yelled at her.

"Why? I just want to see who it is." Meg ran to the window. "It's a truck. Some guy is getting out. I can't see him very good."

"You climb back in this bed, young lady. After all, you're in your pajamas. I'll go down and see who it is."

Bridget tucked Meg back in bed. She went to the window but didn't recognize the truck. Maybe that guy that Claire mentioned, Rich, who raised pheasants. She kissed Meg on the nose and turned out the light in her room. A knock sounded on the back door. She ran down the stairs to see who it was.

RICH LOOKED OVER the heads of all the people in the church and didn't find who he was looking for. He knew that Teddy would have come to the funeral if he had known about it.

Rich decided he should have called him. Darla and Fred obviously didn't think Teddy needed to know about Landers' death. Rich was so mad at them, he wanted to shake them. Darla had been busy being infuriating all her life, or at least as long as Rich had known her. He had known her well when he was growing up.

He had been good friends with her son Teddy, and they often had spent hours reading comics and even making up comics in their basement. Darla hadn't liked that. She wanted the two of them outside playing baseball or something. Actually Rich liked to do that too, but not with Teddy, because Teddy wasn't any good at baseball and thought it was dumb.

The service started, and he tried to pay attention. While they sang the hymns, he calmed down, but when the sermon came he grew angry again about Teddy not being at the funeral. It must have been Darla who had kept him from being told. She had a mean streak.

Rich remembered one time she had gone into Teddy's room and taken the pages of a comic book they had written and drawn together. She had burned them, or at least told the two boys she had when they got home from the Fort. They had gone to get some pop with a couple quarters she had given them. He thought that was awfully nice of Darla, but when he found out she had destroyed all their work, Rich called her a bitch to her face.

The shit had hit the fan at home. He had been grounded for a week and then had to go over to her house with a bouquet of flowers from his mother's garden and say he was sorry.

She had taken the flowers graciously and said she accepted his apology, and then, without stopping for a breath of air, she had turned to his mother and said, "I'm going to have to ask you to keep Richard away from our Teddy for the rest of the summer. These comic books and the profane language they use have just gotten to be too much for the boys. You understand."

The two boys had seen each other in school that year, tenth grade, but they didn't have any classes together. Teddy seemed to be pulling into himself even more, and even Rich found him a little odd. The episode with Darla had left a bad taste in his mouth that made Rich not like doing comics as much and avoid Teddy. And then, of course, Teddy had left town right after high school. He moved up to the Twin Cities and had seemed to have found a way to fit in. He had gone to the College of Art and Design and was making quite a name for himself now.

Rich had been asked to be one of the pallbearers, and he had accepted. He had always liked Landers, a kind old man who had moved through life gracefully. He would miss him. Landers always put in an order for half a dozen pheasant, and Rich would drop them by and then stay for a cup of coffee. At the end of the service, he stood with the other five men, lifted the heavy metal casket, and carried it down the middle of the church.

Near the doorway, he saw Claire. She was sitting with her head bowed and her eyes shut. He hoped to get a chance to talk to her at the graveside. He hadn't seen her since they had gone to the meeting together, but she had been often in his thoughts.

As he left the church, he saw that Darla was still seated, facing the altar. Her shoulders were shaking. At first he assumed she was crying, and then a horrible thought crept into his mind. He was afraid she might actually be laughing.

BRIDGET WATCHED A familiar figure get out of the truck. Her husband, Chuck, was bearing down on the front door. She thought of not letting him in, but she might as well hear the worst and get it over with.

"Where have you been?" Chuck demanded when he came in the door. "You left the house before I even got up."

"Before you got home, you mean." Bridget made him stand by the door. This wasn't going to be a pleasant chat.

"I was home by midnight. You were sleeping on the couch, so I left you there." A smile lit his face. "You looked so peaceful and cozy there, I didn't want to disturb you." He stepped into the room and sprawled on the couch, patting the place next to him.

Bridget stood her ground. "Where did you sleep?"

"In bed."

"I thought you were gone all night again."

"Did you look in the bedroom?"

"No."

She twisted her wedding ring around her finger. She looked down at her husband as he leaned forward on the couch. She believed him. It made sense, and she felt so stupid. She hadn't heard him come home, hadn't looked in the bedroom, and had assumed he was still gone. All that gut-wrenching for nought. Silly, pregnant woman. She hadn't told him about her premonition. She would soon.

"I'm an idiot."

"Sometimes," he admitted. He patted the couch next to him.

She told him, "Claire should be home soon."

"Whatever." He smiled and opened his arms.

She slid into his embrace. Lovely husband. They kissed, and he gently nibbled her lower lip. "Let's sleep together tonight."

"Great idea," Bridget whispered in his ear.

"Hi, Uncle Chuck," Meg yelled from the top of the stairs. "My story isn't done yet."

"Did you know there used to be cougars here?" Bridget asked Chuck, pulling out of his embrace far enough so she could see his face.

"What are you reading her?" They both stood up and walked up the stairs.

"*Little House in the Big Woods.*"

"I'd like to see a cougar."

STANDING IN HER driveway, Claire looked up at the firmament. She picked out the planets, which shone red-tinged light, steady and focused. Other stars hinted at blue and flickered as if a celestial wind blew them. What Claire loved best was the Milky Way, but it didn't look like milk to her, rather salt strewn over someone's shoulder.

Her life was good down here. Claire dropped her eyes down to Meg's bedroom window. She had eight more years before Meg would leave home to go to college. They would be happy years, Claire promised herself. Maybe some nice man would join them. Not to take Steve's place—that could never be—but a man who would be kind to Meg would be so good for her.

Claire had assumed the pickup truck in the driveway was one of her brother-in-law's, so she was not surprised to see him on the living room couch when she walked in the back door. She was surprised to see him in a tight clinch with Bridget.

"Worked things out, have we?"

Bridget sat up, flushed and pretty. "We have indeed. He was there sleeping in bed. He came in while I was sleeping, so he was always there." Bridget looked closer at Claire, then asked, "What's the matter with your eyes?"

"What?"

"Looks like someone punched you."

Claire walked into the bathroom and surveyed her face. Crying always made her look like a raccoon. She turned on the hot water and washed her face. "Never wear mascara to a funeral."

When she emerged from the bathroom, the two of them had their coats on.

"Thanks, Big Sis," Bridget said. "Was the funeral hard?" she asked as an afterthought.

"Yes and no. It is easier when the person has lived a long life," Claire told them as they walked out the door. "Thanks for watching Meg."

Bridget turned around in the yard and yelled back, "I think she was watching me."

CLAIRE STOOD IN the doorway to her daughter's room. Meg was sleeping so soundly that she didn't go in and touch her cheek like she wanted to do.

She wanted to gather her sleeping child in her arms and croon to her all the promises that a mother could make: "It's going to be all right. No one will ever hurt you. I will watch over you and care for you until you're bigger than me. Until the world is your stomping ground. Until you are your own person."

Lately, Claire had had moments of hopefulness. She prayed nothing would happen to take them away.

15

Claire leaned over her desk, reading the paper and chewing a tuna fish sandwich. She made it a point to read the local paper. The headline of the Durand paper was about the opening of fishing season. She usually liked to read what the police had been up to—how many people they had stopped for speeding, if there had been any serious crimes committed.

There had been a fuss in the paper a few weeks ago when one of the deputies escorted a man home after he had fallen asleep at the McDonald's drive-through. The man had ordered and then nodded off. The server wasn't able to wake him, so she called the police. The deputy came, made him move over, and drove him home. He had been called on the carpet because he hadn't given the guy a Breathalyzer test. Claire thought it was sad that even in a small town, helping somebody home was seen as the wrong thing to do.

There was nothing so exciting in the paper today.

Sheriff Talbert poked his head into her office. "Any good news there?"

Claire lowered the paper. "Great deal on radial tires."

"You got a minute?"

"Sure."

"When you're done eating, come on in my office."

As soon as he left, Claire sat up and tried to figure out what she had done wrong. He never wanted to see her in his office. It sounded so official.

The tuna fish sandwich hit the wastebasket with a thud. She folded the paper and swatted a fly with it. Her phone rang, and she picked up immediately.

"Hello?"

"Claire, it's Bruce. Can't talk right now. I got a sniff of someone knowing something about your husband's death."

"What?"

"I'd like to come down tonight and tell you about it. It would be better."

"Of course. Right after work?"

"You got it." He hung up.

She put down the phone and stared at her hand. Her feeling of last night—how safe she was from whoever killed her husband—seemed as far away as the stars. Claire remembered how agonizingly frustrated she had been right after her husband had been killed. The police couldn't seem to get a lead on anyone. No one had seen anything, she had thought. Now she knew that Meg had, and she couldn't stand the thought of Meg in any kind of danger. Out of an urgency to find out who had killed her husband, she had told Bruce. She wondered if it had been the right thing to do.

She rapped on the rippled glass front of the sheriff's office and walked in when she heard his summoning voice. "Yes, sir," she said to tease him.

Sheriff Talbert gave her the once-over, not in a sexual way, more an assessment of an employee. Then he scratched his head. "Claire, I got a call on you."

"What does that mean, sir?" Claire felt her skin flush.

"A kind of complaint." He said the word slowly.

Jenkins rose in her mind's eye, scurvy little fellow stuck to a fence. Claire said simply, "He had it coming."

"What coming?" The sheriff looked over at her and watched her again.

Claire felt as if she had stepped a toe into something sticky. She decided to back up. "Who was the complaint from, sir?"

"Mrs. Langston."

"The property rights woman?"

"None other."

"What was she complaining about?"

"She said you'd come visiting her and her organization."

"I did attend a meeting."

"What you do on your off time is not usually my business."

"Well, I was actually following a lead in the Landers case. His brother is very involved in the landowner rights movement. I wanted to see what they were all about."

"Oh." Talbert leaned back in his chair and steepled his fingers. A smile played on his lips. "Did you find anything out?"

She told him about the figure burned in effigy and the glove. "I just got the glove back from the forensic lab in Eau Claire. The two gloves are a match, which means there's a high probability that the burned glove was Mr. Anderson's."

"Are you planning on talking to Mrs. Langston?"

"Yes."

"Good idea. Maybe you could go apologize in person to her and find out what's going on."

"What do I apologize to her about?"

"You know what I mean. Smooth things over."

"I'm only doing my job."

"I know that." When Claire turned to go, he called her back.

"And, Claire, give her a chance. She's not such a bad old hellion. I actually think you might get a kick out of her."

"WELL, YOU'RE HERE EARLY," Mr. Blounder said, surprise and snideness mixing in his voice like two incompatible medications. He looked exhausted, but that was how he often looked. When they had first started working together a year ago, Bridget had asked him several times if he was all right, with real alarm in her voice. After his grunted assent that he was fine, she quit asking. Now that she knew him better, she realized he never did anything but come to work and go home. He never went outside. His skin was so pale as to seem almost transparent, and occasionally she had the urge to reach over and pet him, just to feel how soft his skin was.

Bridget merely stretched a smile at his comment. She did not need to get into it with him today. Turning and bending down as if she had dropped something, she grabbed a box off the shelf in front of the cash register. Why did they put those goddamn tests there? Right next to the condoms. If you don't wear one, you'll need the other. A kind of perverse morality being practiced right in the store.

Bridget slipped the pregnancy test into her purse, intending to pay for it later. Then she stood up and went to the bathroom. She locked the door and dropped her coat to the floor. Maybe she simply had cancer, some huge growth that had stopped her periods. Time to find out.

Bridget squatted down on the stool and peed on the plastic stick. She closed her eyes and held her breath. The instructions said to wait two minutes. Would it be like Christmas? If you wanted something too much, you wouldn't get it? In her mind she saddled up her horse and rode him hard. The dreams she had welled up in her. She had always wanted to own a small stable of horses. She could see herself giving lessons, riding at the state fair, winning ribbons for jumping. She was saving money from her job to set all that up. Her dreams could be all over, depending on the color of the plastic wand she held in her hand. Wish, wish, no color. Or to see a drop of blood in the water below her.

When she opened her eyes, she saw the stick had turned blue, which meant she was with child. Bridget let it fall into the toilet and then flushed it down. She stood up, adjusted her clothing, and walked to the mirror. Thirty-five—that wasn't too old to be a mom by today's standards. When she was fifty-three, the child would be eighteen. She would still be able to ride. Many people rode into their sixties. Why, she had heard of a woman who had been in the Olympics when she was sixty-four. She would simply put it off for a while; her whole life would go on hold while she changed diapers and wiped snotty noses and told a child to go to bed; she meant it. She could do it all.

For a moment, she considered an abortion. She had had one when she was twenty-three. No regrets. She would have one again, but she knew Chuck would not hear of it. He wanted a child. And he had that odd masculine notion that a child from his seed would be more worthy than all the rest.

Bridget thought of a child as a person, not a belonging. So many of the women she watched who had children acted as if they owned them. It would be easier for her to give in to the prospect of having a child if she could see them that way. As it was, she really wasn't sure she wanted another demanding person in her life. She remembered all too clearly her own childhood, her father being at work all day long, her mother taking loving care of her and Claire and yet wishing they would go on vacation for a few weeks without her. Her mother would lie on the couch in the living room after everyone was in bed just to listen to the quiet. That's what she had told Bridget when she came up the stairs to get a drink of water. Bridget would nod and listen to the quiet, too, and wonder what her mother heard in it. Now, at thirty-five, she understood.

Bridget put her hand over her stomach. It did seem larger to her—harder was the better way to put it. She was with child. One in the oven. Whatever. She had tied her hair back into a knot at the nape of her neck. She'd have to wear it back most of the time so the baby couldn't grab at it and yank her head back. Maybe she should just cut it off. Fat and shorn, that's how she'd look in a few months.

Bridget took a small sip of water and walked out of the bathroom.

Mr. Blounder curled his lips back and said, "Are you feeling okay?"

Bridget stopped in front of him and asked, "Did your mother love you?"

He thought for a moment, then said, "I guess so."

"Did you love your mother?"

For the first time since she had known him, a thin worm of a smile crawled out on his lips. "Yes, I loved my mother dearly."

She stared at him. Maybe it was possible. "Yes, I'm feeling fine."

THE ROAD CURVED up through a wooded hillside to the crest. Claire bumped the police car up the dirt road carefully, feeling the car slide slightly in the runoff caused by the snowmelt. Hidden under the just budding trees were piles of old snow. They would be gone in another week or so, if more snow didn't come. Snow in April wasn't that unusual. Messy and soggy, it reminded Claire of ephemeral East Coast snow, the kind that melted in midflight.

Driving over the top of the hill, Claire stopped the car on the descent, struck by the view. People paid big bucks for this. Lake Pepin spread out below her like a fine, light gray tablecloth. There was no breeze, and it was so calm it seemed possible to walk on the water. Claire compared this view to the one she saw of the lake from her house. All she could make out was a twinkling of silver through tree branches in the dead of winter. By the time the trees leafed out, the lake had disappeared. Here, the blufflands encircled the lake, their contours moving in and away from the water like ripple candy. Way across the lake, she could see another farm. The silhouette of the barn and silos stood out against the light blue sky.

Before the blufflands ordinance, anyone could build right on the edge of the bluff. But in the last century, the farmers had resisted doing that. They sheltered their farmhouses in the small valleys just over the ridge of the bluffs so the houses wouldn't be hit by the winds. However, new developers and owners perched their houses as far out as they could over the water. From the interior of some of these houses Claire sometimes got vertigo, as it appeared that nothing held the house up from the waves below. Charming names were given to these places, like "Eagle's Nest." But since the blufflands ordinance forbade such placement of houses, the far ridge of the bluffs would stay much the way Claire saw it now—the odd barn or two on the opposite side of the lake, but other than that, it could almost give the impression of how the landscape had been a thousand years ago.

Claire let the car ease down the other side of the hill. The road wound into a grove of trees, and she parked next to a station wagon. She reached over and got the charred piece of glove that the forensic lab had sent back to her. As she walked toward the house, a big German shepherd bounded out at her. She stood still and waited for him to come to her; she wasn't afraid of him, just cautious. She held out her hand, and he gave it a sniff, then wagged his tail.

"Good dog," she said and started forward, but he jumped at her. Claire stood still again. He didn't seem to want her to move.

The front door of the house swung open, and a high voice keened out, "Off, Sheriff."

The dog backed up and wagged his tail furiously. Claire walked toward the front of the house, and the dog let her pass.

Mrs. Langston leaned in the front doorway. "I've got him trained," she stated.

"I see that."

"I'm up here by myself now, you know."

"No, I didn't know that."

"My husband passed away nearly five years ago. I got Sheriff two weeks later. Couldn't stand to be alone."

"I know how you feel. My husband died about a year ago." When the words came out of her mouth, Claire couldn't believe it. She had never volunteered that information before. Maybe it was about time she did.

"I'm so sorry. A young woman like you. That's horrible." Mrs. Langston motioned her through the door. "You're in luck. I just put some water on for tea and I baked some brownies this morning."

Claire followed her into a sunny kitchen. A round oak table sat right under a bay of windows that overlooked the lake. A collection of salt and pepper shakers danced around the window ledges: shakers in the shapes of windmills, gas stations, Scottie dogs, and different kinds of fruit.

"What a wonderful collection," Claire exclaimed.

"Oh, the kids are always finding me a new set. They're not as discriminating as I might be. I really like the animals. This is one of my favorite sets." She held up two skunks, their tails raised up high, with little holes in them for the condiments to come out.

When Claire sat down, she took off her hat and faced the older woman. She took a deep breath and began, "Mrs. Langston, part of the reason I stopped by today was to apologize for how my visit to your meeting the other night might have appeared."

"Please call me Edith. You're making me feel older than my sixty-five years. Actually I didn't mind you being there so much, although having the police attend a meeting can be a little off-putting. It's that Rich Haggard. He's been against us from the beginning." She put a cup of tea in front of Claire and set a brownie on the edge of her saucer.

Claire lifted the cup, a simple white one with a scroll of roses on it, and admired it. She brought her attention back to Edith's statement. "How so?"

"You know, I've known that kid since he was born. His uncle was a strange old man, and I've often wondered if brain trouble doesn't run in that family."

"Brain trouble?"

"Oh, you know that mixed bag of depression, schizophrenia, whatever. All the people in Rich's family just seem to think too much."

"That's not always a bad thing." Claire sniffed the tea—the faint smell of jasmine—and took a sip.

"No, but I've not often been on the right side of any one of them, and they're horrible enemies."

Claire almost spit out the tea in her mouth as she laughed. "Well, that's certainly something to hold against them."

"They've always been the outcasts down here. Never fit in, never mingled much. Didn't help any that the Haggards were something like Scotch-English and Catholic to boot."

"What are you?"

"Well, I'm Swedish. My husband was French and German. Mostly German. Lutheran, so that was okay." Edith sat down across from Claire and tapped her on the hand. "I helped form the Landowners of America group because of the strong connection I feel to this place. We in the group love this land. We don't need the government to step in and tell us how to treat it. My grandparents came here from Sweden. They traveled up the Mississippi by riverboat. Landed on the shore of Lake Pepin and claimed this land right here for their farm. We've been here since the beginning."

Claire supressed the urge to mention the Chippewa who had camped probably right where this house sat. "I would like to ask you some questions about your organization and this proposed development."

"Ask away."

"How far along are plans for this development?"

"You've seen the map. We've contacted a terrific developer in Minnesota who's done a contingency plan for us. He thinks we've got a very viable project here, and he's contacting some investors to come and meet with us."

"The development would involve a huge parcel of your own land. How do you feel about that?"

"When my husband died, he didn't leave me any money. Everything we had, we put into the farm to keep it going. He always said to me, 'Edith, the land is our nest egg.' I want to retire too. I'm tired of worrying about getting the crops in. If this development goes through, it will bring in enough money to set me up for the rest of my long life. Who knows, I might live to be ninety-nine like my grandmother, Olga Swenson."

"How are Darla and Fred Anderson involved with the development?"

Edith stood up and bustled around the kitchen. "You can't keep Fred out of anything. He thinks he knows it all."

"Have they put any money in?"

"Not money."

"What about Landers? Had he been approached to sell his land?"

"Of course. If you looked at that map the other night, you couldn't help notice that the whole development borders on his land. To incorporate that ten-acre chunk into our plans would be wonderful. But Landers wasn't interested."

"Who contacted him?"

When Edith didn't answer, Claire prompted her. "Was it Ted Brown who called Landers?"

"Yes, I think so." Edith appeared distracted.

"Who is he?"

"Just one of our major investors. He's been coming down to this area for a long time, picking up small parcels of land and holding on to them. He's ready to make his fortune."

"I hope not at anyone's expense," Claire said. "Was that frustrating to you when Landers didn't want to sell?"

"I didn't see it that way. I'm doing this because I think it will be good for the community. I thought that if Landers could have that explained to him, it might change his mind. If not, I thought maybe Darla could persuade him."

Claire sat puzzled. Of all the people she might pick to persuade Landers of something, Darla would be the last. "Darla?"

"Yes, they go way back."

"But they don't like each other."

"Well, they did. They were going out before Landers left and joined the marines. In fact, Darla and Landers were engaged to be married. Then the war broke out and he left, and she married Fred."

Not knowing what to say to that, Claire reached into her pocket and pulled out the bag containing the burned glove. "The other night at the meeting, you burned an effigy of a DNR man. People put things into the fire. This was one of the items burned. Our forensic lab has matched it to a glove of Landers Anderson's."

Edith Langston stood up and patted her hair. Instead of looking closer at the glove, she pulled back and walked to the window. "I know nothing about that glove. If you're looking for a connection between Landers' land and his death, I think you should look at the man you were sitting next to the other night. Rich Haggard wants that land as badly as anyone."

16

The sun drifted down through the shaking branches and spread over her legs. Meg had her feet stretched out in front of her. The warmth felt good. Only one more month of school, then she got to play all summer long.

From her fort halfway up the bluff, Meg could see the valley and watch everyone come and go on the tarred roads by her house. She saw the red car pull up in her driveway and Bruce get out. He hadn't come over in a long time. Her mom spent too much time alone. Maybe Bruce would make her feel better. Meg liked Bruce because he was from the time of her life before her dad died. He knew her dad, and he always made a point to talk to her. And her mom liked him. Meg ducked under the lookout branch and snuggled down into the old leaves with her dolls.

Mom didn't know she had brought her two dolls up here. Mom didn't know about the fort. No one did. Meg knew inside of herself that she needed this to be a secret. If you had a secret, it gave you power. Her two dolls were a boy and a girl. They were pioneers and very brave. Every day they had new adventures, most of them involved with being lost in the woods and having to survive. Meg gathered mushrooms for them, and berries. Twigs served as utensils, the cap of an acorn was a cup, and the acorn itself was a very good source of food. Meg had read that the Indians pounded it into flour and made pancakes out of it. She had tasted an acorn once, and it was very bitter. It made her mouth pucker up.

Sometimes she pretended that the boy doll was her dad. She would be the girl doll, and they would simply go for a walk in the woods. Nothing scary would happen. It was quiet, and she could be with her dad for a while, tell him about school.

Today, she was playing that the boy doll was his usual self. His name was Jared. She liked that name. It sounded tough. The girl doll's name was Felicity. Such a pretty name. It had loops in the sound of it. Jared and Felicity had gone on a hike and had gotten lost. A snowstorm was coming. They were making a shelter in the trunk of an oak tree; out of the leaves, they formed a nest. Landers had told her mom that oak leaves were the best for insulation because they didn't mush down. They kept their shape and held in pockets of warmth.

The thought of Landers popped into her mind again. She could see him stretched out on the ground. Sometimes, at school, the kids asked her where her dad was. She simply said he was gone. That usually did the trick. Quite a few kids didn't have dads. Their parents were divorced. She poked her head and looked back down at the car. Bruce was walking toward the house. She wondered if she'd ever have a dad again.

CLAIRE LOOKED OUT the window and saw Bruce pull up. He leaned out of the car and then stood up. He looked big down here. Out of context. His suitcoat flapped in the wind. He buttoned it like he was on official business and headed toward the house. She wiped her hands off. He had caught her doing the dishes. She tapped the window, and he looked up. She waved and then headed to the door to greet him.

"Hey, good looking." He smiled and patted her shoulder, but kept his distance.

"Hey, big guy. What's the score?" Funny how the old patter came back automatically. During the years they had worked together, she had spent much more time with him than her husband. Pity, that.

"I'm afraid ten to nothing, and the bad guys are winning."

Claire backed up and invited him in. "So I gather. I hate to hear it. Down here in this part of the country, a speeding ticket is nearly as bad as it gets."

"You did just have a murder across the street. You need to fill me in on that. Haven't heard how it's going."

"You off duty?"

"Way off duty."

That, at least, was a good sign. As he unbuttoned his suitcoat, she asked, "Can I offer you a beer?"

"If you didn't, I'd have to root around in your fridge until I found one."

She laughed as she opened the refrigerator door. "Then you might stumble on some pretty creepy things in there. Long-forgotten casserole." She handed him a Leinenkugel and pulled one out for herself.

"Where's Meg?" he asked.

"She's out playing."

"Alone?"

She heard the sharp tone in his voice. He was a city cop; he didn't know how easy life could be in a small town. "Yes, Bruce, this is the country. She's perfectly safe. She plays close by. I told her she can't go out of voice range."

"And with your holler, that could stretch pretty far." He gave her a quick smile, and they clinked beer bottles.

They sat down at the table in the kitchen, and Bruce shrugged out of his suitcoat. Underneath, his sleeves were already rolled up. He looked tired to Claire. Working too hard and not having much fun. Poor guy. Claire liked seeing him sitting there. Felt good to have a man in the house. End of the day. Talking over what happened. She missed the check-in, she missed having an adult in her life.

His brown eyes looked over at her, and his face broke into a smile. "I'm glad to see you."

"Yeah, you haven't been down here since the end of last summer, when you helped me move in."

"Not because of me."

"No, I know." Claire sipped her beer and then shook her head as if a fly were bothering her. "So what do we need to talk about?"

"Well, I've been thinking about what you told me about Meg seeing this guy. And aside from wondering why I didn't hear this nine months ago, which I kind of know why I didn't, I'm wondering, what do we do with this information now?"

Claire let her head fall forward. She didn't know what to tell him.

"This could get us to reopen the case in a big way."

Claire felt the hair on the back of her neck climbing into her scalp. "What if we just say that someone saw the guy and hint that it was a neighbor?"

"Might work."

"I don't want Meg involved in this. I don't want anyone to know she knows anything. Understood?"

"Of course. Do you think we could get her to talk to an artist and describe the guy so we could circulate something?"

"Yeah, maybe that would work."

Bruce slammed down his bottle of beer. "You can't have it both ways, Claire. You can't completely protect your daughter and still get the guys who did this."

Claire stood up and yelled down at him. She found it helped to be taller than Bruce once in a while. "Why not? Why can't I be both a cop and a mom?"

"Okay, all right. We can try to keep a lid on this. But if you want anything to move forward on this case, you've got to give us something."

"Let me think about."

Bruce set down his beer bottle and shoved back his chair. "Fine, think. But the trail is mighty old and cold. Don't think too long."

Claire sat still for a moment and then asked Bruce, "Do you think these guys are still around?"

"We hear tell of them. I think that drug gang is still operating; whether this particular guy is still with them, I haven't a clue. Although I did get a call about a guy killing a dog in North Minneapolis, and the kid said that he thought the guy was dealing. He might have connections to the gang we're looking for."

"You got somebody watching him?"

"Yeah, they're checking the license plates of the cars that visit him."

"Sounds good. Is that what you came down to tell me?"

"Yeah, I feel like this is heating up again, and I still want you to stay way clear of the case. So say yes, I promise to stay out of it."

Claire squirmed in her chair. "Come on. I promise. That good enough?"

"For me, yes."

Meg came running into the house, then slowed down to a

walk when she saw Bruce. She came up to the table and leaned against her mother, watching Bruce, tugging at her lower lip. Claire pressed her lips together and shook her head, signaling Bruce to keep his mouth shut.

"Hi, Meg." Bruce lifted a big hand and gave her a small wave. He bent his head down to be closer to the girl.

Claire pulled Meg's hand away from her mouth and said, "Say hi to Bruce."

"Hi to Bruce," Meg said and burst into giggles.

Claire tousled her hair. "You goof." She pulled a leaf out of her hair. "Where have you been, my dear? Rolling around on the ground?"

"You've grown about three inches since I last saw you." Bruce looked at her admiringly.

"Four," Meg stated.

Claire nodded over her head and said, "She's in that correcting phase. She never goes along with anything."

"That's not true, Mom. Sometimes I agree with you."

"See what I mean?"

"How is school?" Bruce leaned down as if to hear her answer.

Meg cupped her hands around her mouth and shouted as if he were deaf. "School's fine. I like it."

"Meg, stop being a jerk. Say something nice to Bruce."

"So are you going to stay and have dinner with us?" Meg put her hands on her hips and flirted with Bruce.

Bruce shrugged. "I don't know. Haven't been asked."

Claire hugged her daughter and said, "That'd be nice. Why don't you stay? I don't think it will be anything fancy. Pasta and salad. That might be kinda hard on your digestion—doesn't it require at least a hamburger a day?"

"I already ate it for lunch. I'd love to have dinner with you two charming ladies. I can't stay too late. I've got a busy day tomorrow. Hey, Meg, did you see anything that day that your dad was killed?"

Meg didn't say anything but turned her head up to look at her mom.

"You have any homework to do, Meg?"

"Just math. It's a cinch."

"Well, go do it." Claire shooed her out of the room, then turned and glared at Bruce. She found she was having trouble breathing, both from fear and from anger. "Don't push it, Bruce. Let me decide this in my own way. You know better than that."

THE WOODS SHELTERED him, cool and quiet, the way his mother's hand had felt on his forehead when he was sick as a child. Rotting leaves smelled rich to him, like most wonderful pleasures: cigars, chocolate, a good cognac. They all had that fermenting thick taste. Rich bent and searched and found what he was looking for again and again on the forest floor. The dark sponges, like alien creatures, poked their heads up through the leaves. When his eyes became attuned to them, they appeared under logs and in low places, under his foot as he was about to put it down.

This was his treasure in the early spring; no money could buy such a luxury. He cut their stems neatly, hoping not to injure the living spore beneath them. The morels were one of the many reasons he didn't want any more development coming in down here. Big houses, long driveways, people cutting down trees, mowing their lawns with riding lawn mowers; and with each acre they took, more of the wildness was gone.

When his bag was full, he turned back toward the road and tried not to watch the ground as carefully. He could take no more. He would come back tomorrow and gather them again.

After his long walk in the woods, Rich decided to swing by Claire's house on his way home. He would present her with some of his bounty. A good way to begin to woo her. He would take Stuart's advice. He would take it slow. He would simply be friendly and stop in from time to time. The same way he had tamed the little sparrow hawk he had caught one spring when he was thirteen. Consistent and calm, he worked on that bird, bringing it food. He laughed when he thought of that. Yes, he would feed Claire. Goodies from the woods. Veggies from his garden— the asparagus would be pushing up soon. Pheasants when they were mature. Then, one night, he would invite her for a meal. He was a good cook. He would ply her with delicacies. She would fall into his arms.

He turned up her road and saw that a red Taurus was in the driveway. Maybe a friend from town. Rich thought of just driving by, but he forced himself to stop. If he put it off, there might never be a good time. Plus, he had more morels than he could possibly eat himself. He wasn't ready to dry any; they would be plentiful for another week or two if the rain fell as it should.

He pulled his truck up behind the fiery red car and jumped out, grabbing his basket. He walked around to the back and knocked on the door. A young girl answered it. "Another man, Mom."

"Hi," Rich said.

The girl stood one foot on top of the other and said, "Hi. I've seen you."

"You have?"

"We drive by your house on the way to school. You have all those birds."

"That's right. My name is Rich. What's your name?" He reached down to shake her hand.

She looked at his hand, then gently placed hers inside of it.

"My full name is Margaret. But no one calls me that, except Mom when she's mad."

"What should I call you?"

"You can call me Felicity. I like that name."

"Meg." Claire walked up behind the small girl and dropped her hands on the thin shoulders. "Hi, Rich. What have you got there?"

Rich held up his basket. His offering didn't look as luscious as it had in the woods. When he looked back up to explain to Claire what was in his basket, he saw a man in dress pants walk up behind her and stare down at the basket. "Morels."

"Oh, great."

Rich could tell from her voice that she didn't know what they were. "Do you like mushrooms?"

"Yes, sure I do." Claire reached down and picked one up. "They look like a confection."

The big man looked at them and said, "They look like larvae."

Meg poked at them. "I've seen them before. I feed them to my dolls."

"So you're already a morel hunter?" Rich wished he could disappear. Why had he stopped by? It seemed obvious to him now that Claire already had someone in her life. Some big lug. "Well, I just thought you might like a few."

"I'd love some." Claire motioned back to the man. "Bruce, this is Rich. He's a neighbor. Rich, this is Bruce. He and I worked together in the cities."

"Can human beings eat them?" Meg asked, holding one up.

"Yes, if they wash them and cook them in garlic and butter."

"I'm making pasta. Would they go with that?"

"Perfect. Do clean them well and cut them in half." He handed her the basketful. "I hope you enjoy them."

Claire nodded. "I'll drop the basket by in the next day or two."

"No hurry." He looked at the mother and daughter standing in the doorway, with the man in shadow behind them. Oh, what did he have to lose? "I'll put the coffee on for you. Bye, Felicity."

HE COULD HEAR Claire upstairs, talking quietly to Meg. She had been up there a long time already, putting her to bed. It was quite a ritual: the pajama selection, the bedtime story, arranging the covers on the bed, the kisses and last wishes of the day. He had even been included, asked to bring Meg a small glass of water.

By the time Claire came down from upstairs, Bruce had finished up the dishes for her. She didn't even have a dishwasher down here, had to wash her dishes by hand. What was she doing living in the country? Tonight, he was going to leave as soon as she came down. He wouldn't outstay his welcome. They had had a nice time tonight. She seemed more relaxed around him, like old times.

"Oh, thanks, Bruce, you didn't have to do the dishes." But the smile on her face told him how pleased she was that he had thought of it.

"Good way to get your hands clean." He didn't want that mushroomy smell left on his fingers. He had eaten several of the morels just to please Claire. She had seemed to like them tremendously. He couldn't quite see it himself. They tasted funky to him, like they'd been left out of the refrigerator too long.

"I suppose there's quite a few gays down here," he remarked, thinking of the guy who had come to the door.

"Sure, this is kind of a haven for them." Claire tossed her hair back.

"That explains Rich and his mushrooms, huh?" Bruce laughed.

Claire stopped and tilted her head back. "No, I think he just likes good food."

He was putting his foot in his mouth. Time to go. "Well, Claire, I should head out." Bruce picked up his suitcoat and started to put it on. Claire was watching him, then moved toward him. Gently, she wrapped her arms around his waist and laid her head on his chest. He held his breath and held her shoulders in his hands as if they were breakable. He didn't want to squeeze too hard. He didn't want the moment to end.

Her voice was muffled in his shirt when she said, "You are a rock, Bruce. I know I can always count on you. Thanks." Then she stepped back, and he let her go. He needed to let her call the shots, or he would get noplace.

"Thanks for dinner. Let me know what you decide about Meg."

"Yeah, I'll be in touch."

Bruce turned, walked out the door, and then stopped. "You think you're safe down here, but I'm not so sure."

17

Darla sat in her car on the street in front of Landers' house and remembered better days. She cracked the window so any errant breeze could float in if it felt like it. There was a warmth in the air they hadn't known in months. Spring had settled on the town. She looked over at Landers' garden. Daffodils and tulips were pushing up. He did love his plants. They were pretty, and if you gave them the right amount of water and sun, they grew the way you wanted them to.

Landers had always loved pretty things.

Darla remembered when she had been pretty. Twenty-five and finally come into her own. She had grown up the sixth child in a large farm family. When she was little, her mother had had no time for her. She had always worn hand-me-downs. But that year she had moved away from the small Wisconsin town she had grown up in and gone to live in Wabasha. She lived in a boardinghouse and worked at the dime store. She sewed most of her clothes, copying the patterns from the magazines she bought at work. That had been the one gift she had received from her mother—learning to sew.

One night she went to a dance— the Joe Plummers Orchestra was in town—and she had done her hair in waves and was wearing a new dress she had made. She was dancing with some guy, and Landers cut in. He was a swell dancer. With him, she felt like Ginger Rogers. His hands maneuvered her any way he wanted her to go. A few dates later, his hands had had their way with her in the back seat of his old Ford, parked on a country road. The year was 1941.

Then he invited her home to meet his family. She felt certain that things were getting serious between them. But when he picked her up, he told her he had enlisted in the army. He was shipping out in a week. He drove her to his folks' house and introduced her to his brother, Fred. Asked Fred to keep an eye on her for him while he was gone.

Fred was five years younger than both Darla and Landers. He was cute in his own slow way. Thoughtful. He had really looked up to her and respected her. Fred's devotion became more and more important to Darla when she didn't hear from Landers. He wrote his mother dutifully once a week; Mrs. Anderson would show her the letter. He hadn't even gone overseas yet but was still stationed at Camp Adair in Oregon. Darla wrote him dozens of letters, but never got one back from him.

Once, after he had come back, when she was already married to Fred, she brought it up, asked him why he had never answered her letters. He looked at her kindly and said, "I thought it was better for you if we had a clean break. That way you could get on with your life."

Darla hated him when he said that. She wanted to describe to him what her life had been like at that time, but she decided never to let him know. That would be her revenge.

She persuaded Fred to move away from Fort St. Antoine after that conversation. But after fifteen years of traveling from town to town, Fred unable to keep a job, she gave in when he asked if they could finally go back home. He had written to Landers, who had then offered him a job working at his clothing store. The two brothers had inherited an uncle's farm, so Fred and Darla and their son finally had a place to live. Darla was forced to come back to Lake Pepin and to live near Landers Anderson the rest of his life.

She rubbed her forehead. Eighty-one wasn't bad if you didn't look in a mirror, if you didn't push yourself too hard, if you had a drink or two every night. Fred had just gotten the news from the lawyer that they were inheriting everything that Landers owned. A wave of relief flushed over her. At last, it would all be hers. She and Fred would have money. Maybe Fred would have time to spend some of it. She felt like she didn't have much life left in her, but maybe she was wrong.

Darla had decided that for fun, she would come over here and rummage around in her new house. Look through everything. See what she would see. Who knows what she might find? After all, it was hers now. She could do whatever she wanted to with it. Make a huge bonfire of the photograph albums that documented Landers and his wife's life together.

The two of them had seemed so happy, but it hadn't lasted long after she and Fred moved back to town. Darla had seen to that. Landers never knew what had hit him. She had had a long talk with his wife, Eva, revealing how Landers had deserted her. She laid it on thick, as they used to say. After that, relations had been strained between Landers and Dorothea. Dorothea had died five years later of emphysema, and Darla had been glad to see her go.

She should be gloating, she should be doing a jig with glee. Instead she just felt tired. The sun warmed her where she sat behind the wheel of her car. She'd go into the house in a few minutes. She had been so careful about her secret and now she sat and wondered if that might not ruin everything.

WHEN CLAIRE WALKED out of her house to go to work, she looked over and saw Darla Anderson climbing out of her car. Claire had never seen Darla move so slowly. What was the matter with her? A few days ago when Claire had gone to see her, Darla had been bustling around, cleaning her house. Maybe her arthritis was acting up, or maybe she knew she shouldn't be heading toward Landers' house, and so she was trying to act nonchalant. Whatever it was, Claire ran over to stop her.

She caught up with Darla right at the garden gate. "You can't go in there."

Darla tossed her head up and said, "Oh, yes, I can. I own this place."

That surprised Claire enough that she let Darla get through the gate, but then she pushed after her. "What do you mean by that?"

"We checked with Landers' lawyer. He left no will, so everything is ours. We're the closest of kin." Darla pointed at herself. "We own this house and all the land. So, who knows, we might be neighbors."

"Well, that may be, but this property is still off-limits."

"Until when?" Darla asked.

Claire shook her head. "That's hard to say. I will ask the sheriff what he thinks when I go into work today." Claire knew that she could let Darla into the house if she wanted to, but the idea of this little old lady digging around in Landers' possessions disturbed her. Besides which, she would have to stand there and watch as Darla rifled through the place. She didn't have time to do that this morning. Claire made a note to herself to leave work early today and do some final digging around before she turned the house over to Fred and Darla.

"What if I told you I had to get something in the house?" Darla cocked her head like a robin.

"Then I'd tell you it would have to wait." Claire took a good look at Darla. Something was crooked about her—literally crooked. Then Claire saw that Darla's hair wasn't on straight. Darla must be wearing a wig. Not so surprising; many older women weren't happy with the quantity of hair that grew off their head and supplemented it. Claire had to resist the impulse to reach over and tug the wig straight, but she knew from experience that any patronizing motion would not be appreciated.

"There's none of that yellow police ribbon around here saying stay out." Darla waved at the house.

"We don't always use that. With me living right across the street, it's pretty easy to keep an eye on the place."

"Have you had your eye on the place?"

Claire looked at her, puzzled. "What do you mean?"

"It's a nice piece of land, isn't it? You were getting awful chummy with Landers."

"We were friends, but I have more than enough land to keep myself busy, thank you anyway." Darla came off sounding jealous. Claire wondered if she had been drinking, but Darla didn't seem tipsy and it was not even nine o'clock. Then Claire remembered what Mrs. Langston had told her about Darla and Landers. "I just learned that you and Landers dated before you married Fred."

Darla grew rigid. She wouldn't look at Claire. "Who told you that?"

"A neighbor."

"Gossip. That's all it is. I did meet Fred through Landers, but that's all."

Claire stood there, waiting for Darla to head back to her car, but Darla stood still, staring at the house. Finally, Claire touched her arm and said, "I need to get to work. I'll walk you back to your car."

Darla's head spun around, and she laughed at Claire. "Boy, you really don't trust me, do you?"

"Just doing my job."

Darla pulled away from Claire's touch and continued to head up the walk. Claire watched as she stepped off the path and then bent down and picked a bright yellow daffodil. She spun it around in her fingers and then came back toward Claire.

Darla held the daffodil up high, like it was a queen's scepter, and as she walked past Claire, she said quietly, "Mine."

HER DAY OFF. That was why she was still sleeping in bed and felt swallowed up by it. Bridget had woken up briefly when Chuck had left early this morning; his soft kiss on her cheek felt like permission to keep sleeping, and she had gone under again. She rolled her head on the pillow and cracked an eye open. Even without her contacts in, she could see the clock face. The little hand was on the ten, and the big one pointed at the six. She blinked. Ten-thirty. The shock of it made her sit up in bed. What was the matter with her? She felt her own forehead. Cool and dry. She hadn't slept this late since before pharmacy school. Usually by this time of day, she had eaten and gone for a ride.

Bridget lifted up the front of her nightgown and looked down. Her breasts seemed bigger already. Was that possible? She had studied drugs for over four years of her life, and never had she heard that the hormones of a pregnant woman took on the characteristics of Valium, aspirin, and baking soda all rolled into one.

After a rather long shower, she pulled herself together. She tied her hair up on top of her head, put some makeup on, and dressed. Leaning over to tie the laces of her shoes, she decided she had to tell Chuck. He needed to know. She would walk into the shop and invite him out for coffee. Before she told him, she would first cover his lips with her fingertips and say, "Don't talk now. I want you to have time to think about this. So go back to work, and we'll discuss what we're going to do tonight."

She slipped on the stud pearl earrings he had given her for their anniversary. He loved her. She loved him. They would figure it out. It seemed impossible to her now that he shouldn't know something that so completely concerned him. But then he hadn't noticed when she wasn't hungry last night, or how listless she had been lately, not having the energy to stay up past the evening news.

When she climbed in her car, she gave a longing look to the barn. She would ride Jester this afternoon. She would whisper in his ear that she was pregnant, that she might have a baby, see what he would think of that. If this were the day to tell everyone, she would even give Claire a call. Get it all over with at once. Let the proverbial cat out of the bag. Her stomach jolted inside of her as she drove down the road.

By the time she got to the service station, Bridget was having second thoughts. Maybe she should wait and tell Chuck at dinner. She could even try to cook dinner, something simple like pork chops and potatoes. Oooh, her stomach turned at the thought of food.

When she walked into the shop, Chuck scooted out from under a car on a piece of plywood on wheels. She waved, and he gave her two fingers up, which meant give me two seconds. He went back under the car. She wondered what he was doing down there and how he could stand digging around in the underbellies of vehicles day after day. He was like a doctor, only in surgery a doctor stood above the patient and was very pristine and got paid enormous amounts of money. When Bridget went to pharmacy school, she thought there was a good chance she'd end up married to a doctor. And she had— a car doctor.

Suddenly, she didn't feel so good. The floor wobbled in front of her, and then her stomach turned over. She clutched her belly, swallowed hard, and ran to the bathroom. Pushing the door open, she bolted to the nearest stall, not even bothering to close the door behind her. There was not time. She vomited as soon as she was standing in front of the toilet bowl.

An older woman leaning over the bathroom sink, applying makeup, gave a loud groan. Without even turning around, she said, "I've had five kids, and I threw up through every pregnancy. Good luck, kid. It's only the beginning." Then she walked out.

Bridget dragged herself away from the toilet and cleaned herself up. She decided against putting on any more lipstick. Didn't seem like a good idea. She didn't feel like going out to coffee with Chuck right now.

She would walk out and tell him she stopped by to say hi and go back home. She would tell Chuck tonight, in the privacy of their own home. If she felt good enough this afternoon, she would drive over to talk to Claire, ask her what she was in for the next eight months of her life.

"HOW'S THE MOREL season shaping up?" Stuart asked Rich as they both sidled up to the bar at the Fort. The Fort St. Antoine Café was open seven days a week, sixteen hours a day.

You could buy a box of Band-Aids, rent a video, play a game of pool, or order a shot of whiskey. At least a couple of days a week, Stuart and Rich would meet there for a late-afternoon brew, after Stuart was done baking.

"Pretty good. I made the mistake of dropping off a basket of morels for Ms. Claire Watkins," Rich said.

"How could that be a mistake?" Stuart thought for a second and then answered his own question. "Oh, I bet she doesn't like morels. Not everyone likes them. My mom has never cared for them."

"No, I think she liked the morels fine. But it appears she also likes someone else."

This stopped Stuart for a moment, then he asked incredulously, "Who? Someone from around here?"

"No. This guy named Bruce. Her old partner. He was over for dinner. Looked at my morels like they were a bunch of old condoms."

Stuart threw his head back and laughed. "There is a resemblance."

"You know anything about this guy? Bruce something, didn't get his last name?"

"No, and that should tell us something. You know, I've got my ear to the grapevine, and I haven't heard a peep about Claire seeing anybody."

"Maybe she goes up to town."

"No, she doesn't. I'd know that too."

"God, what have you heard about me?"

"I don't need the grapevine for that. You just come and spill the beans yourself."

"That's true." Rich waved over the bartender. "She sure has got a cute little girl. She answered the door last night."

"Meg?"

"Yes. Insisted her name was Felicity."

"Yeah, she's a sweetheart. I think Claire'd do just about anything for her. You should get to know her."

"Meg?"

"Sure. You know—get an in to the mother through the daughter."

"Not my style."

The bartender took their order. When he delivered their two beers, he asked, "So you heard who's going to get all of Landers Anderson's land?"

"Nope. Haven't heard a peep," Rich told him.

"No big surprise. Fred gets it all, because Landers died intestate."

Stuart looked at the bartender in surprise, then protested, "I heard he died of a heart attack."

"In-test-ate. It's not a disease. Haven't you ever heard that before? It simply means you died without making a will."

Stuart laughed at the bartender's lecture, saying, "I get it. I get it. How do they determine who gets what?"

"Each state has a system to figure that out, some kind of game plan," the bartender explained. "I think first it goes to your spouse; if you have no spouse, it goes to your kids; no kids, goes to your parents; then siblings, then aunts and uncles. Down the line of your relatives. You get the picture.

"All Landers has got is Fred and Darla. Kinda too bad, because they'll just sell it to that development." The bartender pointed to a poster that was pinned to the bulletin board. Beneath an announcement of a tractor pull and a farm auction was an old notice for the town meeting about the new development.

Rich stood up and swigged the last of his beer. "I gotta go. Pheasants to feed."

When he got to the door, Rich reached over, pulled the poster about the development down, and stuffed it in his pocket. He would certainly make an attempt to get that land so it couldn't be developed. He'd have to give it a try. Maybe Claire could help him out.

18

Claire thought of the morel mushrooms while she stared at the floor of the county jail. It was her day on jail rotation, but she only had to stay another hour. A drunk driver was sobering up in the back cell. She could heard him snoring, and the noise sounded like he was grinding through the brick wall. As soon as the next officer relieved her at the jail, she planned to go over to Landers' house and look through it more thoroughly. Having finished her paperwork, read the two daily papers, even completed the crossword puzzle, she was staring at the floor and thinking.

The oil blotches on the cement floor reminded her of the spongelike appearance of the morels. The gift of the morels had surprised and pleased her. A man bringing her the bounty of the land. A strong man with good intent offering her what he had found in the forest. There was something wonderfully romantic about it, and just basically good.

She had found the morels strong and earthy, rich and warm. What did they taste like? How to describe a taste? Like anchovies without the salt, like chocolate without the sweet, but not bitter

either. An undelicate delicacy. Bruce had hated them. He tried
to hide the fact; he even ate them all, but she could tell by the
way he let them sit in his mouth before he swallowed. Bruce was
pretty much a meat-and-potatoes guy, didn't even like ordinary
mushrooms.

She didn't know what Rich was, what he liked to eat, what
he liked to do. She knew so little about him. On one hand, she
found that exciting, but on the other, it scared her. She was a cop;
she knew how weird people could turn out to be. Rich had strong
opinions about what was happening down on the river. Not everyone liked him. But Stuart and he were best friends, and Stuart
seemed like a good guy.

She also had to admit that it had been good to see Bruce last
night and spend some quiet time with him. When they'd met at
the bar in Red Wing the time before, he had stormed off, angry
at her because she didn't want to resume her affair with him. In
their long partnership together, she had watched him go through
so many women. She didn't want to be one of them. She knew
that if they had continued to be lovers and he had dropped her
like all the rest, they would never be friends again. Not a good
way to lose someone.

Claire knew she should never have slept with Bruce the one
time. Right after her husband's death, rather than shutting down,
she had opened up to everything. She wanted to catch the men
who had killed her husband and kill them herself. Shoot them or
strangle them. Anger coursed through her like mercury pushing
skyward in a tube. Hot summer. Bruce had been the only person
in the world she had trusted. She wanted him to work as hard as
he could to catch the guy. In some odd, twisted way, she thought
if she slept with him, he would leave their conjugal bed and bring
her the head of the murderous man on a platter with breakfast
and a rose.

The truth was that when she woke in the morning, she had a great fear that she would lose the only other man she loved by sleeping with him. She had deeply loved Steve. She would always love him. Guilt overwhelmed her, as if by loving Bruce too she had caused Steve's death. She had cut the affair short. Let it go no further. Bruce had been angry, but he kept speaking to her. And last night he was relaxed and pleasant, hadn't put the move on her at all. Maybe she could let down her defenses a bit.

Now, if he would only do the impossible and catch the killer and put him behind bars, she could get on with her life, however she wanted it to be, whoever she wanted to have in it with her.

The phone rang next to her elbow, and she answered, "Jail, Claire."

"Informative." Sheriff Talbert's voice growled over the line. "Listen, it's fine if you want to give Anderson's place one more going-over. I did check with the lawyer, and the brother has inherited the place. So when you're done there, you can let them do what they will."

"You don't think we should keep it under lock and key a little longer? This man was murdered, and who knows what might be hidden in the house."

The sheriff was silent, then he said, "I think this whole case might be a lot easier than you're making it. Maybe someone accidentally killed Anderson."

"Then why didn't the person report it?"

"Scared, not sure what happened, who knows?"

"What if I find something?"

"Like what?"

"A will. A letter. A threat."

Sheriff Talbert harrumphed. "We'll deal with that if it comes up."

After the phone call, Claire got up and walked down to the

end of the cell block. The drunk stirred as she approached him. Without even appearing to wake, he rolled up and stared at her from a sitting position. Maybe he had just been pretending to sleep, but that snoring had been awfully real.

"Keep waking myself up with my snoring," he said. He sounded fairly sober. There was no detox center out in this little Wisconsin town, so they kept the drunks overnight, and if they didn't have a friend in the police department they were charged with reckless driving.

"How are you feeling?"

"Worse than bad." He held his head in his hands and slowly moved it back and forth. "Wish I had never had that last drink."

"You might want to think before drinking the first one next time."

"Is the lecture free?"

"Just part of the package deal, here at Club Jail."

"Wish you'd go away." He curled back up in a ball on his bunk.

Claire walked toward the desk. Her mom used to tell her, "Wish in one hand, spit in the other, and see which gets full first." Claire had quit wishing a while ago. Funny all the things you wish for when your life goes along in a rut, but when calamity explodes in your face and the ground drops from beneath your feet, you wish, you beg to be back in the rut—the feel of solid earth, the same road to take every day, the calm that comes from knowing that the worst you fear is boredom.

ONE OF THE things Red liked about cocaine was it made him see better, he thought, sitting in the borrowed pickup truck. He could see it all: the roads covered with leftover sand from winter, the grass dry and brown, the trees waving their empty limbs like a bunch of old ladies. He took a last puff on his cigarette and tossed it out the side window.

He hadn't driven down to the school today, now that he knew the routine. The little girl either got off the bus or she didn't. If she did, he was parked halfway up the hill she climbed to get to her baby-sitter's. He'd pop out of the car at the right moment, say the right words, and she would be his. Then he'd make sure she could tell no one what she had seen when his truck hit her father.

Nobody was around in this podunk town. Streets were empty. Made his job all the easier. Out here in the boonies, people still left their doors unlocked. He bet he could walk into half the houses in town without breaking a window. 'Course, once he got in, there wouldn't be much there to steal. Unless you were in the antique business. Not him; in his youth he had done a bit of the sleight-of-hand, taking cash, jewelry, small TVs, and stereos. Now he'd go for computers and CD players. Glad he was out of that racket. Nickel-and-dime business. Now he was into the real money.

Coke was where it was at as far as he was concerned. Hardly touched the stuff himself, but he had done a bit today. Thought a little extra energy would help with this job. He could feel it pulsing in him. When he took it, whatever he was doing made sense. He never doubted himself. Great drug. Perfect drug to retail. He had been hearing about these factories where naked women filled glass vials with the white stuff. They kept 'em naked so they couldn't steal any. He had to see that sometime. A roomful of naked women. Just thinking about it got his bone pushing at his pants.

He usually traveled to Miami to get the stuff, then sold it in the Twin Cities. That was his market, didn't want to lose it. That's why he didn't want to relocate. Hawk tells him to get out of town for a year, just too long. Can't stay away from the suppliers that long. He managed to get someone to cover him for a good chunk of time, but now he was back and he was staying back. Hawk was putting the twist on him, telling him they needed him to relocate again. Now, if it was Miami, that would be one thing, but he was talking Kansas City. Cow town. Not his idea of a move up in the world. He'd just as soon stay put and rake in the money they were making in North Minneapolis. He knew the territory. He needed to take care of that guy. He was getting fucking bossy, and Lord knows he was ready for a fall.

Here came the bus. The angle he had set his side mirror at allowed him to see it perfectly. He was slouched down in the seat, so from the road it would look like the truck was empty. The little girl, Meg, waves to the driver as she steps off the bus. Then she trips and sends her books flying. Takes her a moment to collect them all. He can see her in the side mirror. Skipping up the hill. Where do kids get all their energy? He'd take some of the stuffing out of her. Maybe take her to Chicago with him. Go see if he could find the naked ladies. Maybe he could apprentice her off for slave labor.

She was steps away when he made his move. He swung his door open and said, "Hey, Meg, your mom told me to come and get you."

She smiled up at him and took another step. Suddenly the smile vanished. Her eyes dilated, and her mouth opened. She dropped her books again. But this time she didn't pick them up. She ran.

"Shit." Red let the word slide out under his breath as he scrambled out of the truck. By the time he was on the street, she was nearly to the top of the hill.

Red took off after her. She ran like a deer and had quite a start on him. He tried to reassure her. "Hey, hold on. Your mom said I'm supposed to take you home. Give me a chance to explain."

She turned for a moment and looked at him, then ran faster. What was the matter with her? Usually the word *mom* soothed any child. The gravel spun beneath his feet as he dug in and tried to catch her. This hill was fucking steep, and he was wearing these goddamn cowboy boots. He had to grab her before she got to the neighbor's house.

Red ran toward the house, and the little girl veered off. She ducked into a grove of trees, and he followed. She sprinted through the tree trunks, and he was gaining on her when suddenly a branch loomed out of nowhere and caught him under the chin. Gulleted. He went down on his side and heard her running. He couldn't yell, wanted to attract no one's attention. Pushing himself up, he ducked low as he rose and barreled ahead. At the other side of the trees was a field, stubble from corn breaking the soil. He stopped in his tracks and scanned the area.

Shit, she was gone. It was like the earth swallowed her up. Where was there for her to go? She had run out into the field and now she was gone. He took several steps back into the shadow of the trees. Squatting down, he kept his eyes scanning. She was someplace. She would move, and he would see her. He was between her and all the houses. There was only the field, the woods, and the bluff rising up to the sky. She couldn't climb that. He had her cornered; now he'd just have to wait her out. He couldn't let her go. If he did, he'd never get another chance at her. And this time, there was no question that she had seen him.

MEG COULD SEE two ants trying to pull a leaf over a branch. She watched them for a few seconds, and then she knew she needed to move. He had fallen in the trees, and she had climbed down into the ditch that skirted the field and led to the woods. That's where she needed to get to, the woods that hugged the bluff.

She pushed herself up into a crawling position and moved forward slowly, knee by knee. Her socks were ruined, her dress was ripped. Tears fell from her eyes and hit the leaves below her. What if one hit an ant, she wondered, would it be like a huge storm?

She knew who that man was. He had red hair, and he had a wild look in his eyes. The wild look was from killing a person. Once you killed a person, you could never get that look out of your eyes. It was like a badge you always had to wear, and she had seen it. She knew he was the man who had run down her father. And now he was after her, probably wanted to kill her too.

Meg kept crawling forward, slowly and quietly, as low to the ground as she could be. The sides of the ditch were grown up with ragweed and cockleburs. She hated those things; they scrunched up your clothes permanently if they got tangled in them. But Meg had given up on what she was wearing. She could not save herself and take care of her clothes, so she had to forget about her clothes. It was, as her mom told her, knowing your priorities.

She couldn't let the man catch her, because he was mean and there was no telling what he would do with her. But also, her mom wouldn't be able to handle it. Meg was all her mom had left in the world, so she had to stay okay.

Meg could see the woods if she tilted her head up so she was getting close. Right before the woods, there was a little opening that she would have to run through. She would have to stand up in a crouch and scoot along the ground. She reached the end of the ditch. The weeds still grew up to the woods, but they wouldn't completely hide her.

Meg thought back to the movies. She kicked off her shoes and pulled off her white socks, then put her shoes back on. Her sweater was green, and that might camouflage her. She rubbed her face with dirt.

Even if he saw her, she still had a good chance to make it to the fort. If she got to the fort, she would be all right. She could go into her secret hiding place, and he would never find her. She knew because she had looked at it from the outside, and it was completely concealed.

Meg felt her heart scrambling around inside her chest like a chipmunk. Maybe she should roll. Very slowly roll her way to the woods. She inched out of the ditch and lay like a corpse on the ground. She heard nothing. Facing the sky, she could see a plane leaving a white trail behind it. She wondered if anyone up there could see her down below, stretched out on the ground. Hansel and Gretel had left bread crumbs. Meg took off one of the barrettes she was wearing and left it in plain sight on the ground. Maybe her mom would find it.

Slowly, Meg began to roll toward the woods. Her dad and she would roll down this one hill by their old house together, they would have races, their hands tight against their sides, their feet held together, and she would laugh all the way down the hill.

Daddy, she thought in her mind, if you are looking down from heaven, don't let him get me. Daddy, save me. She rolled a little faster until she finally hit a tree. She was at the edge of the woods.

Meg slid up behind the tree and looked back over the field. She knew she shouldn't do that, that it would be better just to run, but she couldn't stop herself. She needed to see where he was. His red hair stood out like a woodpecker's crest. As her eyes found him, his head turned toward hers and he stepped out into the sunlight. She turned and ran through the dark trees.

❦ 19 ❧

Claire thought of picking up Meg from Ramah's while she searched Landers' house, but changed her mind. She didn't need another body tromping around inside this small house before she turned it over to Fred and Darla. It wouldn't look good if Meg played with something and broke it. Although that would never happen with her daughter, she thought with a chuckle.

Claire opened the door to Landers' house and smelled the disuse of it: food rotting in the fridge, stagnant water, old air. She carefully stepped on the mat inside the doorway and wiped her feet, then she stood still and looked around, a scan of the room before she moved into it.

She laughed again, thinking about Meg. No, her daughter was almost too perfect. Meg's room was always clean. Claire didn't know how that girl could slip out of her bed and have it look like she had never slept in it. Meg lined up her plastic horses along the top of her dresser. She folded her clothes a certain way. Meg actually picked up after Claire. Once Claire had told her not to dress her bed, it made her feel too guilty to come home to find her daughter had cleaned her room.

Claire stepped onto the linoleum floor and decided she might as well start with the kitchen. Not the obvious place to store secrets, but you never knew where someone might stick a letter or a note.

Even though it was her job to be in this house and rifle through all the drawers and boxes, Claire felt like an intruder. Maybe she was just being obstinate, trying to keep Darla and Fred out of this house one more day. She hadn't a clue what she was looking for. But it seemed to her there was a history that seamed through this murder, like a streak of gold that would lead to the answer.

She pulled out the first drawer next to the sink. Silverware in top drawer, lift up the silverware box. Nothing. Utensils in second drawer. Phone books in bottom drawer. She pulled those out and placed them on the table. They might be worth a look-through. She would come back to them.

After opening and closing all the cupboards in the kitchen, she moved on to the living room. Claire sat down on the floor and looked at the bookshelves. *The Tontine* by Thomas Costain, *Immortal Heart* by Irving Stone, the whole collection of Sandburg's biography of Lincoln. She pulled a couple of books off the shelves, held them by the front and back covers, and flipped the pages upside down. Nothing dropped out of the books.

Be methodical, she had been taught, when exercising a search warrant. Don't skip anything, because you won't get a second chance. She started on the top shelf and went down through the books. People stuck things in books. That was a fact. She remembered her grandmother kept a zillion newspaper clippings about her dad in the Bible. Report cards from school, the works.

An old photograph album was on the bottom shelf. Claire paged through it. The first few photos must have been from the late forties, after Landers got out of the service. He had a full head of dark hair and was a very handsome man. A wedding picture showed him in a nice suit and his wife in a dark fitted dress with a corsage pinned to her front. She wore a small velvet hat with a net that floated in front of her face, and had small heart-shaped lips. She was much smaller than Landers and looked frail beside his robustness.

Then there were pictures of the department store he owned in Wabasha and pictures of the house she was sitting in, but the trees were smaller, and it was painted a different color; the porch hadn't been added on yet.

Then she came to pictures of Fred and Darla. The date was printed on the side of the picture—1955. Darla had a wonderful full figure, and her hair was done up in a French twist. She looked smashing. Fred looked happy and goofy as ever. And Landers' wife was sitting on the edge of the picnic table with her hands folded and her hair in tight curls on her head. Right next to her sat a young boy with dark hair and glasses.

The last picture in the album made Claire sad—it was of Landers and his wife, just before she died. Eva sat on the couch with her arms folded over her body about a yard away from Landers. He had his arm along the back of the couch and was leaning toward her, but she was staring right at the camera. Her hair had gone completely white, and her face was set hard against him.

Claire went into the bedroom and decided it was time to toss it, so to speak. She lifted up the mattress and found an old comb. She went through the pockets of his suits in his closet and found money and gum, old Kleenex. Just what she might expect. She was running her hand under his underclothes in his dresser when she hit a piece of paper, tucked in a back corner. She pulled it out and found herself staring at the wide face of a handsome forty-year-old woman with light brown hair that she wore in waves around her face. She had quite a bit of makeup on, bright red lips. She reminded Claire of a movie star from the forties. But the photo didn't look that old; it looked quite recent. The colors were bright, not faded at all. At the bottom the photograph was signed, "To Landers, with love." No name.

Maybe this woman was why Landers' wife had hated him the last five years of his life. Maybe he had had an affair with this good-looking gal. Claire wondered if she could find out who the woman was. She didn't want to go around shoving the picture under people's noses. She certainly didn't want to be-smirch Landers' name unnecessarily. This woman certainly had nothing to do with his death—or did she? Claire would be discreet.

Almost done with her search, she looked through the draw-ers of his small desk, tucked into a corner. Checkbooks—she'd take them with her. Taxes—she'd glance through those too. You found out an awful lot about someone by reading their taxes.

Then she saw a small wastebasket shoved way under the desk, a few crumpled papers in it. She sorted through them—old cou-pons from the newspaper, check stubs—then found a document that had been torn into small pieces. She gathered the pieces up and put them into an empty envelope she found in the drawer. One scrap of paper caught her attention, and she smoothed it out on top of the desk. The word *quit* was printed on it. Worth piecing this back together to see what it had been.

She remembered a story a questioned-document examiner had told her about a woman found hanging from a tree out in the middle of a field. At first, they found nothing when examining the crime scene, but then someone noticed a small scrap of blue paper. Police gathered up all the torn pieces of blue paper, spread out over an acre of land. When the examiner pieced the letter back together, he found it was a Dear John letter. The woman's old lover had killed her and then torn up the letter she had sent him, tossing it to the wind.

Claire had ducked under the desk to see if she had gotten all the pieces when someone tapped at the front door. She jerked up, bumping her head on the underside of the desk. "Damnation," she said under her breath. Backing out carefully, she stood up and went to the door.

Ramah waited outside the door, her face sagging with worry.

Claire pulled the door open and asked, "Where's Meg?"

Ramah took a step backward and almost fell off the top step. "Oh, dear. I was afraid that's what you were going to say."

Claire grabbed the old woman by the arms. "What do you mean?"

"I haven't seen her."

Claire shook her. "You haven't seen her. Why didn't you call me?"

Ramah's eyes flew wide open, and she sputtered, "I did. You were gone. She didn't come to my house after school."

"Was she on the school bus?"

"I don't know." The old woman bent over, and now Claire found herself trying to hold her up as she began to cry. "I don't know."

"Did you check my house?"

"Yes, I walked over there, and there was no sign of her."

Claire couldn't take the time to comfort Ramah. Her daughter was missing. That was the only thing that mattered. "Did you call anyone?"

"Yes, I called Stuart. He said he'd go to the park."

"Yes, the park, maybe she went there to play." Claire didn't believe it for a moment, but she heard the words coming out of her mouth. "You go home and wait for her. Maybe she'll show up there. I'll run down to the park and see if Stuart's found anything."

Claire didn't wait to walk with Ramah but ran out of the yard and down the street. Her heart beat a horrible thunder in her chest. Not Meg, she prayed, not my baby.

She ran down the hill and saw a pile of books lying on the side of the road. She rushed over to them, and as she read the name, Meg, hand-printed in such perfect letters on the cover of the blue folder, she reached down and gathered them up.

Claire stood in the middle of the road with her daughter's schoolbooks in her arms, not knowing what to do. Then she knew—she would do everything possible to get her daughter back. She walked over to the side of the road and set the books down in the weeds, where they wouldn't get run over. She and Meg could come and get them later, when all this was over.

THE WIND CAME in off the lake, a brisk wind that whipped up the waves and blew the warmth from the air. Gulls were wheeling in the soft blue sky. Rich looked at the color and thought of how thin Wisconsin air was; not much of the golden color of the sun was held in the atmosphere. The sky was a true blue, the clouds were a solid white, and the gull he watched formed a slight apostrophe as it turned and plunged downward.

Rich looked around and saw no little girl. He and Stuart had split up to cover the park, but they were the only ones walking along the beach, stepping over cast-up driftwood and old tires. Stuart had walked down to the other end of the point, then circled around back and joined Rich.

"This was where I always ran away to. Did you know the steamboat used to land here? That was quite a scene," Rich told

Stuart as they stood along the shore of the lake. "Wonder what got into her, taking off. She doesn't seem like that kind of kid. Did you run away when you were a kid?"

"Yeah, a few times. Once I even made it to the airport by myself. I spent the afternoon watching planes take off and then called my mom with my last dime. Man, was she mad at me."

"God, Stuart, you don't even run away like a normal kid. You actually went to the airport."

Stuart kicked a piece of driftwood. "Well, I wanted to go to France, didn't I? What little fruitcake doesn't want to go to France?"

"I don't think she's down here. You can't walk any farther along the beach." They stood on the end of the sand beach. A gull screeched overhead.

Stuart cupped his hands and yelled, "Meg!"

Rich looked up the road toward town and saw Claire running toward them. He recognized her because she was still in uniform, and her hair was streaming behind her head like a black flag. She ran like someone was chasing her, but she was alone. When she stopped right in front of them, he could see her face was white, as if all color had leached out of it.

She gasped out, "Any sign of her?"

The two men shook their heads.

Claire took a deep breath and said, "We have to find her."

Stuart grabbed her and held her. "Claire, what's going on here?"

"See, this is bad," she blurted out.

"Meg's going to be fine. She probably went for a walk," Rich said to calm Claire down.

"No," Claire screamed. "She didn't go for a walk. Meg doesn't do that. She knows better."

Rich was stunned by the ferocity of her disclaimer.

"Her books, I found her books lying alongside the road. I think somebody's taken her."

"No, no one would do that." Stuart tried to reassure her.

At this, Claire forced herself to stand. "Oh, yes, they would."

"But why?"

"To get at me, to hurt me. They're killing my family."

BRUCE LISTENED TO Claire and almost didn't trust his voice. She had finally called him and was asking for his help. They would be working together again. Her voice held the shrillness of fear. He needed to make sure she was not going to do anything rash. "Where are you right now?"

"I'm in the Fort, that bar in town, using their phone. I can't think. I don't know what to do. I've called the sheriff. He's dispatching some guys down here, but—" Her voice broke. "Bruce, could you come down? Please. Help us find Meg. No one gets how important this is. They don't understand the danger Meg is in, but I know you do."

"I'm leaving right now. Stay in the vicinity. I'll find you." He thought for a second. "Have you talked to the bus driver yet?"

"No, he's still on his rounds. I've put a call through to his house. His wife said he'd call as soon as he got in."

Bruce knew Claire needed something to do, or she would lose it. Give her a task, he thought, any task that will keep her busy and make her feel like she is doing something to get Meg back. "That might be a place to start. See if you can locate him and ask him what he knows."

"Yes," Claire said, "yes, the bus driver. That's a good idea."

Bruce could hear she was panicking. She would be good for nothing if they lost her to that. He needed to snap her out of it. "Hey, anybody there with you?"

"Yes, some of the guys from town have been looking for her," Claire said faintly.

"Put one on, would you?"

A man's voice came on the line. "Yeah?"

"Who am I speaking with?"

"Rich Haggard."

"Listen, Rich, this is Bruce Jacobs, detective from the Cities. Claire's not in good shape right now."

"She's real upset."

"What you've gotta do is put a jacket on her, get her to eat something, and pour a couple cups of coffee down her throat. She's had a real shock to her system, and she needs some attention fast."

"Got it."

"I'll be down as fast as I can come, and that's pretty damn fast."

There was a pause, and then Rich said, "I don't doubt that," and hung up.

BRIDGET DROVE SLOWER than usual. She would be driving along and then look down at her speedometer and notice she was puttering along at forty-five miles an hour. How unlike herself she was these days. She usually pushed the edge of the speed limit into the low sixties.

After getting sick at the garage, she had gone home and taken a nap. When she woke up, she wasn't nauseous anymore, but she still didn't feel up to riding. After walking down to the paddock and feeding Jester an apple, she decided to hop in the car and go talk to Claire.

An eagle soared overhead. She slowed down and drove right underneath it. There was no one else on the road, so it didn't matter how slow she was driving. She leaned over the steering wheel and kept her eye on the bird. Going the same speed, she felt like she was drifting through the same air currents that were holding the bird aloft. That's how life could be sometimes, she decided. Don't fight, just glide in the air that comes your way. Finally the eagle tipped upward and headed up the bluff.

She pushed her right foot into the gas pedal and stared at the tops of the trees that grew along the slough in the delta of the Chippewa. She didn't know what kind of trees they were—after all, she was a pharmacist, not a botanist—but they were budding out red, and it was such a pretty sight. A haze of pink-red floated in the tops of the trees. She couldn't see it directly in any one bud, but taken together they were definitely red. Spring was coming, and she herself was blooming. At the moment, she liked that idea. But sometimes when she stared directly at it—at the fact that she was carrying a living fetus inside her—she felt as if she were looking into the Grand Canyon, and if she didn't watch it, that maw would swallow her alive.

Claire would know what she should do, although she wouldn't tell her what to do. She would just ask the right probing questions until Bridget saw clearly for herself the way her path lay. Claire was a good big sister. They had fought as children, and Claire had taken advantage of her, ignored her, and generally lorded over her, but once they had left the house, they had become best of friends.

Bridget drove into the small town of Fort St. Antoine and felt the rush of pleasure she always did that her sister was safely living there. She had been so glad when Claire had left the police force in Minneapolis and moved away from that big city. As she had told Claire, "Life just doesn't need to be that hard."

Bridget loved the old houses and the quaint storefronts. The town had managed to avoid the horrible disaster that occurred to many small towns—old buildings torn down to make room for new buildings—because the town went from being a prosperous town to nearly dying for about twenty years, until the artists and hippies had come into the town in the early eighties and restored the buildings without ruining them.

For a moment, Bridget was tempted to stop at the bakery for a doughnut and then slip into the bookstore, but she kept driving up the hill to Claire's house. Claire's car was in the driveway, so Bridget pulled in behind it. She stepped out of her car and gave a holler, but no one answered. She walked to the door and knocked. Nothing. She opened the door and stuck her head in and called out, "Anybody home?" No response. Maybe Claire had gone to get Meg or was running an errand. She couldn't be far, with the car right there.

Bridget decided to sit on the front step in the spring sun and get some more freckles on her face. She patted herself on the belly. A little vitamin D from the sun to help her baby grow. Maybe she could get used to this idea that something was living inside of her. The sun felt as if it were patting her all over her body in warm, gentle strokes.

As she was sunning herself, a pickup truck pulled up, and a guy yelled over to her, "Hey."

She waved and hollered "hey" back and then walked over to see what he wanted.

"You waiting for Claire?" the red-haired man asked.

"Yeah, you know where she is?"

"Yeah, she went down to the park. You want a lift down there?" he asked.

This was exactly what Bridget liked about a small town. Everybody knew everybody and everybody's business. Nosy as all getout, but she enjoyed it. "Sure, that'd be great."

Bridget opened the passenger-side door and swung herself up into the cab of the truck. "You live around here?" she asked.

"Ya, sure do," he said and pulled out onto the road.

"I'm Claire's sister," Bridget told him.

"I wondered. You don't look that much alike." He headed the car down the hill.

"Around the eyes we do." Bridget looked over at the man. "Your hair's even redder than mine. Mine's more blond. I suppose everyone calls you Red."

"That's right." He gave a little laugh. "You can call me Red if you like."

"Okay, Red, what's going on here?"

He looked at her sideways. "What do you mean?"

"Nothing, just what's Claire doing down in the park?"

"I'm not really sure. Something about looking for a kid."

"Oh, she's probably still working."

Red pulled up to the intersection of 35 and turned onto the main road. Bridget thought he was making a mistake; the town park was straight ahead. "Hey, the park is right down there." She pointed.

"Oh, she's not at that park."

"Is she at the pullover for the Fort?"

"Yeah, that's right." Red stepped on the gas, and Bridget sank back into the seat. She liked going fast, she just didn't seem to be able to do it anymore.

"Was there an accident?"

"Could be."

"You married, got any kids?"

He looked over at her and squinted. "What do you want to know that for?"

"I don't know. Most people your age have got kids." Now she wondered if everyone had them. She wanted to ask people about their children, if they made their life more full and wonderful.

"Nope, don't have any kids. Or at least none I know about."

Bridget looked over at him, and he was laughing at his joke. The joke kind of gave her the creeps. She didn't like the looks of his teeth. They didn't seem very well cared for. She glanced down at the speedometer and saw that he was going nearly seventy miles an hour.

"What're you in such a hurry for?"

"Got things to do."

"Is this out of your way, taking me to where Claire is? See, I didn't think she was this far, I just thought you were giving me a lift to the park."

"No prob."

When he didn't seem to be slowing down at the pullover, she pointed it out to him. "You can just drop me off."

"No, I'll pull in." He cut the wheel sharply and threw her against the side of the door.

When he stepped on the brake, she pitched forward. Bridget pushed herself off the dashboard and yelled at him, "What the hell do you think you're doing?"

He just smiled at her and wiggled something he had pulled out of his pocket and was holding in his lap. She dropped her eyes down to the black object, and it registered as a gun.

She was sitting in a pickup truck with a total stranger, and he was pointing a gun at her. It was a beautiful spring day with warm sunshine, and she had never been so scared in her life. "What do you want me to do?" she asked.

"Just do everything I tell you."

❦ 20 ❧

Darla walked up to her picture window and stopped, staring at the lake. Not blue today, more steel color. The ice had come off it only a few weeks ago, and it still surprised her to see open water. She was restless in the house, but couldn't go back over to Landers' yet.

They should never have asked Landers for anything. She should have known better, but Fred had thought he could win him over. She needed to get into his house and make sure that the police hadn't found the document. Maybe they would see it and not understand the significance of it, although that Claire Watkins knew a thing or two. City girl with a lot of training. Darla wondered what Claire thought had happened to Landers. And where was Fred? Was he off getting into trouble again?

Dr. Lord had called and given them the results of the autopsy. He hadn't said much, but she knew that man had never liked them. He would only give her the briefest of nods at church.

Darla sat down and picked up one of her beer can hats. She hated the damn things. Only started them because it gave her something to do with all the empty cans Fred had drunk up. That was before recycling. Maybe she should give up making them now. Nobody bought the stupid things at the church bazaar anymore.

The phone rang, and she grabbed it, thinking it would be Fred. "Hello?"

Silence, then a voice she hadn't heard in quite a while said, "Hi, Mom. Dad there?"

"Teddy, is it you?"

"Do you have another son I don't know about?"

She hated it when he was smart with her. A grown man and he still sassed back to his mother. When he talked to her at all. She answered stiffly, "What can I help you with?"

"I'd like to talk to Dad. Is he around?"

"Your father is out at present. Can I give him a message?"

"Just tell him I know what he's up to."

"Your father is not up to anything."

"Yes, he is. Anything you put him up to. It always comes back to you, doesn't it, Mom? You are the troublemaker, and Dad's the one who gets into trouble. Well, I'm onto both of you."

"Would you mind explaining that?" She searched her mind, trying to figure out how he could know anything.

"What a waste of breath that would be. First off, you know what I'm talking about, and second, it wouldn't do any good. I'll talk to you later." He hung up, and Darla held the phone in her hand a few moments after she heard the click, thinking maybe he would pick up again and they could start over. But she hung up the phone when she realized there would be no starting over for her. It was simply too late.

She remembered Ted so clearly when he was a young boy, about ten, when he still would hug his mom. He had soft blue eyes that changed color like the lake, and his skin was smooth and clear. He was a pretty boy and looked like her when she was little.

She had thought he was the most precious thing in the world. She would have done anything for him, and then it all changed.

It had started with that Rich Haggard and his comic books. She had found a pile of drawings and was shocked at what the two boys were up to. She saw pictures of humans embracing aliens; you couldn't even tell the sex of many of the creatures they drew. It appalled her that those two boys could even dream up half the stuff they had written about. Didn't take her a second to split the two of them up, but by then the damage was done to her sweet boy. And he never forgave her. Not for that or any of the differences between them that followed.

Darla walked into the bathroom and stood and faced herself in the mirror. She needed to put some lipstick on. Her skin looked like an old piece of cowhide. This new wig was losing its pluck. She licked her lips and pushed her hair around. It was no good. She was having worse than a bad hair day. Maybe if someone had loved her, she wouldn't be such a nasty old woman.

WHEN CLAIRE WALKED up to her house with Stuart and Rich and saw Bridget's car in the driveway, her heart lifted. To have her sister by her side would help. Bridget would understand. She loved Meg too. Claire knew it was Bridget's day off, and she had probably decided on the spur of the moment to come down for a visit. But when they all went into the house, Bridget was nowhere to be found. Where had she gone to? Probably down into town, and she'd show up in a few minutes.

Stuart helped himself to a drink of water from the tap. Claire felt Rich watching her. She knew her body was moving in a different way. Over the months, she had begun to relax in this village in the country, but now she felt herself falling back into her rigid pose, holding it all in. She kept her arms tight to her body, her fists clenched, her shoulders pushed forward, her chest tucked in, her face empty. The only way to move through the world after you had been assaulted was without points or rumples, or things would catch you up and you'd never escape the pain. Claire knew. There was no way she could explain any of this to Rich, for that would be too big an extension of herself. She needed to stay tight and tucked in.

Rich said, "We've got something here." Claire's heart pounded as she saw him pointing to the front yard. Claire spun on her foot and looked out the front window. No sign of Meg, and then she saw what Rich had pointed at—the bus.

Claire watched the big orange school bus pull up in front of the house and wished with all her heart that her daughter would step off the vehicle. She remembered a couple winters ago a little boy had fallen asleep at the back of the bus and had missed his stop. No one knew he was back there, and it had been twenty below zero. But the bus driver had done his job. When his shift was over and he had pulled the bus into the parking lot, he had gotten out of his seat and walked down the aisles, looking for anything the children might have left behind, before he got off the bus. And so he found the small boy, curled up in the back, and probably saved the boy's life.

Meg liked her bus driver. Claire watched him walk up the front steps. He was young, twenty-four, still lived at home. His folks had a farm near Bogus Creek. Meg told her that she thought he was cute. Bill was his name, and Bill was so good-looking it hurt Claire. She wanted to rush out to him and say, "Why couldn't you have stopped it? Why didn't you keep her with you, where she would be safe? Don't you know how dear she is? How could you have let her step off the bus and into such horrible danger?" But when he got to the door, all she said was, "Thanks for coming over. I hope this is nothing, but Meg hasn't gotten home, and we're terribly worried about her. She never showed up at her baby-sitter's house."

The young man stood on the front steps, and his face twisted as he heard the news. "I knew it was bad when I got the message to come over here. I can't believe anything would happen to Meg. She's such a good kid. I mean, at least you know she didn't take off or anything. She is so well behaved. Best kid on the bus." Bill smiled at Claire.

"Thanks, yes, she's a good kid. Listen, did anything unusual happen today—either on the bus or when Meg got off?"

"Actually, now that you mention it, Meg dropped her books. No big deal, but she's not a klutz and, I don't know, it surprised me."

Claire felt light for a moment. Maybe there was a logical reason why her books were beside the road. Maybe she had gone to a friend's and was planning on coming back for them. "Did she leave them there, on the road?"

"No, she stepped off the bus, dropped her books, and then picked them up. Then she waved at me and started up the hill. I watched her for a second, and then I pulled away."

"Was there anyone around? Any cars? Any people on the street? Did you notice anything?"

"Yes, there was a pickup truck parked halfway up the hill."

"There was? Right in front of Swanson's house?"

"I don't know the Swansons, ma'am, but on the right side of the road as you're going up the hill."

"Was there anyone in it?"

"Not that I noticed. I just figured it was parked there. Somebody doing some work close by."

"Did you notice what color it was?"

Bill thought for a moment. He turned and looked back toward the hill where the pickup truck had been parked. "It was parked in the shade, so it seemed kind of dark. I'd say it was a gray pickup truck. I'm kind of guessing, but that's what I think when I see it in my mind."

"License plates?"

"Sorry, I really didn't notice anything about them. Couldn't tell you if they were Wisconsin or Minnesota. Just didn't pay any attention."

"Sure. Anything else you could tell us?"

"Nope. You want me to help look for her?"

Claire nodded her head. "That would be great. We need to find her." Claire stepped away from the door and waved him into the house.

"I didn't think anything of that truck," he said. "A pickup truck, hell, that's as common as a five-cent nickel around here."

A few minutes later, deputies started to drive up. Most of the squad had showed up, in uniform even if they were off duty. It was a rule in the department. If you were called in to work for an emergency, you still took time to put on your uniform. It prevented confusion when deputies stepped in to break up a fight or help someone. The uniform allowed them to be identified.

Stuart was dividing people into groups of two and sending them out. He had a map of the town and was marking off where people were going. Claire stood by him and watched, but it seemed to be happening to someone else. She hated the idea of not being at the house in case Meg might come home.

Claire looked out the window, as she did every minute or two, and saw that Ramah was walking over. Claire went out to meet her. The thin old woman looked like a crane when she walked, her hip-bones swinging forward from her legs in a very animal-like fashion. She carried a handkerchief that she usually kept tucked in the sleeve of her blouse, close to her lips. As Claire got closer to her, she saw Ramah was nervously patting her face with the handkerchief.

"No news of Meg?" Ramah yelled before they met.

Claire shook her head and yelled back, "Not yet."

Ramah bent low and walked faster. They intersected at the end of Claire's driveway. "I can't tell you—" Ramah started. Her hands were flying around, waving the handkerchief.

Claire grabbed the bony fingers and held them in her own. "No, and I'm sorry I was short with you. It's not your fault, Ramah. You did the right thing. No one could have handled it better."

Ramah looked up and smiled, letting the hand with the handkerchief fall to her side.

"I have a favor to ask of you, Ramah. Would you stay at your house and watch for Meg? Because she might come to your house. She might show up there, and I want you to be there, waiting for her. Maybe she just went to a friend's. I might have to go out again and look for her."

"Your sister came by," Ramah told Claire.

"Yes, her car's still here."

"Someone came to get her."

Claire was puzzled. "What do you mean?"

"A man in a pickup truck."

Claire let go of Ramah's hands. She felt as if someone had poured another bucket of ice water down her back. What was going on here? "A pickup truck. Was it gray?"

"A dark color. She got in the truck with him, and then he drove away."

"HOW CAN YOU see when you're fucking crying like that?"

Bridget wiped the tears away with the back of her hand while keeping her other hand on the steering wheel. He had made her drive the truck so he could keep the gun trained on her. She was on 35 heading north, going back toward the Twin Cities. A few cars passed them on the road, and she thought of swerving out in front of one of them and causing an accident, but it seemed too risky. She didn't want to endanger anyone else. "I often drive and cry at the same time."

"Well, for Christ's sake, quit."

He hadn't said much since she had started driving, and she decided it would be good to keep him talking. She needed to be a real person to him, not just some woman he picked up. "I can't," she told him.

He raised the gun, then seemed to think better and lowered it to his side.

Bridget decided to tell him the worst of it. "See, I'm pregnant."

"Shit," he said. "You're pregnant? You don't look pregnant."

"Well, I'm about seven weeks along. My hormones are doing wild things to my brain. I'm sick, I puke, and I cry a lot." She turned and looked at him. He was awful skinny. She bet she could take him in a fight, but not when he was holding a gun in his hands. Bridget glared at him. "You made a mistake when you picked me up."

"You made a mistake when you got in the truck."

"Your mom made a mistake when she gave birth to you."

At that, Red stuck the gun into her ribs and poked her. Bridget drew in her breath. He said, "You leave my mom out of this."

Okay, she thought to herself. You've got one of his weak points. Back off. "Sorry," she said with a half-smile. "I'm sure she's a nice lady."

"None of your business." He pulled the gun away and turned and stared out the window.

"So what are you going to do with me?" Bridget asked.

"I'm just doing what I was told to do. You'll see."

"Someone told you to pick me up. But no one even knew I'd be at Claire's. Did you come to get Claire and get me by accident?"

"Not exactly."

"Then what?"

"What the hell are you doing asking all these questions?"

Bridget watched the road slide under the truck. He was awfully nervous. Then she asked, "You on something?"

He jerked up in his seat. "What's it to you?"

"Well, you seem irritable, and your pupils are large. I would assume that you've been taking some form of a stimulant, possibly cocaine. Am I right?"

"What're you, a doctor?"

"Yes, as a matter of fact, I am."

"I don't do much of that shit."

"But you decided to take a little snort today, huh?" She wanted to know, because it would help her assess what she needed to do to handle him. "It seems like it's made you a little jumpy."

"Shit no, coke don't hardly touch me."

There it was—coke. Bridget went over what she knew about the street form of cocaine. It was a fairly pure form of the coca, often cut with a little strychnine, which caused a little paranoia, but maybe she could use that. "How pure is your stuff? You cut it with anything?"

"It's the best stuff on the market."

"So only a small amount of extraneous material goes into it."

"What the fuck is with you? If you don't shut up, I'm going to tie you up and toss you in the back." He reached out and touched her hair. "Pretty hair. I like long hair. Gives a guy something to hang on to when he's bucking away on top. Know what

I mean?" He wrapped a lock of her hair around his fist and yanked at it.

"Hey, I'm trying to drive here," Bridget snapped at him.

He let her hair go and then stroked her shoulder. "We don't have too much farther to go."

Bridget drove quietly for a while. Not too much farther. They were getting close to Prescott, she thought. Maybe that's where they were headed. She needed a plan. She glanced in the rearview mirror. There was already a pile of something covered with a tarp in the back. She wondered what was under there. Her eyes leaked a little more, and she snuffled up her tears. She really didn't understand why she was crying. She was scared, but that wasn't it. It felt like she had a lot of pressure building up inside, and maybe that just forced the tears out. Let this jerkball think she was a wimp. She'd show him. She was getting herself and the little life growing inside of her out of this mess.

"So how did you come to know Claire?" she asked him.

"Your sister Claire fucked up my life, and I don't mind returning the favor."

◆ 21 ◆

Bruce stopped in the doorway of Claire's house to watch her. Claire was still in her uniform. Bruce hadn't known her when she was working as a uniformed cop in Minneapolis. They hadn't met until they were partnered up. This tan-colored uniform didn't do her justice, and yet there was something about seeing a woman in a uniform, seeing her breasts squeezed into the same shirt that the men wore, that he liked.

She was directing two other deputies, and they were listening to her. Claire had always been good at giving orders. Bruce had loved to have her order him around. He didn't always follow her orders, but it was as much fun to thwart her. The years they had worked together were such good times for him. He wanted it all again. He wanted her back in his life on a daily basis. Seeing her working made that even clearer to him.

He could hear her telling them to put out an APB on a gray or dark pickup truck, possibly heading north. One of the men got on the phone, and the other asked her what they should do next.

Two dots of red stood out on her cheeks. Claire was on a jag, definitely. He knew her well like this. It wasn't good for her, she would crash in a day or two, but while she was up, she was incredible. He watched to see if she was falling apart, but she wasn't. She was funneling all the anger and energy this loss of her daughter had brought into organizing her rescue.

He stepped inside the doorway, and she saw him.

"Oh, Bruce, thank God you're here. No time to meet everyone." She waved her arms. "This is Detective Bruce Jacobs from Minneapolis Police. He's here to help out." Men nodded at him. Civilians were mixed in with the tan Pepin County uniforms. Bruce was wearing a blue-and-white-striped shirt, a tie, and a blue blazer, his slightly dressed up spring uniform. He didn't like to have to think in the morning when he put his clothes on, so he always laid his clothes out the night before.

He moved up next to the table and saw a spread-out map with sections marked off on it, the town of Fort St. Antoine and the adjoining township. The blue areas showed the wetlands along the river. He wondered if they had checked through there yet. "What about these slough areas?"

"We've got a couple of people in boats and canoes down here," Claire answered. "They're not very deep, and they're thick with reeds around them. Hard to get to. But we are looking there."

"What're you doing about the possibility that she was picked up?" He had to bring it up to Claire. After all, it was more than a possibility.

"A dark pickup truck was seen in the vicinity by two witnesses. Unfortunately, neither of them saw the driver. But we've put out a call on that truck. She's been missing two hours. But Bridget's only been missing an hour."

"Bridget?" Bruce was stunned. "What about Bridget? Was she with Meg? What is going on here?"

Bruce watched Claire's face drain. She closed her eyes and

pressed the back of one hand to them as if to press back tears, but when she spoke, her voice sounded calm. "No. All we can figure is she came over to see me, and the guy grabbed her too."

Bruce slammed his fist on the table. He wanted to take Claire in his arms and promise her that no one would be hurt. What was going on here? "Shit. Claire, I'm so sorry."

Claire pulled her hair back from her face, which cleared of any emotion. It was an expression that Bruce had never seen on her before. "No time for sorry. I need you to get right back in your car and drive back toward the Twin Cities. If he's one of the guys we think he is, that's the way he'll be going. I'll go with you. I don't think we're going to find them around here, but we have to keep looking."

CLAIRE CLIMBED INTO the car, and Bruce took off. He turned the squawker on and they both listened as the car dropped down the hill and he turned onto 35 going north.

She reached out and grabbed his hand. His big fingers wrapped around her wrist. "Bruce, I don't know what—"

He squeezed her hand and then held it gently in his. "Don't waste your breath. We've got one thing we've got to do right now, and that is find Meg and Bridget. I've been kicking myself. I should have checked in with you on my way down. What if he drove right by me?"

"Let's not go there, as we used to say when we worked together. We've got to move forward on this one, and fast."

"Listen, we've got more information than this guy can imagine. We know what color truck he's driving, we've got a good idea of the direction he's headed in—hell, that's more than we've had to go on most of the time. You put out that all-points bulletin. We'll hear it on the squeal box if anything is reported."

Bruce pushed down on the accelerator, and the car sped down the road. He still held her hand, and Claire didn't let go of him. The sun was dropping into the edge of the earth on the far side of the lake. Soon it would be dark, no moon. The last light of the sun poured molten red along the shore of the lake, and the lake blazed up in answer.

With Bruce next to her, she felt calmer. They had worked so well together as a team, having the highest success rate of any detectives on the force. When she faltered, he knew and said the right thing to antagonize her or whatever it took to pick her up again. She had done the same for him. Right now, she was relying on him more than she ever had when they worked together. He had to help her find Meg before it was too late.

As they drove by a farmhouse, a golden dog loped across the yard in the twilight. He was running for the fun of it, not chasing anything. Claire watched him, and he seemed to represent a way of life she could vaguely remember but hardly hoped to achieve again. A run in the wind just to feel air on your skin, not because someone was chasing you, not because you were trying to catch someone. A way of moving in the world, moment by moment.

Claire lost the dog as they turned a corner in the road, and the loss pulled at her stomach, at her bones.

RICH WALKED HOME from town. It was only a half a mile, and he watched the road as he walked, looking for anything that might tell the story of a small girl wandering alongside the highway—a ribbon, a piece of paper, a small shoe print.

He didn't hope to find anything. It was getting too dark, and he didn't think she had walked down this road. He was afraid she had been spirited away. Just as Claire had been. This big, hulky guy had taken her, and they had sped away into the dangerous night, while the Pepin Police Department traipsed around town looking down alleys for Meg. But the consensus was, Meg was gone. The men were disheartened. Stuart was still out looking, checking back at the house every half hour or so. Rich told him he'd come back after he fed the pheasant.

Rich felt like there was a whole huge story lurking behind Claire, and they were just seeing the edges of it. She reacted too strongly to everything. She was too brave, too scared, too aggressive, and too removed. He had watched her go away when he was standing right next to her in the kitchen. It was as if her body stood by itself without moving as the inner part of Claire—the soul, the spirit, the unconscious—had flown away. He had stayed close to her, ready to catch her body if it too dropped away, but then someone had come to the door, and she had returned.

How do you ask someone where they are when you were standing right next to them? How do you ask them what has happened in their life that they jump to the worst conclusions?

He hiked up the hill of his driveway. His house was dark and probably cold, as he had left no heat on today. He would check his messages, feed the pheasant, and go back to wait for Stuart and pray a little girl, the quintessential apple of her mother's eye, would return so that he could get to know her mother better. So that her self would return and make a home of her body once more.

"I HAVE TO PEE." Bridget slid the words out of her mouth, emphasizing the last one like a kid.

"Can't you wait? We're almost there." Red slammed his fist against the dash, and Bridget focused on keeping the truck on the road.

She decided to get even whinier. Who would suspect that

someone who was whining was up to something? "No, I can't wait. That's the problem. When I have to go, I have to go. I'd rather not piss in this truck."

"Okay. Pull over. You can go squat in the bushes. But I'll have to keep an eye on you."

That's what Bridget was counting on. She slowed the truck down and stopped it near a thicket of scrub trees. They had turned off 35 a few miles back, and she was afraid of what would happen to her when they got to where they were going. She would give him a little show. And see if he wouldn't go for it. She was remembering her aikido from her years that she took it at the university. Move into the aggression. Make it a dance. She had to try something.

Red got out his side and then made her climb out right behind him. The gun, which she had studied a bit, was in his right hand, but he wasn't gripping it tightly. It was a revolver with a long barrel, and she knew it was loaded because she could see the bullets in the cylinder. He was using it more like an extension of his hand, pointing the way for her with the barrel. "Get over there." He pointed to the clump of trees.

Bridget walked to where he pointed and watched that he followed behind. She turned her back on him and unzipped her jeans and pulled them down. She crouched, leaning over her pants, and hoisted her butt up in the air so she didn't pee on them. She knew he was watching. That's what she intended. He was razzed enough to go for her now. She could feel it. If she waited any longer, she might not have another chance. When she was done, she stood up and pulled up her pants. She wanted to get him to make a move for her while it was just the two of them.

When she turned around, he was only a few feet away. "How'd you like the show?"

"You've got a great ass."

Bridget backed up a step, and he followed. When he reached out to grab her neck, she was expecting the move and stepped into him. She slipped under his arm, grabbed his wrist, and threw her hip into his side. He grunted and tried to scramble, but she had the advantage. She knew what she was doing, as she had done it thousands of times in aikido class. But what had worked in class did not happen in the woods. When she tried to flip him, he pulled her down with him. She kicked him away and scrambled up. He landed on his side and then bounced up, the gun still held in his hand.

This had not been her plan. He still had the gun. He wouldn't get close to her again. Her only chance was to get away from him now. She turned and ran. She had decided he could shoot her if he wanted to; she'd rather get shot and killed than be subject to his idea of fun. Dropping down and into the woods, she grabbed tree branches and flung herself through the underbrush. This early in the year it was easy to move through the woods.

She heard him behind her. He sounded a fair distance back, but she guessed he was a sprinter. If he was going to catch up to her, it was going to be soon. If he was going to shoot her, he'd have to stop to aim. She was counting on that to get away from him.

In the dim light of dusk it was hard to see where she was going. She wasn't trying to watch her footsteps, just run as fast as she could and not hit a tree. She was running like a horse; she even changed her pacing, galloping through the trees, breathing in lunges, and going faster than she could ever imagine herself running. Branches grabbed at her, her feet tripped over roots, but she kept charging forward.

Bridget could hear Red behind her. His were the other feet in the woods, the breathing that was coming up behind her. However fast he ran, she would run faster. She didn't want him to touch her, to touch what was growing inside her. She would never go in that truck with him again. Nothing could make her get back in it and go anywhere. She would make it out of these woods and find safety. She had to believe that to keep running.

She ran even harder, and then she heard a shot. It sounded like a huge wind blowing over her, and then she felt the sting on her arm, electric like a wasp bite, only an enormous wasp. She didn't stop running. Her hand flew up to her arm and came away wet. The woods were darker and deeper than she would ever have imagined. She kept running away from him.

Even while she was moving forward, trying to run in a straight line, the woods circled around her. Another shot rang behind her, but it didn't touch her. She was counting them. One, two. He had six bullets. She knew blood was running down her arm, but she couldn't take time to look at it. If she looked, she would stop running. She would give up. She needed to sail through the forest and get to the clearing that was waiting for her. She thought of Jester and how he loved to gallop down the path in the woods, she tried to imagine riding him, and then she felt him falter. Her horse was getting tired.

Another shot cut through the trees, and she was afraid that it had hit her horse, because something seemed to have gone out of her. Don't quit running, she told herself. Don't count the bullets. That was three. Count your steps. She slowed down to a trot, but it was constant. She grabbed at tree trunks and pushed off them to help her keep going.

And finally she came out of the woods. Just when she thought it would never end, she broke through into a field. She ran into it and saw it was freshly plowed. The ground pulled at her feet. She stumbled and caught herself and kept running.

A bullet tore past her face, and she felt covered in sweat. That was four. The field shone black in the night that was falling. She stood out in her white shirt. She couldn't disappear, and he would follow her with those last bullets.

She couldn't run anymore. Her legs were burning, and her arm was on fire. Her throat rasped raw, and she was whinnying with fear. She turned and saw him on the edge of the field. He lifted the gun, and she knew another bullet was coming.

IT WAS DARK out. When she had crawled into her hidey-hole, she could still see light filtering through the screen of tree branches she had built. But now it was pitch black in her hole. She must have slept. Meg remembered curling up and closing her eyes and praying that she would be all right. She wasn't sure it was okay to pray for something like that. She wondered if you weren't supposed to just pray for the poor people in China, but she decided to send out a prayer so it would keep her mind busy. The prayer had melted into sleep, but she didn't know how long she had slept.

She blinked her eyes, and it didn't get any lighter. She shrugged out of the leaves that surrounded her and poked her head up. Dark all around. Meg came out of her hiding place and let her eyes grow into the darkness. She wouldn't move forward until she was sure that the man wasn't around anymore. She figured if she hid long enough, he'd have to go away. Her mom would catch him otherwise, and she was a cop and could put people in jail.

Rocking in the dark, her knees tucked right in front of her, Meg hoped that her mom would put that man away in jail. Otherwise how would she ever go to school again, or anything? She'd have to be watching all the time, and that would take away all the fun of walking around by herself.

Meg could see through the tree branches now. There was a light on in her house, and there were cars parked around it. She needed to go down there and tell her mom she was all right. She stood up and took deep breaths. Her feet felt like they had gone to sleep on her, but she kicked the needles out of them.

Meg walked slowly down out of the hillside, holding tree limbs as she went. She walked as quietly as she could, like the Indians moved through the forest, not making a sound. When she got to the edge of the woods, she looked carefully. There were some pickup trucks. She'd have to walk in slowly and make sure it wasn't a trap.

Meg dropped to her knees and moved across the ground like a woodchuck. They snuffled through the grass, and she wouldn't make the noise they made, but she moved like they did, rocking gently back and forth, wiggling forward. She made her way down to the fence line, and then she froze. Someone was standing on the side of the road. She could see the tip of a cigarette floating up and down, and she heard a cough.

Then Meg saw the white hair on the person's head. It was a woman, an older woman. She was watching Meg's house. A woman had to be okay, especially one this old.

Meg said, speaking from among the weeds in the field she was lying in, "What are you doing here?"

The cigarette dropped, and the woman spit out, "What the hell?"

Meg stood up. "I'm sorry I scared you, but what are you looking for?"

The woman came and took Meg's face in her hands and then shone a flashlight on it. "Probably you. Like half the town here. Where have you been?"

"Who are you?"

The woman turned the flashlight on herself, and Meg stared up at the ghostly face that appeared. Bright red lips, hair that looked like cotton candy, and a face with wrinkles that ran the wrong way. "I'm Darla. Landers' sister-in-law."

"Oh, you live down on the highway."

"Yes, I do." Darla turned the flashlight back on Meg. "Now I've answered your questions. You answer mine. Where have you been?"

"Hiding."

"Why?"

Meg remembered what her mother had said to her, "Never tell anyone what you know, Meg. It's too dangerous."

"I fell asleep in my hiding place. I was just playing."

"I don't believe you."

Meg didn't know what to say. Everyone always believed her. This old woman looked like a witch—*hag* had been the word used in one of her fairy tales. But she could be a good witch. There were such things. And maybe it would take a good witch to see the truth in Meg.

Darla lit another cigarette and looked at Meg. "What's going on?"

"Somebody tried to get me."

"A man?"

"Yeah."

Darla stiffened. Meg felt Darla's body go tense as she stood next to her, then she asked, "An old man?"

"Not so old. Medium old. He had red hair."

Darla relaxed. "Red hair, don't think there's a guy in town with red hair. Maybe not one in the county, come to think about it."

She asked Meg, "Did you know him?"

Meg shuffled her feet on the ground. This was what she

wasn't supposed to talk about. But she had to answer the older woman. "In a way."

"But you got away from him?"

"Yes. I ran and hid. He didn't find me."

Darla put an arm around the girl and started walking her back to the house. "You did good, kid, real good. Your mom will be proud of you."

22

ilence hung over the field. Bridget held her breath inside her body, willing herself to lie still. Pain seared her left shoulder and her right leg. Electric and burning, it felt like energy was pouring out of the holes the bullets had made. More than blood, she was losing her strength of will to go on.

She was lying facedown in the dirt. There was no reason to get up. If she stood, he would see her and shoot again. She couldn't run away from him. She wasn't sure she could stand. The tilled earth was soft beneath her, and she pressed into it, wishing to disappear.

Then she heard him. He was grumbling to himself. Cursing. Probably mad that he couldn't find her. For a second, she thought of jumping up and running again, but decided it was too late. She was so deeply in the mess she was in, she could go no farther. She thought of the soldiers who lived because the enemy thought they were dead. That was the best thing that could happen to her.

Bridget kept her eyes closed and quieted her breath. She let the pain wash over her in waves. She concentrated on feeling it so it wouldn't overwhelm her.

He was coming closer, no longer cursing. She heard his legs move through the field. Like an animal, her sense of hearing had opened wide up with the adrenaline that was pumping through her. As a pharmacist, she understood what was happening to her, but she could neither stop it nor control it. Ride it out, she thought. Last moments on earth, and she was filled with pain and fear. How many people died like this?

She wished she had told Chuck she was pregnant. He would lose something he never knew he had. The sound of the footsteps were closer. He stood right over her. She waited for the last shot. If it killed her, she might not even hear it, the sound traveling slower than the bullet itself. That would be a relief, not to hear the sound of her own death. Then he nudged her shoulder. She didn't move. He pushed, and she rolled over. She waited for the final bullet, but it didn't come.

She felt him lean down close to her, and her eyes popped open.

She screamed and screamed. Her enemy had a different face.

RICH TUCKED THE pheasant chick in the crook of his arm. He wasn't sure why he was bringing the small bird with him. Admittedly, it needed attention, as it had been severely pecked by another bird. Bird cannibalism happened from time to time, but usually it meant that the birds were feeling some sort of stress, such as overcrowding or cold weather. He knew neither was a problem in his pens. Rich hoped the birds weren't still getting harassed by someone lurking out in the woods. He hadn't seen any evidence of his pheasant stalker lately. Every once in a while, cannibalism happened for no reason, and this time he had been lucky and got to the chick in time. He would keep it separate from the other birds until its wounds were healed and then reintroduce it to the flock.

After feeding all his birds, he had called over to Claire's and found Stuart manning the phones. Most of the search crew had gone home. Claire and her partner were nearing Prescott, according to Stuart's latest report from them.

It was going to be a very long night for everyone. Rich decided that if he was going to stay the night at Claire's, he might as well have the little chick near him to feed and to watch over.

The chick struggled in his arms, and he stroked the silky back of the bird. The down on a baby bird was so soft it reminded him of a woman's cheek. It had been two years since he had kissed a woman, and that had happened by accident at a street dance when he had had too much to drink. He never saw the woman again. She might even have been married. Most of the women he knew were married. He had been married once for a short while, to Jenny. He had met her in college, and they had married in her hometown of Minong, Wisconsin. Their marriage had lasted for about fourteen months. Long enough for him to feel pretty hurt when she left. But that was years ago. As far as he knew, she was living out in Los Angeles now.

He had wanted to get to know Claire, but with the abduction of her daughter, he wondered what would be left of her. Claire already seemed so removed from life, very watchful of all around her.

A sliver of moon crested the bluffs as he walked up the hill. Not enough to see by, but a wonderful shape to look at. Rich found the waxing moon intriguing. He loved to look beyond the lighted part and make out the outline of the rest of the moon in shadow.

When he walked down the street toward Claire's house, he saw two figures leaning up against the fence, one average height, one fairly short. As he came closer to them, he could hear them talking. The slight breeze of the night air carried their voices to him: an older rusty voice, weathered like the siding of a barn, and the other one, young and feminine, a pitch of energy he had heard before. Meg. It sounded like Meg. She must be all right. She was talking to old Darla Anderson.

What was Darla doing up here? She could mean trouble when she wanted to. Cranky old woman who never had a good word to say about anyone. That's what his mother had always said about her. Then she'd shake her head and say, "But maybe she has reason." Rich had never followed up that odd statement, and now he wished he had.

He stood still and listened to the young girl and the old woman talk, taking in the feeling that was flushing through him—the world turning again into a place of possibility. Claire's daughter had returned; Claire would come back; he had a chance to enter their lives, as a friend at least.

Rich quickened his pace, stroking the back of the bird he held in his arms. Maybe Claire and Meg needed a pet. They didn't have a dog or even a cat. A pet pheasant might be just the thing they needed.

CLAIRE AND BRUCE were gliding through Prescott when they heard an emergency call come through on the shortwave: ambulance on its way to the hospital, picked up a thirty-year-old woman, bleeding from gunshot wounds, found in a field by a farmer.

Claire turned to Bruce and said, "Maybe—"

He answered, "We'll check it out. I wonder where the closest emergency room is to here." He got on the CB and called to find out where the ambulance was going. When the answer came back, "River Falls," he cranked the vehicle around on the bridge going over the Mississippi and headed upriver to the hospital.

"Why is this happening, Bruce? Why has someone tried to kidnap Meg and then taken Bridget? Do you think they thought Bridget was me?"

"Possibly."

"I thought leaving the Twin Cities would take care of it. If it's the drug gang, I'm no longer a threat to them. What is going on?"

"We'll find out."

Claire would always remember that drive. She kept thinking of her sister as a deer, caught in headlights, not knowing what was going on, shot in a field, a farmer finding her, a fairy tale where the kiss of life comes in time and the woman lives. She imagined her sister, standing and walking out of the field, the moon shining on her hair. She hoped for the best ending to this horrible story and wondered if the wounds would turn into red flowers decorating her shoulders and neck, flowers that would fall onto the field and grow. Claire told herself these stories as the night whipped by them on the drive up the river and her hands clung to her seat belt.

THE EMERGENCY ROOM shone brightly with metal trays and white curtains and gowned patients, but it was much quieter than the emergency rooms in the Cities. A reverential peace of people whispering. As Claire and Bruce strode up to the admitting desk, Claire could feel the wake of attention they created: she in her uniform, Bruce by his sheer presence. People knew something was going on, or about to happen. Claire pulled out her badge, slapped it down on the desk, and asked the attendant about the young woman who had just come in.

"Is she alive?"

"Yes, very." The male nurse leaned back in his chair behind the desk and waited for the next question. He had a hank of dark brown hair pulled up high in a ponytail, and under that his hair was buzzed short. His big brown eyes smiled at her, and she took this for a good sign.

"Who is she?" Claire dared ask.

"She said her name was Bridget Watkins."

Bruce reached forward and rubbed her shoulder. Claire thought it odd she hadn't given her married name, but told the nurse, "That's who we're looking for. Where is she?"

"In surgery."

"Why?"

"Bullet in her arm has to come out. Patch up the hole in her leg. Could be a domestic."

"Her husband doesn't own a gun. Believe me, this is not a domestic. Is she okay?"

"What do you mean by that?"

"How is she going to be?"

"She'll be sore for a while. She'll have a significant scar. I'm sure we'll want to keep her in at least overnight." The young male nurse smiled his admiration. "She kept insisting that we not use a general anesthetic but rather a local. They checked her over, and as the bullets had hit neither bone nor major blood vessels, they agreed to it. They also sedated her." He laughed. "Of course, in her condition, she's absolutely right." He said no more.

Claire waited for him to go on, and when he didn't, she nudged him. "Her condition?"

"Well, a general anesthetic isn't recommmended for pregnant women." The nurse snapped his chair down on the floor and stood up.

Claire took a step backward and ran into Bruce, who was still right behind her. He was being awfully quiet. "Pregnant? My sister?"

"She's your sister? You two don't look much alike."

Claire nodded her head and said, "We're not much alike."

The nurse pointed to an old man in overalls, sitting in the waiting room. "He brought her in. Said he found her in his corn-field. Lives between here and Prescott. Probably saved her life. His name is Mr. Ferguson."

Claire looked over at the man. She guessed him to be in his seventies, but it was hard to tell, with the weathered life he had led. His face was toasted a deep brown, and deep in the wrinkles were white lines, the color his skin used to be. His hands curled in, taut with arthritis. He drummed on his chest with them.

The old farmer looked up at her when he felt her gaze on him, and Claire was amazed at the lightness of his eyes, an eerie green color, like new-sprouted wheat. She and Bruce walked over and introduced themselves.

The old man pushed back his hat, which had "Wayne Feeds" written across the front of it. "Once I found her, I couldn't carry her, so I got the wheelbarrow. That worked good. Got her out of the field and to the car."

"She couldn't walk?" Claire asked.

Ferguson considered the question, shifted his jaw from left to right, and then answered, "Not so good."

"How did you find her?"

"The shots. I heard the shots. Goddamn it, I hate it when the kids shoot at the deer that come in to eat my corn. I went out to give them what for. Dumb little shits. And then I found her."

"Did she tell you what happened?"

Ferguson wrapped his fingers around the straps of his over-alls. "She wasn't in very good shape. I didn't ask her many ques-tions. Seemed like the best thing to do was get her to a doctor."

"Did she tell you anything?"

"She said the word 'five' a couple times, and it seemed to scare her."

"Five?"

"Yup." The old man rubbed his cheek. "Then she roused herself when the ambulance came and told them what to do. Is she a doctor?"

"Yes. Of pharmacy." Claire looked down at the man and asked him, "Why did you come down here?"

"Well, she's got one of my shirts on. And I was worried about her."

"She was shot up that bad?" Claire asked.

The old man cleared his throat. "I've seen worse. In France, 1944. No, that wasn't it. She was just so scared of something. Hunted looking. Whoever did that to her should be horse-whipped past an inch of his life. You know what I mean?"

"Yes. I most certainly do."

STUART PICKED THE phone up on the first ring and said simply, "Hello," but Claire could tell by his voice that he had some good news. His voice was lighter and higher and happier.

The floor of the hospital moved away from her as she stared down at it, but Claire managed to say, "Meg, is she there?"

And he answered her, "She is. Sitting right at the table. Right as rain."

"She's fine?" Claire felt tears splashing on her cheeks. She held on tightly to the line of the phone, not wanting this news to be pulled away from her. Her sister safe in the hospital, her daughter back.

"Couldn't be better. Some guy chased her, but she got away and hid in the woods."

"Oh, my God." Claire felt a river of fear run through her. Then she stood up straight and wiped her face. She breathed in deep and said, "Can I talk to her?"

"Of course."

A pause, and then Meg's sweet, clear voice came on the line. "Mommy, where are you?"

What a question! "I'm a ways away. Aunt Bridget has had an accident, so I'm in the hospital helping her out. She's fine, but I might have to stay here for a while. I'll be home as soon as I can. Are you okay, sweetie?"

"Yeah, I'm good. I was scared, but I didn't let that man get me. Just like you told me. Guess what?"

"What?"

"Rich brought a baby pheasant over. He let me hold it. Can we keep it? He says it's okay with him. He's going to teach me how to take care of it and everything. Not very many kids have pet pheasants."

Claire laughed. Anything and everything, they could keep a pet gorilla, but she was the mom. "We'll see, honey. When I get home we can talk about it. Who's staying with you now?"

"Stuart, Rich, and Ramah. We're making popcorn. When will you be home?"

"I hope soon. I might have a little more work to do."

"Can I stay up until you get home?"

Claire found herself saying easily, "Yes, you can stay up as late as you want."

Thinking, I want to tuck my daughter into bed tonight myself. Fluff the pillow. Pull the sheets up around her shoulders. Kiss her white forehead. Touch her before she goes off to sleep. Tell her that nothing will ever hurt her again, and really mean it this time.

23

ridget was stretched out on a hospital bed in a white room. She had a bandage on her left shoulder. Her right foot was elevated and swathed in cotton. She had never felt so alive. The pain had left her, swirling away in a mist of painkillers. She had given in to them. Bless doctors, bless farmers, bless pharmacists. As she requested, they had not put her out, but they had given her a light sedative. That and a couple good shots of Novocaine, and she came through the surgeries feeling fine, and remembering little.

Claire walked into the room, and Bridget waved her fingers at her. Claire looked so impressive in her uniform. Trustworthy, like a Boy Scout.

"Hi, big sis," Bridget said to Claire as she leaned in close.

"You pretty out of it?" Claire asked.

"Now, that's all relative."

"What day is today?"

Bridget thought hard. She knew the information was someplace in her brain and retrievable, it just seemed hard to find the right path to wander down and find it. Which didn't mean she couldn't answer the question. "My day off."

"Quite a day you've had."

"Is it still the same day?"

Claire looked at her watch. "Fifteen minutes to midnight."

Claire pulled up a chair and sat down, resting her arms on the crisp white sheets of Bridget's bed. "What happened?"

A big man walked in behind Claire, and Bridget felt afraid. She didn't want him in the room. She would make him go away. Having decided this, she simply closed her eyes, and he disappeared.

"Hey, Bridget, it's just Bruce. You remember him, don't you?"

Bridget shook her head no and kept her eyes closed. He looked hulking and dangerous to her. She didn't know him. She wanted him to go away.

Bruce said, "I saw you at Steve's funeral."

Claire whispered to Bruce, "I think she needs peace and quiet. She's still recovering. Let me talk to her for a minute. Then I'll be ready to go."

Bruce left the room, and Bridget opened her eyes when she heard the door close. "I don't like him." Claire took her hand, and Bridget thought of their mother. When they were sick, she would come and sit next to them and hold their hands. She wondered where their mother was now, if there really was a heaven. Would Mom have been waiting for her by the white tunnel if she had died?

"Well, he worked hard to find you. He's probably why I'm here right now. You don't need to like him. What happened to you? Who shot you?"

Bridget's eyes wandered up to Claire's face. She wrinkled her brow and then let her face relax. "I don't remember. It's so far away. The shock and the drugs are making me woozy."

Claire's hand gripped Bridget's harder. "You really don't remember anything about this guy?"

"Not much."

"Why did you get in the truck with him?"

Bridget thought back to how it had all started, the feeling she had about the safety of the small town. "I think I thought I was going to where you were."

"Do you remember anything about the man? Was it just one guy?"

"I think it was only one, but I really can't picture him. He's a blur."

"What did he want?"

Bridget picked at the sheet and then said, "I think he had seen me before."

"Where?"

"I'm not sure, but he knew who I was." She wasn't sure what she should tell Claire. "He liked me."

Claire's face grew large as she leaned in toward Bridget. Bridget felt the urge to push her away. "Bridget, did he rape you?"

"No, he didn't get that far. They checked here at the hospital."

"Would you recognize him again?"

"I don't know. I don't want to talk about him anymore. Does Chuck know where I am?"

"I've tried your house a couple times. He's not home."

"Probably at his brother's. He'll be home soon." Bridget rubbed her stomach. She remembered something else she had to tell her sister. She pointed at her belly and announced, "Claire, I'm pregnant."

Claire moved away and sat on the edge of the bed. "Yes, so I've heard. How do you feel about that?"

"I think I want it. Will you help me?"

"Absolutely." Claire patted her leg, and Bridget felt safe again. "First we have to get rid of this guy."

"I'M GOING TO call him King Tut," Meg announced as she placed the small bird in his new home.

Rich felt a laugh bubble up in him, but he coughed it down. "King Tut? That's a pretty important name."

"Hey, he's a pheasant. The royalty used to keep these birds in China. He should have an aristocratic name."

"King Tut it is." Rich had found a packing box, cut the sides down, and lined the bottom of the box with sawdust and pebbles. A bowl of water would keep the little bird through the night. He'd bring feed in the morning. Meg had agreed to go to bed only if the bird could sleep in her room. She was falling asleep, so he said that would be fine. She had brushed her teeth and washed her face, and changed into pajamas with dancing girls in hula dresses on them. She was stretched out on the bed, looking over the edge at the bird.

"Why did that other bird peck him?"

"It's hard to say. Maybe the other bird felt like he was in a tight spot and took it out on Tut."

Meg thought about that for a moment. "Maybe Tut grabbed the biggest piece of corn and the other bird wanted it."

"Possibly."

"What if Tut would have died?"

"He would have gone to bird heaven. But I got there in time."

"Did the other bird know it might be killing him?"

"I'm not sure what goes on in their bird brains."

Meg laughed at that. "Bird brain. I get it."

Rich looked down at her smiling face. Her small teeth looked like pearls in her mouth. Her bangs were swept back off her face, and her hair spread out on the blanket like a dark halo. There were bits of her mother written on her face, but she was coming into her own as a person.

"Well, I think his royalness, King Tut, needs to catch a little shut-eye." Rich reached down and stroked the pheasant. It would be interesting to see what a pet pheasant would be like, how personable it would get.

Meg scrambled under the covers. "Will he sleep all right without his brothers and sisters? Will he be lonely?"

"Not with you here."

Meg tilted her head back into the pillow. "Could you stay for a while and watch and make sure that he falls asleep?"

"Sure. I could do that." He turned off the light in the bedroom and sank down into an easy chair in the corner of the room. He thought of saying something about sleeping tight and not letting the bedbugs bite, but he decided that Meg was worrying about more than bedbugs tonight.

AND NOW HE was bringing Claire home. They had sent off a squad of cops to find the pickup's tracks near the field where Bridget was found. Everything had worked out this time. Her sister, although injured, was safe, her daughter found, and a thin sliver of moon shone on the lake as they drove alongside it. Bruce thought of the really happy ending this could have, where he swooped her up in his arms and she welcomed him. Claire had been very quiet since they left the hospital. Bruce wondered, as always, what she was thinking, where she went sometimes when she was sitting next to him in the car but seemed to disappear.

"What are you going to do next? Do you consider Bridget's kidnapping your case?"

Claire's voice broke as she turned to him. "Of course I do. I couldn't give it away if I wanted to."

"Bullshit. The Pierce County police looked pretty comfortable sitting in the lobby, guarding Bridget."

"That's exactly it. No room for comfortable in this case."

"My guess is that the guy who took her is not from Pepin County, so you're going to need a liaison with the Cities."

"Am I? Who's going to know if I go look around?"

"Claire, this isn't about looking around. This is about catching the bastard. Now, stop playing coy with me. We don't need to talk tonight. I know you want to see Meg. But I want to hear from you tomorrow. And we need to plan this out."

Claire hesitated. Bruce didn't like her hesitation. What was she up to? "Fine. I'll call you tomorrow."

"Did Bridget have anything interesting to say about this guy?"

"Not really. She was pretty out of it. I'll try to pull more out of her when I see her tomorrow."

Bruce pulled into her driveway. Lights were on all over the downstairs. "Do you want me to walk you in?"

"No need. I'm sure Stuart is still here. His truck is in the driveway." She turned and touched his shoulder. "I'll blink the lights at you."

He laughed. "Great. Then I'll know you're safe." He reached out and slid his hand around her neck. "Claire—"

She turned toward him and let him pull her in closer. "Thanks, Bruce. You're my best pal." When he kissed her, she didn't resist, but she wasn't really there. He let go of her before she could pull away.

. . .

THE FIRST THING Claire did once she was in the door was call Chuck again. She had tried a couple times from the road and from the hospital, but he hadn't been home. Finally he answered the phone. She told him briefly and minimally what had happened to Bridget.

Chuck hadn't even missed her. His voice splintered as he tried to explain why he hadn't been worried. "I just thought she was with you. She left me a note saying she was going to visit you. Here she's been kidnapped, and I didn't know anything. What should I do?"

Claire told him to go to River Falls. She told him where the hospital was. She told him how Bridget would be. But she didn't tell him that Bridget was pregnant. That she left to her sister.

Stuart had cleaned her kitchen. He was drinking a cup of coffee and doing the crossword puzzle in an old paper. The sink had been scoured, all the dishes put away. The kitchen was cleaner than she had ever seen it since she had moved in. Was she such a bad housecleaner, or was Stuart the best?

"Thanks for straightening up."

"Had to do something with myself. Amazing what a little soap and water will do for the dust that collects on your shelves." Although Stuart's voice was lively, Claire knew he must be beat. After all, he got up at four-thirty to bake.

"You cleaned my cupboards too?"

"It's been a long night."

Claire nodded toward the stairs. "How does she seem, Meg?"

"Fine. A little frantic. I actually think she's rather proud of herself. But I don't know if she let herself think about what might have happened to her. I certainly wasn't going to point it out to her. I figure that's your job, Mom."

"Let me go take a peek at her. I assume she's sleeping?"

"Haven't seen her in an hour. I assume so."

Claire climbed the stairs quietly. She didn't need to wake her darling daughter up, just cast eyes on her. She peeked into the room and realized that there were a couple other creatures sleeping in it.

Next to Meg's bed was the baby pheasant. Claire peered into the box, and the bird ruffled its feather, its head tucked under its wing. Meg's head was facing the bird, and she had a hand draped off the bed, falling into the box. Claire could see Meg's face clearly in the light of the hallway. She seemed perfect, without a wrinkle, a scratch, a worry. After she was done visually inspecting her daughter, she turned to the last sleeping creature in the room—Rich.

He was slumped into the small easy chair, his feet stretched out in front of him, his chin on his chest, his hands on the arms of the chair. He looked younger, without concern. Claire stared at him. When again would she get the chance to examine him so unself-consiously? He was a striking man, dark hair, thick eyebrows, high cheekbones, not pretty but nearly handsome. She didn't blame Meg for wanting him to stay with her a little longer.

Claire felt the desire to touch him rise up in her. Since her husband died, she had not felt such a longing, and it surprised her.

24

Chuck didn't like hospitals. His mother had stayed in one for six weeks before she died. He had been twelve, just old enough to visit her. So he had to go and see her every day with his father. She had changed from the woman he loved and thought was beautiful into a skinny, breathing machine whose lips puffed in and out as she tried desperately to stay in the same world he was in. She had loved him, and she had left him.

He stopped just inside the doorway of the main entrance. He swore there was a distinctive smell that hospitals had; blindfolded, he would know when he entered one. He didn't want to see Bridget in here. He should have asked Claire to go with him. He was a brave man, a football hero, but walking into a hospital was almost more than he could do.

He leaned over and took some deep breaths. What was the matter with him? Some husband he was—out fixing cars while some hoodlum grabbed his wife and nearly killed her. The thought of Bridget dead almost floored him. A soft voice right above him asked if he was all right. When he managed to stand, a young nurse guided him to a chair.

"What's the matter?" she asked him. She looked about sixteen years old, her hair pulled back in a tight bun, round red cheeks and a big smile.

"My wife is here."

The nurse smiled. "First baby?"

Chuck sat up straight. "No, I wish. She was shot."

Her cheeks deflated, and she looked as if she'd been smacked. "Lord, that's awful. Where is she?"

"I don't know."

"Gunshot wounds would put her on three west. Do you see the elevators?" she pointed.

"Yes." Chuck stood up.

"Go up to three and then turn left."

He walked into the elevator and then looked down at his empty hands. He hadn't brought Bridget anything. No flowers, no candy. But it was three in the morning, and she wasn't just convalescing. He would do better next visit. Maybe, if he stayed with her tonight, she could leave in the morning. Claire did say she was not in that bad shape. But still—bullet holes.

The nurse at the station on the floor told him it was past visiting hours.

He stood in front of her and explained, "But this is an unusual circumstance. My wife was shot."

She looked him up and down, obviously checking him out.

"And I didn't do it," Chuck told her. "I wasn't even there. We live in Wabasha. I was working on a '78 Chevy."

"I didn't think you did it." She nodded down a hallway. "See the cop. Check with him."

Chuck had to show ID to a policeman stationed at her door. Claire had called ahead and said he was coming and that he should be let in to see his wife. The cop looked like he was about sixty years old. His arms folded over his chest, he stepped aside for

Chuck to enter the room. "I'll be right here," the cop told him in a deep, labored voice.

When he walked into the room, Chuck winced. Bridget was asleep, and the light was turned to the wall so he could only see her face in shadow. She looked different, as if some energy had drained out of her. He checked to see if blood was seeping from the wound on her arm, but the dressing was a clean, snowy white.

He didn't think he should wake her. God knows what she had been through. He stood by her bed and breathed in and out as she did. This thread of breath connected them. Suddenly, she turned, curled up, and gave out a small yelp. When she saw who it was, she loosened up and whispered, "Oh, Chuck."

He was afraid to touch her, but leaned in close so she didn't have to strain herself to talk. "Oh, sweetie, are you okay?"

"I think so. The drugs are pretty good." She spoke as if the words were falling out of her mouth.

"Do you hurt?"

"I do, but it's like it's far away. Very distant."

"Good, we'll keep it that way."

Bridget roused herself. "No, I can't for much longer."

"Why?"

"Because. I have to tell you something. I'm sorry. I should have told you before." Bridget gripped the edge of the sheet and looked as though she was going to spit something out of her mouth.

On the drive down, Chuck had tried to prepare himself for this. He was truly afraid of what had happened to her, didn't know if he could handle it if the kidnapper had molested her in any way. When he thought of that man touching Bridget, he felt as if the top of his head would blow off. "What?" he asked.

She took a deep breath and said, "I'm pregnant."

What she said was so close to the last thing he had imagined that Chuck didn't even know what the words meant. He scrambled to say something and ended up asking, "With a baby?"

Bridget actually giggled. "I sure hope so."

He moved in to hug her, but she stopped him by putting out her hand. He took her hand and kissed her fingers. "Do you want to have a baby, to be pregnant? I thought you weren't sure."

"I wasn't sure. I'm still not completely. But after all I've been through, I'd kinda like to see what it looks like."

"WHY'D YOU TAKE the sister?"

"She was there." Red turned down the TV with his big toe. The real question was, why had he bothered to tell Hawk what had happened?

He was stretched out on the couch, watching Oprah ask smart questions of dumb people. She should have him on her show sometime. God, a real ex-convict and full-time dealer. That would blow people's minds. The phone had been resting on his stomach.

Hawk's voice came out of the receiver again. "You fucked up."

"I went to a lot of risk to take her. Hell, I'm in deep shit now. She can ID me. I left her for dead, but she rose again. Saw it in the paper today."

"You fucked up. How did that little girl get away from you?"

"She should try out for the Olympics. One hell of a sprinter. Right into the woods. It was like the ground ate her up."

There was silence on the other end of the line. Then Hawk's voice boomed out: "You didn't catch the girl. But you let her see you. You took the sister, which was the stupidest idea in the world. Then you didn't finish her off. And she knows what you look like and probably everything about you."

"What do you mean?"

"You got a fucking big mouth, that's what I mean. You can't keep your trap shut. You keep your pecker in your pants?"

Red scrambled up off the couch, and the phone fell off his chest and hung down to the floor. "Shit. Of course I did."

"Didn't get a chance, huh? She took off on you."

Red said, "Let me explain."

"That's what I want. I want you to explain. That will make it all better. Especially after you say you're sorry."

So Red told him all that had happened when he had tried to catch Meg and ended up with Bridget. At the end of recitation, the voice on the other end of the line said slowly, "I want you to disappear."

Red didn't say anything.

Finally Hawk cleared his throat on the other end of the line and asked, "Did you tell her about me?"

CLAIRE SQUATTED IN the dirt, weeding her garden. It was ten o'clock in the morning, and the sun was a full orb in the sky. She needed the quietness of the plants simply being green and new to settle her. Landers had helped her plant most of the perennials; many of them had come from his garden. The hosta were amazing, their spears of new growth twirling out of the ground with green delight. She could see ferns just starting to push up, their fronds all tightly curled, like little green fists aimed at the sky.

She sat back on her haunches and looked around her—her small house snugged into the bluff, the black walnuts and maples that sheltered it. She had thought she was safe down here. But yesterday had proved her wrong. She had tried to run away and hide in this small town, and it hadn't worked. That was clear. The two people she loved most in the world had almost been killed by this evil that haunted her. Why didn't they just come after her? Was the answer that they wanted her to live? For what? What would she be worth without her sister, her daughter? The question she didn't want to face was, what could she have done that was so horrible that someone wanted to completely demolish her life while leaving her trapped in the ruins?

She had checked in with the Prescott police this morning and would go up and review their information later on today. They had gathered a lot of evidence from the scene of the assault: shoe prints, tire tracks, bullet slugs. The fresh, wet earth of April held prints easily. Now, if they could just match them up with something. No pickup truck had been reported missing that matched the description of the one the kidnapper had been driving.

She returned to her weeding. The soil crumbled under her fingers, so soft and sweet from the spring thaw. Many of the weeds she pulled out of her garden, she ate. Landers had taught her to recognize purslane, the loopy succulent that grew everywhere, and lamb's-quarters, the silver-green plant that tasted like spinach. But it was too early for either of them, and she wasn't sure she was ready to tackle nettle soup, although Landers claimed it was one of his favorites—a spring tonic, he had called it.

A hand landed on her shoulder, and she flew to her feet, knocking Meg over as she stood.

"Mom, it's me."

"I see it's you." Claire reached down and hoisted up her daughter, still in her nightgown. She had let her sleep in this morning.

"What about school?" Meg asked.

"I decided you could skip school for a day. It's the weekend tomorrow. You needed the rest." Claire bent down and hugged her daughter. "You want some breakfast. Something special like pancakes."

Meg nodded her head, then looked serious. "I need to tell you something, Mom. I think it was the same guy."

Claire couldn't stop her intake of breath, even though she had guessed as much. "The same guy?"

"Yeah, the same one who ran over Dad."

"BRUCE, I HAVE a question for you. Have you had any luck tracking down the pickup truck? You know they got the tread marks; we could match it now if we could just find the frigging truck." Claire spoke close to the phone. Meg was upstairs playing dolls.

God, she was a bulldozer sometimes, but he did love to hear her voice, Bruce thought as he leaned back in his chair and took his time to answer. Then, as if she had called him to chat, he said, "Hi, Claire."

"Hi, Bruce."

"We've got almost nothing on the truck—maybe a dark color, that's not enough."

"Are you going to give me a hard time here?"

She had a real edge to her voice. She didn't need him to be pushing her. "No, last night was pretty awful. I checked this morning's listings of reported stolen vehicles. Nothing that sounds like our buggy." There was a pause, and a thought occurred to Bruce: "You've checked with Prescott?"

Claire told him what they had found.

Bruce thought maybe, if he played his cards right, he would get to see her again tonight. "I have an idea. Why don't I pick up some Chinese takeout and come down, and we can sit down and go over everything that they've gathered?"

Claire's answer was all too quick. "Not with Meg around. I don't want her to be involved, and I need to spend time with her right now."

Bruce reluctantly said, "I understand." He would not win Claire by competing with her daughter. "How about on Monday?"

Claire said, "Great. Monday would be good. I think I work the late shift. You want to come down for breakfast? Could you bring some bagels?"

He definitely liked the sound of that. Claire in the morning, cream cheese and bagels. Maybe things were starting to work out the way he wanted them to. "Sure. Have the coffee brewing."

BRIDGET KEPT A hand on Chuck's thigh as they drove down the river. She had never been a clinging woman, but she didn't seem to want to let go of him. The sun was blaring away above them, and a light spring breeze was stirring the new growth of leaves in the trees. It was a gorgeous day, and she felt as if a piece of winter ice had lodged in her chest. Maybe it was still in her shoulder, a sliver of bullet they had been unable to extract from her, but wherever it was, it left her feeling cold and scared.

This morning, they had done an ultrasound on the growing fetus. They let her see it on the monitor, a small mass inside her with a beating heart. Even though she wanted to have it now, she was surprised at how little affection she had for it. This growing organism would definitely have to prove itself. Her wounds ached; she felt sick to her stomach again. Because she was pregnant, she couldn't just dope out on pain pills until she felt better. She had to be a brave mother already.

"What if I'm not a good mom?" she asked Chuck.

"Are you planning on beating our child?" Chuck smiled at her.

"No, what if I neglect it?"

Chuck grabbed her hand and squeezed it. "Listen, I've watched you with Jester. You lavish attention on him. Why would you do less for your kid?"

Bridget thought about that. Maybe she had been going at this all wrong. Maybe she should just imagine she had a young animal growing inside of her, a wonderful new creature that no one had ever seen before—part horse, part wolf, part human. She could handle that. She would love such a being. She felt better already thinking of this growing life as utterly new. Her child didn't have to be like anyone else's kid. It couldn't possibly be.

"I want to see Claire."

"Of course." Chuck swerved to move around a truck. "I knew that. I can read your mind."

Bridget saw the pullover where Red had made her start driving the truck, where she had seen the gun for the first time and realized what danger she was in. The air swam with needles. "Chuck, I was really scared last night."

"I know."

"No, I mean I wanted the earth to open up and swallow me. I thought it was going to. I thought I'd never see you again."

Chuck wrapped an arm gently around Bridget and pulled her even closer than she was already sitting. "I don't know how, but you got through it."

He turned the corner without disengaging from Bridget, and they cruised up the hill to Claire's house.

They found Claire sitting on the front steps of the house. She told them Meg was inside, sleeping. "Again. She's exhausted. How are you, Bridge?"

"I feel like pure poop." Bridget sank down next to her sister and leaned her head on her shoulder. Claire rubbed her neck, and Bridget felt all she needed to tell her well up inside like her like a dammed river. She needed to get rid of Chuck. She had remained vague with him, hadn't give him any information about the guy. She trusted Claire to take care of that bastard. Didn't want Chuck to go off half-cocked.

Bridget looked up at Chuck and said, "Could you go get us some ice cream down at the Fort? I really feel like ice cream."

Chuck looked surprised and then smiled and said, "Sure. You going to be all right?"

"Hey, my sis is a cop. Of course I'm going to be all right."

When he had left, Bridget turned to Claire. "I remembered what happened. I can see the guy clearly now. He told me everything while we were driving. It came back to me this morning."

"Did you tell anyone? The cops who were there?"

"No, I don't trust anyone but you." Bridget leaned forward and held her head in her hands for a moment, then emerged and said, "Claire, you have to get rid of this guy. He's a mean fucker, and he's not going to stop until he's killed us all."

Claire looked at Bridget and said, "What do you know, Bridget?"

"First of all, he blames you for fucking up his life."

"How so?"

"I guess you had him thrown into jail on a minor offense about six years ago, something to do with beating up a hooker, and as a result he got raped in jail. He's never forgiven you."

"Six years ago. God, I was just working the street then. I didn't think it would be anything from so long ago. We've always thought it had to do with this drug gang."

"I think it's both. I think he's dealing now. I know he was high on coke yesterday."

They both sat silent for a moment, then Bridget started

laughing. "Do you remember when we were in our early twenties, I think just getting used to the idea that we were on our own and someone could actually hurt us, and we were sitting at the table in your apartment, and we decided to try to scream?"

Claire stared out over the yard and then slowly nodded. "Yeah, I think I remember that."

"I keep thinking about that. I couldn't scream when I was with this guy, there was no one to hear me. It wouldn't have done any good."

"But it sounds like you ran like hell."

"I did. But I need to know this guy isn't around anymore. I don't want to have to start practicing my screaming again." Her voice quavered, and she ran a hand down her face.

"Yeah, I hear you."

"Can you find him?"

"I think so."

"Can you put him away again? I'd really like him to be gone before the baby is born."

"I promise, Bridget."

Bridget picked up a pebble from the sand and then picked up a bigger rock. "I don't think he's in this alone. He told me he's got connections in the police force. And then he said something about a guy named Hawk."

25

"Are you sure it's all right?" Fred asked again as he pushed the door open.

"Of course I'm sure. It's yours now. Or ours. Your brother's dead, and you've inherited his house. It's about time. Who's going to keep us out?" Darla pushed Fred so he would keep walking forward. He hadn't wanted to come up to the house, and Darla had had to force him. He was still afraid of Landers, even though he was dead.

Fred looked across the street at Claire's house.

"Don't worry about her. She's the one who said we could go in the house. You leave her alone, Fred. Don't go hanging around her house or anything."

Fred walked into the kitchen and sat down. "I don't like this."

"You don't have to like it. Sit still and watch TV for all I care. I'm going to look for that damn paper. He told you he wouldn't sign it, didn't he?"

"Yes, I told you he did."

Darla stood in the middle of the kitchen floor with her hands on her hips. "It still makes me mad just thinking about it. What right did he have?"

"Well, the way I see it is—"

"Don't start, Fred. We'll be here all day. Just sit, and I'll look."

Darla wanted to do more than look, but now was not the time. She would come back on her own and take this place apart slowly, throwing away all the memories that Landers had gathered so carefully over the years. It would be a pleasure. But for the moment she wanted to be sure that nothing remained that could tie Fred and her to Landers' death.

Darla looked where she knew Landers might keep such a document; after all, he wouldn't have hidden it, no reason to. Landers had always been very organized, so she looked on his desk, in the drawers, in his file cabinet, but she found no sign of it. The wastebasket was empty, the shelves were clear of clutter. She started to feel desperate. The police had already been in here; maybe they had picked it up already. But why? Would anyone even know what it was? Would they figure out the connection?

She didn't know why she had brought Fred with her. He wouldn't sit still. He wandered around, picking up framed pictures and putting them down. Finally he stood and stared out the window, looking at Claire's house. "I see her out there in the yard. With her daughter."

"Fred, I warned you."

He stared out the window, the way she imagined him gazing in on women when he went for his long walks at night. There was no lust on his face. She never felt the peeping was sexual with Fred. He had just always felt so left out of everything—it was the way he caught up with the rest of the world. It was his secret time.

She had never bugged him about it because she thought it was rather innocent, as long as he didn't get caught. That's when the trouble started. If he stood in the dark and stared at people, he captured something. If the women were naked, so much the better, he saw more of them.

He turned and looked at Darla. "I think they have a pheasant over there, a baby pheasant." He turned back to the window, and his hands were moving in front of him as if they were holding something.

Darla sank down into a chair and held her head in her hands. "You leave them alone, Fred Anderson." She lifted up her head and stared at him. "You leave them alone, or I'll call our son and tell him what you're doing."

RICH HAD BEEN putting off walking up to Claire's, but not in a bad way, more the way he would eat his cake first, and then the frosting. All through the day, he had felt the promise of seeing Claire and Meg in front of him. He caught himself humming a tune as he fed the pheasant, and when he sang the words to himself, he realized the song was "Penny Lane," by the Beatles. The song was both unbelievably sweet and from a time in his life when he had been truly happy. The truth of the matter was, he hadn't felt this giddy since he had been a teenager.

Last night, he had woken up when Claire walked into Meg's bedroom. He watched her through hooded eyes while she checked over her daughter. Then he had feigned sleep while she stood and stared at him. He didn't know why he had done that, why he hadn't let her know he was awake. But he felt like he was bait in a trap and hoped she might be lured in closer. She did take a step toward him and bend down, then she whispered his name and he opened his eyes.

Finally, at four o'clock the next afternoon, he caught himself thinking again about Claire as he finished his chores. He decided he better get up to their house or his little pheasant would have eaten all his feed, and Meg might start to fret about that. So he filled up a quart container of food, enough to keep them going for a couple days—that way he'd have to stop by from time to time—and walked down the road toward their house.

As he walked, he thought about what his next move should be with Claire. She reminded him of a forest animal—not one specific animal, a deer, a fox, but rather the embodiment of them all, the soft way they moved through the forest, the sure way they saw and smelled danger, and the decisive way they acted when it was upon them. He decided he would give Claire time to get to know him. The worst thing he could do was rush her. She would run, and he would never see that opening in her eyes again. He knew how she could vanish while remaining in the middle of a room. He didn't want that to happen.

So he decided he would drop by every few days, let things develop naturally between them. The next move would be more like an amble. If he hung around, she might invite him over for dinner. He could ask her to stop by his house and have a cup of coffee.

As he walked down their road, he could see Claire and Meg out on the front lawn and watched the two heads lift to the sound of his footsteps—both of them projecting fear, then attention, and quickly, gladness. Their faces showed they were happy to see him. Meg left little doubt as she ran out to the road to greet him. Her face shone, and she was prancing as she came up to him.

"He ate some food right from my hand," she told him.

Rich dropped down to her level and gently tweaked her nose. "I'd probably eat food from your hand."

She giggled and danced alongside of him. "Like popcorn?"

"Something like that." He stood, and they continued up to

Claire. When he saw what they had made for the pheasant, he roared with laughter. They had brought out an old doll crib, and the pheasant was curled in the crib in a bed of straw. Then they had made a fence around it, with an old lace curtain as the covering. "This is quite a fancy castle King Tut has got here."

"Nothing's too good for our Tut," Meg said, looking down possessively at the sleeping bird.

They set up a water and feed tray for King Tut, and then Claire asked him to join them on the porch for fresh lemonade and brownies. Rich stayed for an hour and then decided it was time to leave. He was working hard not to become a pest. Claire told Meg to stay in the house, and she walked out with him.

"Could I ask you something?" Claire said as she walked Rich to the road.

She seemed embarrassed, and Rich smiled to make whatever she was going to say easier. Nowadays, he had heard, women often asked men out. That was something he would give up with gladness. He had always hated putting himself on the line. Rather stay home with his pheasants than ask for something he might not get. So he smiled and said, "Sure."

Claire looked down at the ground and kicked at a rock. "You know, Meg really likes you. She talked about you a lot today. Giving her that pheasant was about the nicest thing you could have done for her."

Rich wasn't sure where this conversation was going, but he tried to keep smiling.

"So I was wondering if it would be possible for you to come and stay with her for a few hours tomorrow while I run into town."

"Stay with Meg?" Rich wasn't sure he had heard right. "You mean, like baby-sit?"

"Yes," Claire nodded. "Usually I ask Ramah, but with all that has happened, I'd feel a lot more secure knowing you were with her."

Rich nodded and said sure. "What time would you like me to come over?"

"Late afternoon."

"What are you going to do?"

Her eyes dropped from his face, and she kicked at the dirt. "I have some shopping I need to do."

He nodded again and said, "See you."

As he turned to walk home, he decided that Claire might be good at a lot of things, but she was a lousy liar.

CLAIRE HAD CALLED in that morning and asked for the day off. Sheriff Talbert had said, Of course, don't even think about it. After a couple harrumphs, he asked how everyone was. Claire cleared her throat too and told him. Then she thanked him for the day off and said she'd see him next week.

"You've got one precious little girl there. You take as much time off as you need to make sure she's all right. And if you need anything, Claire, you don't hesitate to call. Anything in this sheriff's department is at your disposal. You know that." He fell silent, as if the words had emptied him.

"Thanks, Sheriff. I needed that."

She and Meg had gone grocery shopping, she had caught up on all the laundry, and Rich had stopped by to show them how to care for the pheasant. Such a normal, safe day. Claire made a nice dinner for the two of them—all Meg's favorite things, spaghetti and corn and blueberry muffins. They had even walked down to the lake after dinner. Their sunset walk. Each day the sun was setting later.

Meg had climbed into bed at a reasonable hour, only to come

popping down the stairs again to check on Tut. They had compromised and put him out on the back porch for the night. Meg had wanted him in her room again, but Claire explained that little birds needed to be closer to nature than that. However, Claire couldn't bear the thought of anything happening to the bird, and she knew coyotes and foxes skulked in the woods above their house. So they moved his castle to the porch, and Claire latched the door to the porch. Claire checked on the pheasant as he roosted on the edge of his cardboard box. Then she walked up the stairs to check on her daughter. Meg sprawled across the bed, her covers wrapped around her limbs like sea foam. Her little night swimmer.

Outside the window, the darkness swelled. Claire stood by the window for a moment, feeling the night press against the glass, and then decided it was time to go to work. She worked, as she always had done, on the kitchen table. No matter where she set up a desk for herself, she was drawn to the kitchen table, the center of the house.

Claire turned on her working light and laid out all the scraps of paper she had picked out of Landers' wastepaper basket. She had loved working jigsaw puzzles as a kid. Usually over Christmas her mother would buy one with a thousand pieces, she and Bridget would set up the card table in the living room, and they would all work away on it. Her mother always started with the edge pieces, trying to frame in this world of chaos.

And so Claire started with the edge pieces. They were harder to discern than in a cutout puzzle, but anytime she saw a straight edge, she put the piece in a pile. In the Cities, if she was working on such a case, she would turn these pieces of paper over to an official questioned-document examiner. It was their job to put such documents together again. But she didn't want to send it to Eau Claire and wait to get it back. If she couldn't easily solve it tonight, she would send it off.

There must have been some anger in Landers when he tore up the paper; he had ripped it into rather small pieces. She had gathered over a hundred scraps, some of them only the size of a dime. Her eyes were drawn to the words, and she could make out lines running through some pieces, but she kept looking for the straight edges. Do it methodically, in the end it will be faster and more successful, she had been taught.

When she raised her head to look at the clock on the stove, it was after eleven. She had been piecing the paper together for over an hour, but it was almost done. The problem was, she was missing some pieces. Still, with what she had she would be able to go to a legal stationery and find out what the document was. It appeared to be something about property.

This did not surprise Claire. She couldn't help but feel that Landers had been killed because of his land. There was such a greed for it down on the lake these days. People wanted land with a view, hopefully of the lake, preferably off the bluff. Landers' piece of property commanded a view of the lake from the second tier of land, about one hundred feet up from lake level. Far enough away from the lake to not be bothered by the highway and the railroad tracks, but close enough to have spectacular views.

Something Mrs. Langston had said kept niggling at Claire. Something about Darla and Landers.

Landers owned ten acres. They all extended off an alley and could be cut into quarter-acre lots. That would mean a lot of money for Darla and Fred. She had noticed them over at Landers' house today. It irked her to see them pawing through his belongings. What a funny word. She had never thought of it before, *belongings*—that which shows that we belong. She wondered if they would have a garage sale. Maybe she could buy some knick-knack of Landers and keep it in her house so that he would in some way continue to belong.

But in reading over the document, she could make out a lot and block number: Lot 12, Block 1–4. She wasn't sure, but she didn't think they were Landers'. As she recalled, all the lot numbers on this side of the town were single digits. She would ask Stuart to open up the village hall and check it out tomorrow.

Claire taped the document together as best she could, with special tape that was easy to peel off again. She walked out to check on King Tut once more and stood in the dimness of the porch, listening to the shriek of an owl in a dark tree under the bluff.

She remembered the memory Bridget had of the two of them screaming as loud as they could. Claire longed to do it again, to step out into the darkness broken only by a spattering of pinprick stars, throw her head back, and howl at her own fears. If she could scream loud and long enough, maybe she could empty herself of all her fears. It would be her battle cry, for as sure as she was of anything, she was going to find the red-haired monster and stop him.

26

laire realized she'd been sitting at the kitchen table just feeling the sun fall on her. Her coffee was cold, and she hadn't gotten anywhere with the crossword puzzle. Time for the day to begin. "Let's go examine a map."

Meg looked up from where she was sitting on the floor, cutting out a paper doll, and asked the perennial question of children: "Why?"

"Because I'm trying to figure something out, and a map would help."

Meg stood up and brushed her jeans off. "Where's the map?"

"In the town hall."

Stuart had said he would meet her at the town hall at ten-thirty. Meg had to brush her hair before they could leave, and then she had to check on King Tut to see that he was happy in his castle.

As they walked down the hill to town, Meg babbled on, the sound of her voice like a brook to Claire, happy and full of life: "Only four more weeks of school left, Mom, and then what are we going to do for our vacation this year? We hardly have to go on one, because now we live in the country, plus what would we do about King Tut? Maybe Rich would watch him. I want to take swimming lessons this year. You promised last year, but it never happened. I need a new swimsuit anyways. My old one is too tight. It pinches me on my bottom."

Claire nodded and clucked in appropriate places, feeling for all the world like a mother hen, herding her little chick down the hill. As they rounded the corner at the bottom, the town opened out in front of them—a row of old clapboard buildings in yellows and white, some with awnings, looking much as it did a hundred years ago. Except the streets would have been dirt, and buggies would be tied up where the cars were parked. The lake glinted through the trees in the park. The bluffs on the far side of the lake offered protection and gave a sense of the world they lived in as having a clear boundary, sheltered from the rest of the world. That was why it worried Claire even more that someone had dared to come down here and try to kidnap her daughter and harm her sister. She needed to make this place safe again.

Stuart was already in the town hall, a small square cement-block building with a vault. "They needed the vault because they used to put all the deeds in here," Stuart explained, "but now they are kept at the county seat in Durand."

He had the town map used for zoning stretched out on the conference table. Claire leaned over it and oriented herself. The lake was marked with blue, the railroad tracks with a crosshatching, the elevation marked on the bluffline. She ran her finger up Main Street until it intersected High Street and located her property: Block 6, Lots 3 and 4. Across from her was Landers' piece—Block 8, Lots 1 and 2—and then the field across from that, which wasn't platted. Looking at the map, she could see clearly that the property in question on the document was not Landers'.

250 | MARY LOGUE

"What're you looking for?" Stuart scrutinized the map, then twirled it around on the table in front of him.

"Block 12, Lots 1 through 4."

"Oh, that's Fred and Darla's." Stuart pointed over to the other side of town, just up from the railroad tracks.

It didn't surprise Claire that it was their property. It just confused her. Were they thinking of giving it to Landers? That didn't make any sense. She had seriously misread what she had taken to be a clue.

"Who pays taxes on that land?" she asked.

Stuart looked surprised. "Darla and Fred, of course. Late, of course. That's how they handle everything. Why?"

"Just wondered," Claire said, then asked out loud, "Why would they want to give it away?"

IT MADE A kind of horrible sense to Bridget that two days after her attack she felt the worst she had ever felt. Her shoulder burned to the core of its bone; she felt bruised from head to toe; and she was terrified. She sat in an easy chair in the living room and looked at catalogs of clothes and food and gardens and housewares; anything to keep her mind off her pain.

Chuck brought her a grilled cheese sandwich. He had been waiting on her in a way that was foreign to him and disturbing to her. He stood in front of her, staring down at her.

"There's nothing in the house," he said.

At first she thought he was trying to reassure her, but then she realized he was telling her they had no food. That wasn't good. Even though she was still nauseous, she was hungry all the time.

"I want some ginger ale," she commented after taking a bite of her sandwich and swallowing it.

"I need to go grocery shopping."

Without hesitation, Bridget said, "I'll come with you."

There was no way she was staying at home by herself. She had told Red nothing about her life, but he still might be able to find her. After all, he had seen her before, and she never found out where. He knew who she was.

Being out among people made her feel better. She felt safer, as if no one could grab her in public. And walking seemed to make her body feel better too, as if doing something physical stretched out and soothed the sore muscles.

She held on to the grocery cart and pushed it slowly through all the aisles while Chuck pulled things off the shelves and put them in the basket. They were a good team. She should always let him do the grocery shopping; he was a natural at this. He bought items in larger quantity than she did. Where she would buy two cans of tomato sauce, he grabbed five.

When they had snaked through most of the store and were coming into the cosmetics and paper items, she remembered something else she was craving. "I'd really like some yogurt."

Chuck turned back for it and left her standing there, staring at diapers. She had no idea they came in all these different forms now. Diapers for boys and diapers for girls. Every month or two the baby needed to change to a whole new shape. She remembered the soft, thick white cloth diapers her mother had used on them and then used for years after to clean the windows of their house. Maybe she should use cloth diapers. She had read conflicting arguments on the environmental advantage of each. Yet another big decision she would have to make.

Just then, out of the corner of her eye, Bridget saw a man walk by the aisle she was standing in. He had red hair. Her blood drained into her feet, and she broke out in sweat on her back. She left the shopping cart and started to back up the aisle, away from the end she had seen him pass. She needed to get to Chuck. She reached out a hand to grab onto something and managed to knock a row of formula to the floor. The sound the cans made clanking down would draw everyone's attention in the store. She turned and ran. Reaching the end of the aisle, she couldn't remember where yogurt was. She stood still and yelled, "Chuck, I need you."

An old woman walked by her and clucked. Bridget was ready to bolt past the butcher's counter and go out the back way when she saw the red-haired man at the far end of the store, browsing in the produce. She turned in the opposite direction and ran. Her heart had bolted in her chest and her feet were flying when she ran into Chuck full tilt, coming around a corner.

"He's here," she whispered at him as he held her in his arms.

"Who?"

"The man who did this to me."

"Where?" Chuck asked as he pushed her off him and looked around. "Show me where he is."

"In produce."

"You stay here, and I'll go check him out." Chuck turned back to her. "Point him out."

"He has red hair. I'm coming too."

As they walked toward the red-haired man, who was testing tomatoes, Bridget grew less sure of his identity, but she picked up a cantaloupe just in case she needed something to throw at him.

Chuck walked up to him and tapped him on the shoulder. When he turned, Bridget got the same relieved yet horrible feeling she had had in the field, when the man kneeling over her had a different face from the one she expected. He wasn't Red. He was just a normal man, doing his grocery shopping.

Chuck looked at her, and she shook her head to indicate it wasn't the man who had hurt her. Then she felt faint, too heavy to keep standing. There was only one thing to do. She dropped the melon, and it broke open on the floor, spilling orange seeds on her tennis shoes.

CLAIRE STARED AT the big reddish-tan fortress she had worked in for ten years and felt as if she were entering a monastery—the holy order of the fraternity of cops. Taking up the whole block of Fourth Street and Fourth Avenue, the stone building had a clock tower in it and at one time had been one of the taller buildings in the city. But that was almost a hundred years ago.

She walked into the building and felt the coolness of the stone brush her face. No need for air-conditioning in this place; the marble and limestone kept it cool all summer long. The Father of the Waters statue in the atrium waved at her from his throne of turtles.

Claire hadn't been in this building since she had left the force. She wondered if she would run into anyone she knew and hoped she didn't see Bruce. She hadn't told him she was coming in, and he would be mad at her. He rarely worked on Saturdays, so there was a good chance she wouldn't.

She walked down the white hallways, devoid of any art, but now and then a plaque of some distinguished nature would appear. She turned the right corners and walked in through the glass doors of the police department. She told the woman at the desk that she wanted to go into the archives. She pulled out her deputy sheriff's badge for Pepin County and said the right words. The woman let her pass.

Claire kept feeling like she was breaking and entering, but she reminded herself she was here on official business.

The archives were empty, which didn't surprise her for a late

Saturday afternoon. She knew the woman, Bonnie, who pulled the files, and when she told her the years she wanted, Bonnie looked annoyed. Claire had given up trying to please Bonnie years ago. What really surprised Claire was that Bonnie didn't even remark on the fact that she hadn't seen Claire in over a year. But nothing surprised Bonnie.

"You want to go back to eighty-seven and pull four years' worth of files?" the woman asked in a snotty tone of voice.

"Yes." Claire said the word clearly. "I don't think it's that unusual a request."

"Usually people are a little more specific. It's going to take me three hours just to gather that."

Claire suggested, "Let's start with 1992 and work backward."

"It's a deal. I can pull that for you pretty fast."

It took her fifty-five minutes. Claire sat on one of the hard chairs in the waiting area, trying to reconstruct that year in her mind: Meg was five, and Steve had just gotten a new job, they had bought their house in the suburbs, and by the end of the year, she had been taken off the streets and had started working with Bruce. A good year, as she remembered it. Claire had thought at the time that she was aimed in the right direction.

Memories could do her in. She would think back to the time before her husband had been killed, and the light in the air seemed more golden. She had been another woman—open, excited, more alive. When her husband had died, part of her had died with him. More of her would have gone, except Meg needed her. She wondered if that part of her would ever return, if she would one day be whole again.

"Here you go."

Methodically, case by case, Claire went back over the year. She had arrested shoplifters, pickpockets, johns, disorderlies, drunks, psychos, but no guy beating up a prostitute.

While she had been going through the year, Bonnie had gone and gathered another file.

Claire went through this year—1991—and found the guy. His file was in order, and there was a black-and-white mug shot. But she could tell just from reading the description that she had found the right man. Clarence Dudley Warren, alias "Nickel," alias "Jesus," alias "Red." Picked up for beating the crap out of a prostitute working Lake Street.

"Bonnie, could you pull this guy's record?"

"Deputy, I'm off in fifteen minutes."

"Just bring it up on the screen for me. Let me sit and stare at it."

The woman thought about it.

Claire looked at her and asked, "Bonnie, do you have kids?"

"Yeah, little boy and little girl, and they're home waiting for me."

"Well, this guy tried to kidnap my ten-year-old daughter Meg and shot up my pregnant sister."

"Say no more." She leaned into the screen, and Claire watched the green light aura her face. After several commands, she turned the monitor to Claire. "It's all yours. I'll let Joe know you're in here. You can stay as long as you want. I'm outta here."

Claire read the biography of the man who she feared had killed her husband. Warren was thirty-five years old. She would have popped him when he was twenty-nine and impressionable. Beating up the prostitute wasn't his first offense. He had been picked up several times on dealing charges, two before she had arrested him and one afterward. She scrolled down to get the information off that latest arrest. It had been made by Bruce— several months before she had partnered with him.

That struck her as odd. Why this connection with Bruce?

Just chance, a coincidence? She would have to ask Bruce about it, see what he had to say about Warren.

THERE WAS ONE more place she wanted to look for information on this guy Clarence; she hoped Joe Howard was still on duty. He had been a police sergeant for as long as she could remember. He ran the office, knew everything that was going on. She found him making coffee in the back room.

"Hey, Claire. Look at you. You sure are a sight for sore eyes. It's been way too long." Joe beamed at her like a proud parent. He had raised her in this building.

"You're right, Joe. It's good to see you."

"I heard you're on another force these days."

"Yes, I'm a deputy for Pepin County down in Wisconsin."

"Quieter?"

"You can say that again."

Joe laughed. "That probably suits you these days, huh?"

"Gives me time to garden."

"Good for you." Joe offered her a cup of coffee. "Fresh brewed."

For old times' sake, she took it. It was always bad, but it gave the cops something to complain about.

"Wow, this is worse than I remembered."

"See what you been missing." Joe slurped a mouthful of coffee, gargled it around in his mouth, and swallowed it. "Speaking of missing, old Bruce hasn't been the same without you. You guys were quite a team. He hasn't even partnered up with anyone since. He's going it alone these days. Do you ever see him?"

"Yeah, we keep in touch."

"What brings you here? Not to reminisce, I assume."

"I'm just checking up on an old felony I sent away about six years back. A guy by the name of Clarence Warren. You know anything about him?" Claire showed Joe the picture of the guy.

Joe pulled out his reading glasses, which he had tucked in his breast pocket, and looked over the picture and information. "Seems to me he's somebody's informant."

Claire didn't say anything, watching Joe spin through his amazing mind. He could remember anything; he actually had the gift of a photographic memory. Suddenly, he gave out a hoot. "Sure, I remember now. Bruce had him under his thumb for a while. Informing on some drug dealers. Left him stranded at court while one of the dealers got off scot-free, and this Clarence guy almost peed his pants. Bruce came and picked him up in a squad. But that was quite a while ago. I haven't heard anything about him recently."

Joe folded up his glasses and looked at Claire, his bottom lip hanging open, and then he sucked it in. "What're you doing messing around with this guy? He down in your area? Get rid of him. He's a case and a half, and liable to go off at any moment."

27

ou remind me of my dad a little bit."

Rich was stretched out on the bed next to Meg, and they had just finished reading a section of *Through the Looking-Glass*. He hadn't read the book since he was a kid, and he hadn't realized how funny it was. He loved the part where the White Queen told Alice that when she was a child she sometimes thought of six impossible things before breakfast. He needed to work on that exercise himself. "How's that?"

"You do voices."

"I do voices?"

"Yeah, you know, when you read. The queen sounds different than Alice, and I really liked the way you did Tweedledee and Tweedledum."

Rich dropped his voice and drawled a lazy English accent. "I'm delighted that my performance amused you, Your Majesty."

Meg giggled and looked very sleepy.

"Do you want me to sit in the chair while you fall asleep?"

"Oh, no. That was just for King Tut. But could you check on me from time to time? That's what my mom does. She says I fight with my blanket all night long, so she has to come in and break it up and straighten it out."

"I think I can do that."

Her eyelids were fluttering, and she was almost under. "You won't leave?"

"No, absolutely not. That's beyond impossible. That's completely impractical."

Her lips curved into a slight smile, and she turned her head into the pillow. He left the door open halfway and the light in the hallway on as he had been instructed. Meg struck him as a girl who knew her mind. She knew what she wanted, and she knew how to ask for it. He really liked her and admired her. Someone was raising her right.

Once Meg was asleep, he didn't quite know what to do with himself. He wandered from room to room downstairs, looking for clues as to who Claire was. She was an organized housekeeper, but not particularly tidy. She didn't dust often, and he was fascinated by one loopy cobweb in the corner of the bathroom. But her cookbooks in the kitchen were neatly arranged, and her spices were in a row and looked like they actually got used.

There were a few pictures: a great one of Claire when she was in her teens, and a gorgeous younger woman who he guessed was her sister Bridget. Claire looked all sparkly and had long, straight dark hair parted in the middle. Her teeth looked too big for her mouth, but her lips were also full. She was flirting with the camera, and she looked like a handful. It made him sad to think of all that had happened to her since then. When Meg had mentioned her father, he had been tempted to probe, but decided he would rather hear about the man from Claire.

He sat on her couch and read a copy of a magazine called *Country Journal* and learned how to rustproof your gardening tools. He might borrow that from her. Rich realized he didn't know when Claire would be getting home. She had said something about not being too late, but he hadn't an idea what that meant to her. He tended to angle toward bed around nine-thirty, ten o'clock. It was after nine, and he hadn't heard anything from her. He wondered what she had been up to, and if she would let him know.

He decided it was time to make the rounds. He checked on King Tut out on the porch. The little bird was definitely prospering, which he hadn't been sure would be the case. Maybe it was just so relieved to be away from the chick that had been pecking it that it didn't mind all the attention it was getting from these strange humans.

Next, he climbed the stairs and peeked in at Meg. Her mother was right. The covers looked like they had been strangled, twisted in her hands while the ends drooped to the floor. He gently untangled them and covered her again. She stirred, but just a whisper.

Then he went and stood in the doorway of Claire's bedroom. The hall light shone in, illuminating a patch across the floor and over her bedside table. On the table he saw what he had been looking throughout the house for—a picture of her husband. It was actually the whole family—Claire with Meg in her arms, and her husband behind her. He looked like he wouldn't give up life without a struggle. He was a big man, like that cop Bruce. Maybe that was Claire's type. He looked away and saw that the rest of the room was spare. The bed was dressed simply with white sheets and a comforter. The bedroom smelled clean and sweet, with just a hint of musk.

Rich walked down the stairs and then went outside and sat on the steps. The wind blew through the trees, and up the hill he heard an owl hooting. What the hell was he doing baby-sitting for a woman with whom he was falling in love? But maybe Stuart was right; maybe the way to Claire's heart, at least right now, led through her daughter. No matter what came of it all, he would be glad for the sweetness of his friendship with Meg. He had grown up without younger siblings and didn't think he knew what to do with kids. But she was truly a small person, surprising him with her odd ways.

He heard the sound of gravel crunching up the hill, then lights cut across the lawn, and finally Claire's car turned into the driveway. She didn't see him at first, and when she turned off the car, she simply sat still for a few minutes, staring straight ahead at the bluff. Must have been some shopping trip. He wondered if he should ask her what she bought. When she got out of the car, he decided not to. She looked stupefied, as if something had hit her in the face and she still didn't quite believe it. He decided he would let her do the talking.

He stood up and yelled, "Hi," to let her know he was watching her.

"Oh, hi. What're you doing out here?"

"Nice night."

Claire looked around as if she were presented with the night for the first time. "It's not too cold."

"No, not too cold. Definitely springlike."

She walked up to him and tried to smile, but it was a sham. Her hair was loose and hung over her shoulders like a veil. Her eyes were only dark in the light from the house. "Would you like a drink?" she asked him.

"Yes. I would love a drink."

"I mean a real drink," she continued as they walked into the house together.

"How real?" he asked.

"A single-malt Scotch." She walked up to the spice rack and pulled the cupboard door behind it open. From behind the boxes of macaroni and cans of tomato sauce, she pulled out a long-necked bottle.

"Sounds good."

She showed it to him. "I have this bottle that I only bring out when I really need a drink."

"Well, I am honored."

She didn't say anything. She went to the next cupboard and brought out two juice glasses. "Do you want Wilma or Fred?"

"We're drinking with the Flintstones?"

"They were handy."

"I'll take Wilma."

Claire pulled off the cork and poured him a healthy swig. "Good choice. She's smarter than Fred."

She poured herself a drink and chugged it, then poured another shot. They sat down at the kitchen table.

"How was Meg?"

"Meg was fine. She's a good kid."

That brought a smile out of her. "She is a good kid. She likes you."

"I like her."

Claire looked down at the drink she held in her hands and swirled the golden liquor around in her glass. "I like you."

He didn't know what to say. He knew he should say that he liked her too, but he felt like that wasn't enough, and would sound like he was simply copying her. He took a sip of the Scotch. Then he felt fortified enough to say, "It's mutual."

Claire turned her hands up. "I'm not really available to be liked."

Rich took another sip. "That's okay."

"I mean, my life is a mess."

Rich didn't argue. He had learned that didn't work. He watched her, waiting for a clue as to what she wanted.

"I have been trying to run away from my life. That's why I moved down here. I thought it was only in the city that life was truly evil. But it's followed me."

"I'm sorry. Is there anything I can do?"

She smiled and said, "You've been doing it. Helping out with Meg. Making me feel like I can trust someone again."

He finished his drink and asked, "What kind of trouble are you in?"

Claire looked at him, and it was as if her eyes opened wider in the dim light they were sitting in. She stared at him, examining his face for something, and Rich wanted to reach across the table and touch her, tell her she could tell him anything. Then she started, "It is such a long story—" The sound of her own voice scared her, and she shut her mouth. Then she said, "Some other night. I can't go into it right now."

"I understand," Rich said, not understanding at all. He stood up. He didn't think he should stay much longer. It was late for him, and Claire was ever so slightly drunk and completely lovely. "Well, you know, if things get too bad—"

She looked up at him. "Yes?"

"I am available." He turned and let himself out the front door.

AFTER CHECKING ON Meg, Claire poured herself one more shot. She had let Rich leave. What else could she do? At this moment in time, she was a suck hole. Anyone who came close to her was in danger of their life. There was no one that she could turn to anymore for help. She shut off the light in the kitchen and walked into the living room to sit in a rocking chair in the dark.

It scared her how small and alone she could feel. She had to remind herself to take deep breaths, because she caught herself holding her breath. Waiting. She felt frozen with knowledge of how horrible the world could be. Just when she thought that her life could get no worse, she would turn another corner and see just how much worse it could get.

She needed to find out what Bruce knew about Warren. If he used him as an informant, he would surely remember him, might even be in touch with him. This could be the breakthrough they were looking for. Conceivably, Warren had even used Bruce to get to Claire. Who knows what Bruce might have let slip, not knowing that Warren had it in for Claire? What was scary to Claire was that she didn't even remember the guy. Maybe she would if she saw him. She had arrested so many scumbags, after a while they all blurred together.

She needed to quit thinking about this, or she would never sleep tonight. She wanted to have another drink, but three was already over her limit. She would have to bring the crossword puzzle book to bed and puzzle away until she couldn't see straight.

The house seemed so quiet and safe around her, but she knew how penetrable it was. Anyone could get into this house if they wanted to. She would call and get someone to come out this week and put in an alarm system. She had resisted before, feeling strongly that she didn't want to live with so much fear. But now she felt like she needed to know that she would hear someone before they got to her in her bed.

She would also sleep with her gun. She always locked it away when she came home so that Meg would never have access to it. Too many stories of children playing with guns and killing themselves or others.

Suddenly, a rasping noise came from the back porch. She froze in her rocking chair. Was it the pheasant chick? Did pheasants make some strange noise that Rich hadn't warned them about? The noise stopped and then started up again. But this time she could tell it was no animal noise. It sounded metallic.

Claire stood, holding on to both arms of the rocking chair so it wouldn't rock back and make any noise. Then she crept over to where she kept her gun locked and pulled it out of the drawer. Quietly, she took off the release and crept to the back door.

Her eyes were already adjusted to the darkness, so she could see the shape of the back porch. It was empty, and she knew the door to it was latched. She had told Rich to do that. Meg would have insisted that he see to it. Nothing moved in the back. She stood staring through the window in the back door, and then she saw something. It was next to the door. A large man was sawing through the screen next to the door.

Claire waited. He didn't know she was there, so she had an edge on him. She was armed and ready to shoot. She would let him get into the porch. She wanted to see him before she did anything.

A hand reached in through the hole in the screen and unlatched the door. Then the door slowly swung out, and in walked a large man. He walked toward the pheasant's crate. Claire made out who it was and slammed open the back door, switched on the light, and said, "Freeze, you idiot. Get your hands up. What the hell are you doing on my back porch?"

Fred Anderson swung up his arms as if he were doing a jumping jack. His mouth dropped open, and his eyes bugged out of his head. When he saw the gun in her hand, the front of his pants darkened. "Oh Lord," he moaned. "I didn't do it."

"Well, yes, you did. You cut my screen and walked into my porch. What're you up to? Were you going to steal my pheasant?"

"Sort of."

Claire heard Meg call from upstairs. "Mom?"

"It's all right, honey. Somebody just stopped by. I'll be right up." Then she swung back around to Fred. "You've frightened my little girl. You better start talking, or I'm taking you in."

"Taking me in?"

"You bet, breaking and entering. That's a felony offense." Claire lowered the gun and motioned that he could drop his arms. "What are you doing here?"

"I just wanted to see your pheasant."

"Why?"

"I like to hold them."

Claire felt exhausted. She had cornered an old man in her back porch who wanted to hold her daughter's pet pheasant. It felt like a low point of her career. "Then what do you do with them?"

Fred looked confused, then he seemed to come through a tunnel, and the light shone on his face. "I must hold them too tight. They die."

Worse and worse. He killed pheasants. "Not a good idea. Have you been over to Rich's house, holding pheasants?"

"Yes. Are you going to arrest me?" He seemed excited about the idea.

"I'm thinking about it, Fred." Claire looked him over. He definitely needed a psychiatric evaluation. She would get on the phone and have someone pick him up. She backed into her house and picked up the cordless phone. Without taking her eyes off Fred, she dialed the sheriff's department. "This is Claire Watkins. Send a squad down to Fort St. Antoine, my house. Yeah, that's right. I've got someone who needs to go in for the night, at least."

"I could pay for the pheasants," Fred suggested.

"That might be a start." Claire let him stand there for a few moments while she was thinking. She had often found that a little thinking time made a suspect more compliant. Fred, in her mind, was still very much a suspect in the death of his brother. And since he seemed to be telling the truth, she might as well ask him a quick question. "Tell me, did you see Landers the night he died?"

Fred licked his lips, looked down at the pheasant, then back at Claire. "Maybe."

"Maybe. What kind of bullshit is that?"

He cringed at her tone and squinted his eyes like he was going to cry. "I'm not sure."

"We need to talk about that night, Fred. You need to tell me what happened to Landers. You better start remembering, or I could make it tough on you about breaking in here tonight. You're going to spend the night in jail. That will give you time to think it over. I'll be down to see you tomorrow."

His eyes grew big, and his hands flew up from his sides. "I haven't done anything."

"Yes, you have, Fred. Breaking into someone's back porch is against the law."

"No one ever told me that."

"You haven't been talking to the right people, then, Fred." Claire figured she might as well dump it all on him.

She didn't want to ask him any more right now. She needed to get it on tape. She didn't want him to tell her something and then have to try to get it out of him again. Get him into jail tonight, and then she wouldn't have to worry about him. "Well, we need to talk about Landers soon."

"Okay."

"Don't tell Darla," Claire warned him; she wasn't sure why.

"I don't tell Darla everything."

"That's probably a good idea."

"I try."

Claire nodded. "I guess we all try." She motioned him to sit down. They sat waiting for the police to come.

28

Claire stared at the jigsaw-puzzle piece of paper she had taped back together again. She read the number of the lot and block to the man over the phone. She said yes, she'd hold the line while he went and checked. While she waited, she stared at the faucet dripping in the sink. It probably needed a new washer. Maybe she could pick up a washer in Durand, when she went back to work. The drops of water fell regularly, every two seconds.

Minutes later, the man from Durand County was back on the line. "That piece of property is actually owned by Landers Anderson. He holds the deed on it."

Claire could hear the man rustling pieces of paper on the other end of the phone line. "Since when?"

"Since his uncle died in 1964."

"But Fred and Darla Anderson pay the taxes?"

"I don't know about that, ma'am."

"Thanks." Claire hung up the phone and stared down again at the piece of paper she had taped together.

So this was the missing piece. Darla and Fred didn't own

their house and property. They couldn't be part of the development without Landers quitclaiming the deed over to them. He wouldn't do it. Fred probably went over to talk to him about it; they had words; and Landers died. Now they owned everything—both their land and the house they lived in and Landers' property. But if she could prove they killed him, they would own nothing. After what had happened with Fred last night, she realized he was a loose cannon.

She would talk to Fred as soon as she finished up what she had to do with this Warren guy. That crazy old man on her back porch. She had called to check on Fred this morning and learned that he had been taken away for psychiatric evaluation, as she had requested. She knew, even if he were released today, he wouldn't leave town. He had nowhere to go that would make any sense to his life. She would have to have another conversation with Fred—this time with a tape recorder going. It would take about a minute to break Fred in two. He didn't have the backbone of a snake. She wondered, as she had before, what Fred and Darla's son was like.

"WHAT'S MOM GOING to do while I'm gone?" Meg asked.

Bridget patted Meg's skinny legs. They were lying stretched out next to each other by a swimming pool in the Best Western motel in Rochester, Minnesota. Meg was wearing a tight blue bathing suit with stars, left over from last year. Bridget wore a two-piece that she had just bought last year, but she felt like her stomach was starting to stick out too much already and felt self-conscious. The wound on her leg had healed nicely, but the one on her arm still looked a bit raw.

Chuck had gone to get them drinks; they had both ordered

Shirley Temples. Bridget had always loved them when she was a kid, and decided that she could take advantage of her pregnancy to order them again. "Oh, she just thought you needed a break. We all needed a break. She had a good idea, don't you think? This is going to be a lot of fun, staying at a motel."

Meg twisted her head around for a moment, wrinkling her nose as if an odd odor had risen up from the depths of the pool. "You don't need to be careful around me, Aunt Bridget. I know when Mom's up to something."

Bridget stared down at Meg's carefully coiffed little head. This was what scared her. Meg was more adult than Bridget felt she herself would ever be. What if her child turned out to be that way? "Well, since you know so much, what do you think she's going to do while you're gone?"

"Well, she showed me a picture that might have been that guy. The same one she showed you. I told her it could be. It wasn't a good picture. So I think she's going to get that guy. Arrest him. Throw the book at him. Lock him away forever and ever. Throw away the key. Then we'll all live happily ever after." Meg said it all very matter-of-factly. Then she added in a more worried tone, "I just hope King Tut is all right. I hope we left him enough food."

Bridget suddenly felt a sense of relief that Meg knew it all: how Claire had called up early Sunday morning and asked Bridget if she had any vacation time coming, how she then persuaded Chuck to take time off too and whisk them both away to a town where no one would even think to look for them. Meg obviously knew that Claire wanted them safe and out of the way so she could take care of business.

Bridget felt a slight chill run through her. Meg knew it all except the last thing Claire had said to Bridget. Claire had asked Bridget to take care of Meg if anything happened to her during the next few days. Bridget had promised she would, but prayed that she would never have to keep that promise.

She ruffled Meg's hair just so she wouldn't continue to be too perfect, then said, "I'm sure you did."

CLAIRE SWALLOWED A gulp of coffee. Bruce would be here in a bit. She had the coffee ready—nice and strong, the way he liked it—and the table set for two. She knew he had wanted her to stay out of the way in finding Red, but she couldn't do that. He had to understand.

Claire went to the window and looked out across the fields to the bluffs. A perfect day; already it was nearly sixty degrees. She could see hawks soaring off the bluffs. She wished that she could spend the whole day in her newly growing garden, clearing away the old plants from last year, giving the sprouts pushing up more room to grow. The ground would be warmed by this sun, and it would feel so good after the long, hard winter they had had.

Claire wondered what Rich was doing. She hadn't talked to him since he baby-sat Meg. She would need to do something special to thank him for that. And she should tell him that she might have caught his pheasant poacher. What was the suitable punishment for that old guy? Maybe Rich could make him shovel pheasant manure for a few days.

Bruce drove up the driveway as she was standing at the window. He was early. Claire watched him step out of his car. He was so tall, he unfolded as he stood. He looked the same, big guy moving toward the house with an easy roll. Claire took two deep breaths standing there in the sunlight and then started to put out plates for them. They had work to do.

"Hello," he hollered from the door.

"Come on in," she yelled back.

"Stopped at your favorite place, Big-Time Bagels." He looked happy and awake. His hair combed straight up from his forehead, he reminded her of a young football player, ready for his big game. As he handed her the bag, he smiled at her, and his eyes glinted with pleasure. "Two cinnamon bagels for you with plain cream cheese. That's your favorite, right?"

"You're a pal." She smiled back at him.

"I'd like to be more than that," he cracked back, not too serious.

"Any trouble getting off work today?"

"Hey, don't ruin my alibi. This is work." He laughed, a big, generous guffaw. "Don't you know, I'm reconnoitering with the Pepin County Police Department, deputy sheriff."

"So you are." She poured him a big mug of coffee, held it out to him, and then asked as he took it, "How many cups have you had so far this morning?"

"A 7-Eleven special. Grabbed it when I got gas. Might have got the two liquids mixed up. The taste was a cross between Styrofoam and car fumes. You know, it had that nice little oil slick on it that let you know it had been a brewing a long time."

"Yuck."

Bruce took a sip of her coffee. "So I guess I can truthfully say that this is my first real cup of the day."

Claire poured herself a cup and sat down to fix up a bagel. "This looks great."

"How's Meg doing?" Bruce asked, sitting down across from her.

Bruce caught Claire's eyes as she answered, and she forced herself to look him in the eye and give him a slow smile. "You know, I'm surprised, but I think she's fine. She didn't get much of a look at the guy. She really couldn't describe him to me. I think she took off running right away. So nothing bad really happened to her. It's Bridget I'm a little more worried about."

Claire ate a bagel with relish. This was one of the things she missed about living in the city, access to good ready-made food.

"What did she have to say about the guy?"

Claire pointed at her mouth and finished chewing. "She's the same as Meg. Couldn't give me much information. Actually I'm afraid with her it's more a case of real trauma. She really doesn't remember much that happened. The one thing she told me, though, was that he said I had arrested him at one time." Claire wanted to set this up right. See what Bruce had to say. "So I went and pulled up some old files of mine. Just to see if any of them would be likely suspects."

Claire laid out the copies she had made of the files on six of the perps she had had dealings with before she partnered with Bruce. Last night she had decided to play it cool and watch him pick out Red. Let it be a surprise for him that it was a guy he had worked with as an informant. "Could you look these over and see if any of them ring a bell to you?"

Bruce glanced at them and then asked, "Why are you going so far back?"

"I don't know where else to go. One of the things Bridget remembers the guy did say. She said the guy claimed I had arrested him. Said I pulled him in off the street. So it must have been before we worked together. I thought I'd look over all the potentials. Who knows, this guy could have been incarcerated someplace for the last five or six years, holding a grudge. So he explodes at me when he gets out of prison."

"Sure."

Claire finished off her bagel and then poured both of them more coffee.

Bruce took his time, reading over the files, really looking them over. He was being his usual, thorough self. He never rushed when he worked. It had bugged her when they sat next to each other and she was waiting to read something after him. There was no hurrying him.

Maybe she was completely wrong about it, but when he came to the file on Red, he looked it over like the rest and passed on to the next one. She felt herself tighten up in the chair. Why hadn't he said anything?

Finally, he stacked them all up and pushed them across the table toward her. "Nope, none of them mean anything to me. Don't know any of these guys. My guess is, it isn't one of them. I think you've gone too far back."

Claire stood and gripped the back of the chair, wanting to give him one more chance. She couldn't look at him, amazed at how easily he lied to her. How often had he told her lies? Was it possible he didn't remember an informant? Maybe Joey was wrong. Or maybe he was lying in order to protect her. She couldn't stand not knowing, yet she didn't want to show her hand. She pointed at Red's file. "What do you think about this guy, Bruce?"

He shrugged, hardly gave the file a look. "Not much. Looks like a real loser, penny-ante stuff."

"I don't know. He beat up a prostitute."

"That's nothing." Bruce picked up a different case. "The one that looks more interesting to me is this guy."

Claire looked over at the file of Tyler Anthony, who she had picked up on possession in 1991. "Why?"

"Just the range of activities. Starts with possession. He could be into heavier stuff, have access to some big guns, and not want you to recognize him again. Offhand, I'd say this is your guy." He held up the sheet on Anthony. "Have you shown these guys' profiles to Bridget or Meg?"

"I did. Neither of them was sure. Bridget didn't think either one was the guy, but she just isn't remembering it well enough."

"Interesting. We might want to try hypnosis on her. Maybe she could remember something else he said to her."

Claire nodded. "Yeah, that's a possiblity." She looked up at Bruce and smiled. "In the meantime, could you check Anthony out for me? I am going to try to stay out of this. If I know you're taking care of it, I will feel much better." Claire decided she had to back way off of this with Bruce. Let him think she was completely dropping it again.

"Don't worry about a thing. That's exactly what I'm here to do. Take care of you." He stood and walked around the table and took the dish she was holding from her hand. "Claire," he murmured, and ran a hand over her hair. He stood separate from her, but she could feel his desire.

She couldn't help the shiver that ran through her, but she didn't want Bruce to kiss her, so she leaned into him. "I just don't know—" she said, her face muffled in his clean, pressed white shirt.

At this slight hint of acceptance, Bruce grabbed hold of her and pulled her close. "I have the whole morning off," he told her.

She hugged him tightly and then gently extracted herself from his grip. "I wish I did, but I don't. I have to go check out this other case I'm working on—I told you about the murder case."

Bruce tried to pull her back in to him, but she resisted. "Come on, Claire. Don't play with me."

"I'm not playing. I've never played with you. I have only ever been honest and true to you. Yes, I have strong feelings for you. But I need to be a whole woman again. I need to understand what has happened to my husband. Don't you understand that?" She tried to speak calmly, but the anger and fear she had felt for the last day kept spilling into her speech.

"What do you want me to do? Can't we see each other

again?"

"I can't think of anything else but who took my sister and threatened my daughter. If you can find that guy, maybe we can start over again. I've gotta get going now. I need to be up in Durand by noon."

"I'll check out this guy for you. I think you might have something here. Then you won't ever have to worry about him coming after any of you again."

"That's what I want, Bruce."

He stood over her, took her head in his two large hands, and then leaned down and kissed her.

After a moment, he pulled away and held her tightly by the shoulders. "Well, I want you, Claire. That's all I've ever wanted from the moment I met you. I'd do anything for you."

Claire wondered how far he would go; she was afraid of what the answer could be. Would he kill her husband to get her? Would he hurt her pregnant sister, have her daughter kidnapped? If so, he would stop at nothing.

He walked out of the house and left her sitting at the table. She didn't move until she heard his car pull out of the driveway. Then she stood up, went to the sink, and leaned into it, feeling sick. Turning the water on full force, she washed her face and hands. A shriek came out of her, and she spun around. "Not Bruce. Please, not Bruce." After grabbing the coffee mug he had used off the table, she hurled it to the floor. Black drops of coffee speckled the floor in a gunshot pattern.

29

ed cracked open another hard-boiled egg and popped the whole thing in his mouth. He ate eggs that way because it reminded him of that gritty scene from *Cool Hand Luke* where Paul Newman swallowed fifty hard-boiled eggs. Red never pushed himself to see how many he could swallow; he simply ate them that way as an homage to the man. He didn't really like eggs, but he knew they were full of protein, so when he was dragging he'd swallow a couple eggs whole. That way he didn't have to taste them.

Unfortunately, they did kind of remind him of what happened to him in jail, having to go down on a couple guys, and sometimes that memory would make him feel like heaving the egg back up, but he'd tough it out. He wasn't ever going to jail again. Hawk had promised him that if he did what Hawk asked, he'd be safe.

That's why it was making him a bit tense to have Hawk snapping at him and telling him to get out of town. The last conversation he'd had with Hawk, Hawk gave him the deadline of Tuesday to leave town. Not possible, he had told him, he had a big shipment coming in, which Hawk knew. Hawk was in this thing up to his neck. Plus, didn't they want to finish off that Claire's sister, Bridget?

"You stay away from her!" Hawk had freaked on him. They were talking on the phone, but Red felt like he could see the veins popping out on his neck. He had once felt Hawk's hands around his neck when a deal had turned sour, and he never wanted to be there again. The man had the strength of a Mack truck.

"Jesus, what's with you?"

"I want you outta here, or I might need to take you down." Hawk had sounded like he was playing the tough-guy cop in a movie, but he certainly had the deep, gravelly voice for it.

Red didn't say anything for a while, let Hawk hang on the line like a fucking hooked walleye. What the hell did he think he was doing, threatening him like that? Didn't he know that they were deeply in this thing together?

Red thought maybe it was time to remind him, so he said, "Who's going to take who down?" He waited a beat, then another, then spit out the words. "I've got more on you than you would even want to think of."

"Who'd believe you?"

Then Red used the one name that he knew could send Hawk over the edge. "Claire. She'd believe me."

"Don't you ever—don't even think—"

Before Hawk could completely blow sky-high, Red cut in. "Hey, I would never do that. But I also know you gotta understand that I got a deal happening here. After it's over, in a couple weeks, I'll clear out of here. I promise, man."

"You little slug, don't you 'man' me."

"Hey, hey, hey—"

"Make it as fast as you can." Hawk ground the words out. Red could tell he was trying not to lose it again.

"Will do."

"Stay away from those women."

"Absolutemento."

Red hadn't known where he had come up with that last word, but he liked it. He was going to try to work it into conversation from now on. It could be like his signature. Hawk had hung up, and Red had needed to eat a few eggs.

RICH CALLED CLAIRE and heard the phone ring and ring. It was after six in the evening, and he thought he would find her there, making supper for Meg. He hadn't talked to her since they had had a few drinks together, and he didn't want that conversation left dangling in the air too long. It needed a follow-up, even a simple "How are you?"

That's what he had planned on asking—only, How are you? no presumptive, Do you want to get together? But when she didn't answer the phone, he started to worry. This was a very foreign feeling to him, but Claire was a woman walking around with more troubles than anyone he had ever known.

Growing up in this small town on a big lake, he had always had such a strong sense of security, that nothing could harm him. That didn't mean people didn't die or fight or drink—but this was different; he had a sense of real danger shimmering around Claire and Meg. He wanted to put them in a bubble, like that man in a TV show when he was growing up. He wanted the two of them safe.

But no one was there, and Claire didn't appear to have an answering machine. The phone ringing on and on was a sad sound, so he hung up the phone. He sat at his kitchen table and wondered about dinner. He could always have pheasant, but he was more than tired of it. A hamburger was what he wanted, with all the fixings—tomato, lettuce, even a strip or two of bacon. A big hamburger that he could sink his teeth into and feel like the meat was going straight to his muscles. They would enlarge simply from the protein burst.

That's what he had thought as a teenager, but he had also thought that you found one woman when you were twenty, you had sex, and you got married in some kind of order, and that was that. No way did he dream that when he was in his forties, counting his chicks as they were hatched, he would find a woman fraught with trouble who would fill him with passion. But it had happened, and maybe a hamburger would help—make him feel he was up to what was now on his plate.

"BRUCE, I'M GLAD I caught you." Claire's voice sounded close over the phone line.

Bruce was glad too. To hear Claire's voice at the end of his day was a real treat. "What's up, babe?"

"I think I found the guy."

What was she talking about? He had looked up more information on the Tyler sheet he had taken. The guy looked perfect for a setup. He was out of town, but had been here and not in jail when her husband had been killed. "I think you picked the right guy, all right. It all checks out with that Tyler guy."

"It's not him. Bridget remembered some more. It's that other guy, Red. I got on the phone, and I think I located him."

Bruce looked down at his watch. He had to fix this, and fix it fast. All of a sudden he wondered if he had enough time. He needed to get to Red before Claire talked to him. "Claire, are you sure?"

"Bridget remembered his name. It all fits. I arrested him six years ago, and he's pissed at me. Bridget said he's been carrying a thing for me. He was out of jail when Steve was killed." Claire stopped for a moment, then she added, "And he told Bridget there was some other guy in on the deal."

"Oh?" Bruce held his breath.

"Yeah, a guy named Hawk. The big man in their drug deals. I think that's who we were getting close to when Steve got killed."

"Hawk, huh?"

Claire talked fast and punchy. "I think we should move on this, Bruce."

"Where are you?"

"That's why I'm calling. I'm still down in Fort St. Antoine, but I'm on my way up. I found Red's most recent address through his parole officer. He lives in Minneapolis. Can you meet me there?"

Bruce held his breath. "Where is that?"

Claire told him. "North Minneapolis. Buchanan and Hennepin."

Shit, thought Bruce, she knows where he is. He had to stall her, put her off the trail long enough to take care of everything. "Yes, but let's not meet there. How about the Union Bar on Hennepin? We can figure out how we want to handle this. I'd actually like you to stay out of it."

"That's a good idea," Claire agreed. "What do you think? It'll take me about two hours to get up there—do you want to say eight o'clock?"

"Yeah, I'll meet you there at eight." That gave him enough time to take care of the situation. He should have done this long ago, and now it was being forced on him. That goddamn Red was going to have to go. In many ways, it would be a total pleasure, and now he could come out looking nothing but good.

"Great. I have a good feeling about this, Bruce."

Bruce leaned back in his chair and smiled at the tone in her voice. She sounded like the old Claire, the woman he had fallen head over heels in love with when she would saunter into the office and say just such a phrase to him. "I have a good feeling about you, babe."

CLAIRE HUNG UP the phone and slumped against the side of the phone booth. "Mike loves Cheryl to suck him off," she read, etched into the glass. Nice neighborhood. She had called from the Dairy Queen two blocks away from Red's house. He was in the house right now, some old beater car in the driveway. Now all she had to do was wait. She had rented a car so Bruce wouldn't recognize it. Rental cars were not unusual in this neighborhood. She wore a black jacket over her deputy uniform and a painter's cap with her hair pulled back into a ponytail. Cops were not particularly welcome in this neighborhood, but at the right time, she would shed her disguise and become a cop. She needed the security of her uniform to try to pull off what she was going to do.

She had thought very seriously about going to the police about this, tell them what she suspected, but she knew nothing would come of it. She could pin Bridget's kidnapping on Red, but she needed to find out what Bruce had to do with all this. Red had more to fear from Bruce than he did the legal system, so he'd never give him up. She had nothing concrete that tied Bruce to Red. Sure, he had been an informant, and Bruce had lied about that, but he could easily claim he simply didn't remember right then. What proof was that? All she had was her own deep, dark suspicion that had grown like a lake inside of her, flooding all avenues of hope. She had become clear about what she needed to do.

Claire parked down the block from Red's house, shaded by

some trees that allowed her a perfect view of the house. She would wait and see if Bruce drove up. If he did, she would follow him into the house. The three of them could have it out together.

It could turn out one of two ways: either she and Bruce would bring in Red and find out who this guy Hawk was, or she would bring Bruce and Red in. She had surprise and powerful anger on her side. She also had the belief that Bruce would never hurt her.

She thought of Meg for a moment and hoped she was having a good time with Bridget. Meg had looked at her so gravely when she had tried to act cheerful about her mini-vacation with Bridget and Chuck. After Claire had gotten done telling her how much fun she would have, she looked at her mom and said, "Just be careful, Mom."

30

ifteen minutes had passed. Claire knew, because she had watched each one of them tick by on her watch. She felt like she couldn't catch her breath. She hated waiting. Especially hated it when she was so scared. She figured it would take Bruce at least fifteen minutes to get to Red's house from work, if he was coming. If he didn't show in an hour, she would go down to the Union Bar to meet him. They could plan out the strategy together.

She tried to distract herself by watching the little girl playing in the dirt at the end of the driveway across from her. The girl must be about three. She was digging a hole. Odd, the fascination kids had with holes in the ground.

Claire remembered Meg trying to dig to China; she remembered Steve encouraging her, telling her that when she got there, she would see people walking upside down. She remembered the life she used to have and wondered how she got to be where she was, hunched over in a car. Then she saw Bruce's car pull up, and knew this was it.

. . .

BRUCE HATED DRIVING into this scuzzy neighborhood. When he had first been a cop, he saw this side of town as kind of exciting. He could feel people bristle around him when he wore his uniform and pulled them over to check their driver's license. But that wore off pretty fast. He realized it was truly dangerous around here, although not particularly for cops.

No, he came to see that living in this neighborhood was dangerous for the people who lived there. Their kids got shot and killed on their way home from school, riding their bikes, going for a walk.

He turned at the Dairy Queen and slowed down as he approached Red's house. He could see a car in the driveway. He hadn't been by to see Red since the kid called about him killing his dog. Man, he had reamed him out for that. What a brainless crud Red could be. Tell him to keep a low profile, and he kills a dog. Certainly engender good feelings in his neighbors. Time for Red to go. No doubt about it.

Bruce tapped his gun. He had set up this deal before he left the office, told the desk sarge that he'd gotten a call on an old informant, and it sounded like the guy might have been into some bad shit. Joe told him to watch his back, asked him if he wanted to take someone with him. Bruce shook his head no, explained that he thought he could handle it better on his own.

Then he stopped and turned back to Joe. "Hey, you remember Claire, right?"

"Hell, she's hard to forget." Joe had laughed silently, his shoulders shaking like an earthquake was happening inside of him.

"If she calls, tell her to sit tight. Tell her I'll be right there."

"Sure, no prob, Big Bruce." Joe had turned away and then lifted a big hand and said, "You know she was just in here a few days ago."

That had stopped Bruce in his tracks. No, he hadn't known. Why hadn't he known? She hadn't told him she'd been to town. "What was she doing here?"

"I'm not sure. Looking through some old files."

Bruce thought she'd said she took those files when she left the force, but maybe not. "Oh, sure. I think she told me about that."

Joe gave Bruce a long look. "Not the same without her around here. Bet you miss her."

"Who knows. Maybe we'll get her back."

Bruce thought about that as he checked out Red's front door. Wouldn't that be something, having Claire working on the Minneapolis police force again? But if they were going to be as tight as he hoped they would be, she probably shouldn't work with him. It wouldn't be approved by those in command. Plus, he wasn't sure he would like it. He knew one thing for sure. He'd much rather feel her in the night than see her all day long. Maybe after this was all over, he could persuade her to stay in town. That would certainly be the cherry on top of the whipped cream. What a sweet, luscious cherry she could be!

Bruce opened his car door and noted the activity along the street. Small girl left to play in the driveway. What was her mother thinking? Car parked midway down the street, but it looked empty. Nice quiet evening, sun just setting. Perfect time for an execution. He strolled across the street and walked down the broken-up sidewalk to the house. Piece-of-shit building. Metal screen door hanging half off its hinges. He knocked and waited to hear someone moving around inside. The wood door had a peephole, so he knew he would be screened before Red opened the door.

He heard loud music playing, a guy singing over and over again, something about being a loser, and wanting to be killed. Appropriate lyrics, Bruce thought. The level of the music dropped, and he saw the peephole go dark. A moment later, the door moved open, and a lanky figure appeared behind it.

"Hey, Hawk, what're you doing here?" Red asked.

"Just in the neighborhood. Wanted to say I was sorry about our last conversation."

With that the door swung open, and Red waved a beer bottle at him. "Don't think a thing about it. You want a hard-boiled egg? I made a whole bunch of 'em."

RED HAD BEEN having a nice afternoon. The eggs sat well in his stomach. He drank a few beers and then decided to take a 'lude. Hadn't done a 'lude in a long time, but seemed like the right kind of day. He was feeling fine, and it would slow everything down. Then he had stretched out on the couch, turned on the radio, cranked it up high, and thought about masturbating, but about all he could manage on the 'lude was to think about it. To actually put his hand down there and start to move it up and down was way too much work.

So he had lain on the couch and tried to remember that new word he had come up with. Then he had thought about Bridget, a special memory he pulled out for moments like this. He wished that he would have gotten a little further with her, although it did kind of weird him out that she was pregnant. Maybe he would visit her again, without Hawk having to know anything about it. Maybe he should get Hawk in trouble, like plant something in his car, then call in an anonymous tip on him.

God, that creamed him just thinking about it. It would be worth a gram or two just to get Hawk popped for drugs. He could say Hawk stopped him on the street and lifted the dope off him and then let him go. He could ask, had Hawk ever turned in those drugs? He knew what Hawk's car looked like. Wouldn't be that hard to do. God, it'd be nice to have that guy out of his life.

Then the doorbell rang. Just as his hand had been crawling down his chest. He grabbed the beer off the coffee table and peeked through the hole. Hawk-o-reeno in person. His sudden appearance made Red feel as if he could read his mind. Hawk did seem like he had extrasensory powers sometimes. He was spooky that way.

He opened the door for Hawk and invited him in, offering him an egg.

Suddenly he noticed that there was a uniformed cop strolling down the sidewalk toward them. Hawk turned but did nothing. The other cop came walking toward them and motioned them both into the house. She had a gun in her hands. It took Red a second to realize that the other cop was a woman and, most importantly, *the* woman—Claire Watkins. What the fuck was she doing here? Red could feel the edges of his brain slightly fizzing. He didn't need this. What did Hawk have cooked up now?

Hawk was asking her what she was doing here, but it could be a trap.

"I wasn't actually that far away when I called. You seem to know Red, Bruce. You had no trouble finding the place?" she asked, and her eyebrow lifted up at the end of the question. The gun she was holding was steady on Hawk.

Red cursed inside himself. His fucking gun was in the bedroom. What good was it in there?

"What are you getting at, Claire? We're both here for the same reason."

Hawk had raised his voice, and it made Red's ears feel warm and tingly. It was too loud. He didn't like it.

"Don't shout!" Red yelled at Hawk.

"Do you understand what's going on here, Red?" Hawk had turned his back on Claire and was facing Red.

Red didn't like what he was seeing in Hawk's eyes—a shifty look that meant trouble—or what he was hearing in Hawk's voice—blame.

"We've figured out who's responsible for one murder and a very nasty kidnapping. Claire found you out and tracked you down. Her sister has fingered you and said you killed Claire's husband too." Hawk reached into his holster and pulled out a huge gun, pointing it right at Red.

Red felt like the eggs were doing dodgem cars inside his belly. If things didn't quiet down, he was going to blow pretty soon. He backed up as the gun came toward him. He couldn't help it. The gun was black and ugly, and he knew what size hole it would leave as the bullet traveled through his body. Red pushed his feet backward until he hit something. He was up against the wall of the living room.

"Hey, I didn't do a thing. I haven't been feeling too well this last week or so. I haven't left the house. You've got the wrong guy."

Hawk laughed. "You are the right guy, my friend. And if you don't confess to what you did, I'm going to shoot you right here and now."

The gun moved in closer and seemed like a cobra snake ready to strike. Red didn't like the way it zoomed in toward him. He put up a hand to hide the end of the gun. "Don't, Hawk," he asked. "Please don't."

"Tell this lady what you did, then," Hawk demanded.

"I did it. I killed that guy. Put the gun down. Please."

"See," Hawk said, and turned to look at Claire.

Red followed Hawk's glance, and that's when he saw that

Claire still had her gun out, and it was still pointed at Hawk. She was standing over across the room.

"Claire, you got the right guy," Hawk told her.

Claire kept staring at Hawk and said, "I know. Bruce, he called you Hawk. Hawk was the guy that Bridget said was behind all this."

"It's him." Hawk pointed at Red.

Red felt the gun dip and decided he should take his chance. "Hawk told me to do it."

Hawk turned all his attention back on Red, and the gun pointed toward him. Hawk yelled, "You don't know what you're talking about, you lying fuckhead."

Claire didn't move. She kept her eyes on Hawk.

Red screamed. "Shoot him. It's all his fault. It was all his idea. He killed your husband to get you."

Hawk's hand jerked, and Red felt something explode inside his body, the room jolted red, then white, then nothing.

CLAIRE NEVER TOLD anyone what happened next. She took the moments that followed and dug a deeper hole inside of her than her husband had been buried in, and she vaulted the moments inside. The gun went off in Bruce's hand, and she knew she had to decide. She saw the body of the skinny man called Red turn very red in his chest, and his arms flew out and his body caved in and he started falling. She knew she only had a moment or two.

Bruce was still aimed toward Red, but then he started to turn, a slow spiral. And she was never sure if Bruce would have been able to kill her. She was never sure. When he turned toward her, his gun pointed at her, she knew she only had a moment to decide what to do. He wasn't looking her in the eyes; his eyes weren't smiling. He was staring at her shoulder, right where a shot might go.

She thought of Meg walking through a field, gathering flowers, she thought of Bridget holding a new baby in her arms, a sweet handful, she thought of her husband going out to get the evening paper and dying on the grass. Bruce's gun lifted toward her, and she pulled the trigger.

He didn't die immediately. He twisted and he slumped. His hand rose to his chest and came away bloody. His eyes dimmed, and he tried to find her with them. His mouth opened, and he said one word that she heard, he said, "Why," but didn't even have enough strength left to make it a question. The word didn't rise at the end. It fell with the rest of him to the floor.

Claire stood in the silence that filled the room and left her own body for a moment. She felt the world black around her, dark and despairing. She saw down a long, dark hallway with no doors and knew it was her life and she would have to keep on walking, that there would never be any way out of it. Then she fought her way back into it. The world took shape again, and she felt light, as if something evil in her had flown away and was gone.

Two men were dead in the room, and neighbors had probably heard the shots. She had work to do. She had to take care of Bruce and save herself. She wiped off the gun she had inherited from her dad and that there was no registration on, and put it in Red's hand. She rubbed her right hand on Red's, so he would have some of the powder residue from the shot on his hand.

Then she walked over to Bruce. She was on automatic. This all had to get done, and quickly. He was so big and so heavy, but she needed to move him. She turned Bruce so he faced Red, and then she moved in on him. She put her hands on his chest as if to stop the flow of blood. She tried to resuscitate him. She slapped his face. Her hands were bloodied, and she had polluted the crime scene horribly. Just what she wanted.

When she was sure that the men were just the way she wanted them, she went to the kitchen sink and scrubbed her hands down with the Scotch Brite sponge. If it would scour pans, it should take care of her hands. Then she walked to the phone. She called directly through to the desk and got Howard. "Officer down, Joe. Shit, it's Bruce." Her voice broke. She gasped. "I think he's dead. Send over a squad and an ambulance." She gave him the address.

Then she sat very still on the edge of the couch and waited. When she heard the siren, she made herself think of all the people she loved who had died, Bruce among them, and she cried. The police found her hysterically sobbing, bent over near the man she had worked with for years, her partner.

❧ 31 ❧

I don't know how he did it." Claire spoke the words through sobs. "He was shot, but he still pulled the trigger and killed that guy. He saved my life. And now he's dead."

The atmosphere was tense and sober in the small, dark living room that Red had occupied. But there was also a sense of pride and justice in what Bruce Jacobs had managed to do before he went down.

The bodies were still in the house. They had been photographed from every angle. Plastic bags had been taped around their hands. No one had even suggested that Claire be checked over. She had apologized for making a mess of the crime scene. No one had been critical. Everyone had treated her like she was porcelain. She wasn't sure they were wrong.

Clark Denong, a homicide detective whom Claire didn't know very well, was taking her statement. He had still been in the ranks when she left and, at twenty-eight, was fairly young to be made detective. With his slicked-back black hair and eyes that were too wide apart in his head, he had the demeanor of a bull but was actually, from all she had heard, a very nice man.

He told her, "I remember a cop telling me a story like this—you know, where a guy managed to get a shot off before he caved—but I never thought I'd see anything like it."

Claire just shook her head. She figured she had said enough. She had been questioned off and on for two hours. She had said the same things over and over again. Bridget had identified Red as her kidnapper; Claire had called Bruce and asked him to meet her here; he had gone in before her; when she saw he was in trouble, she had gone in. Red had shot Bruce, and Bruce, in a superhuman moment, had in turn shot Red before he died.

She would add nothing to it. Less was always better when you were lying. She had learned that from the felons she had worked with. Now that she had given them the framework, they could piece the picture together, and for a dead officer, it would be as pretty as they could make it.

"Let's get you out of here." Denong helped her up. She had been perched on a metal chair they had pulled in from the kitchen. "I've got your statement. This is no place for you to be."

Claire let him walk her out of the house and then ask her where she wanted to go. "I need to get home," she told him.

"Sure. Are you going to be all right to drive? You live down in Wisconsin now, on the river, right?"

"Yeah. I'll be fine. I'll go get a cup of coffee, and I'll take it easy." Claire looked up at the sky. It was dark with the orange cast of the city's ambient light. "You'll keep me posted."

"You better believe it. I'll call you right after the chief."

She laughed, then snuffled. "Okay. Take care of him."

"We try to take care of our own," Denong said back to her. It struck her as sounding as awkward as what she had said. They were both babbling, trying not to show how bad they felt about what had happened.

She walked down the street and crawled into her car. She

headed to an old familiar spot, the Perkins on Lake Street, open twenty-four hours a day. Bruce and she had gone there often. She slid into a booth and ordered what she always ordered: a short stack of pancakes, a side of bacon, and coffee. But when the food came, she stared at it and then shoved it around her plate. She managed to eat a few bites of the pancakes, feeling she needed some sugar in her for the ride home. Trying to distract herself, she picked up the paper. She couldn't go back and change what she had done.

At this thought, the paper started to shake in Claire's hands, and she stopped eating. She put the paper down and stared at the spot Bruce should be sitting in. She understood so little of what he had done to her. How had she ever thought she had known him? What had made him think he could get away with it? Because he was a cop, did he come to believe he was above the law?

She sat in the booth and made herself think about what she had done. She knew after this night that she would try to push it out of her mind, but now she needed to face it. Once she had worked on a case that involved horrible child abuse. A father was beating and raping his little girl. When Claire questioned the girl, it was clear that the seven-year-old loved her father. All she would say was, sometimes he was mean, but she talked as if that were a different person.

Claire now knew how she felt. There was Bruce, and there was Hawk. There had been a terrible evil in her life, and she had killed it. That was Hawk. There had been a man who had loved her and was her partner, and she had saved his reputation. That was Bruce. They were both dead, and she would mourn the passing of Bruce. It was over.

Trying to take another bite of the pancakes, she found they had turned to sawdust; the coffee she was pouring down her throat was acid. She pushed the plate away from her and stared out the window. Dark stared back in at her. The road home would be winding and shadowy. Somehow she needed to make her way home. She threw more than enough money on the table for the check and a tip. She would make one phone call, and then she would drive down to Fort St. Antoine.

BRIDGET WAS SURPRISED to be paged at poolside, and then she was panicked. Only one person knew she was here, so did that mean Claire was all right? She bolted across the tile floor, slipping and then trying to slow down. She didn't want to fall. The clerk showed her to a phone at the edge of the checkout counter she could use.

"Are you all right?" Bridget asked as soon as she picked up the phone.

Claired seemed to think about the question before she answered quite solidly, "Yes, I am."

"What happened?"

"Two men died. One was Red. So you need never worry about him again." Claire spoke very fast, words like darts on the telephone line.

Bridget felt relief sweep over her like a hot flash. "Oh, God, thank you."

"You need to thank Bruce. He's the guy who put him away, and unfortunately—" Claire's voice broke.

"Claire? No."

"Yes, unfortunately, Bruce died in the line of duty."

"I'm so sorry. Your best friend." Bridget wished she could take the words back when Claire didn't say anything for a moment. Maybe they had been a lot more than that. Bridget had always suspected a more intimate closeness between the two of them. She waited for Claire to answer.

A sigh, then Claire said quietly, "No, you are my best friend."

"You know what I mean."

"Yes, at one time, Bruce meant a lot to me."

"You sound funny."

"Does that surprise you?"

"Where are you?"

"At a Perkins."

Bridget could feel relief rising up her body in bubbles. "Do you want to come down and join us?"

"No. I don't. I want a day to myself. Can you keep Meg like we'd planned—overnight?"

"Sure." Bridget wasn't surprised that Claire wanted time alone. She had always been like that. When they were growing up, even if something good happened, she'd often go to her room to savor it in solitude.

"Don't tell her about Bruce. Just tell her about Red. I'll tell her about Bruce."

"That sounds good."

"Tell her I love her." This time Claire's voice broke straight through, and Bridget heard the tears behind it.

"Of course."

AFTER AUNT BRIDGET told her in no uncertain terms that that horrible Red guy who tried to kidnap her was dead, Meg decided it was time to go for a swim. She hadn't wanted to before, because she felt like she had to keep thinking about her mom so nothing bad would happen to her. But now she could relax. Mom was on her way home. She would see her tomorrow.

Meg slipped into the water slowly. She hated to jump in. It seemed so rude to her, such a shock to the body. She inched in a short step at a time. The part she hated was when the water reached her belly button. That seemed like the most cold-sensitive spot on her. Usually she let the water reach slightly above that, and then she would do a jump-dive. That's what she called them anyway. She skipped up in the air, flung her hands over her head, and aimed toward the bottom of the pool. If the chlorine didn't burn her eyes too much, she opened her eyes underwater. She swam better underwater than on top. Her swimming instructor had told her that was because she was too skinny, so she didn't float, except the tip of her nose stuck out.

She was glad Aunt Bridget was going to have a baby. It could be like a little sister to her. Of course, she hoped it was a girl. A boy, what was there to do with a boy? But a girl you could tell secrets to, dress up, comb her hair, play dolls with. Although she hardly played dolls anymore. Now she was getting old enough to where she was supposed to care about boys. With that thought, she popped to the surface and started to do the breaststroke. She wondered if the stroke really helped your breasts. Hers were starting to slightly lift off her chest. She hoped and prayed they didn't get too big. They seemed like they would just get in the way, like when you were trying to do the breaststroke.

After swimming around the pool for a while, Meg did her favorite thing. It was kind of silly really, but she loved to go all loose in the water and hold her breath and let the water hold her up. Again, her floating wasn't much good, but the water cradled her, and if she closed her eyes, she felt like she was in heaven or at least in the sky. Then she talked to her dad. Now she told him that Mom was okay and that the guy that had killed him was dead. News might not travel from heaven to hell that fast. She wasn't sure she really believed her dad was in heaven, wearing white robes and playing a harp. She thought maybe he was sitting around a table playing cards and smoking a cigar. That's what he'd like.

Suddenly, Meg stood up in the water. She would always keep her dad in her heart, but now that his killer was gone, she could let go of him a little. She wouldn't need her dad as much as she had. He didn't have to watch out for her anymore. And more important, nobody was going to hurt her mom. Because if there was one thing in the world that had worried Meg, it was that something would happen to her mom. She hadn't wanted to let Aunt Bridget know, but she had been awfully worried about her.

32

A week later Claire was finally ready to interview Fred Anderson. She had the tape recorder sitting on her kitchen table, a list of questions, a lawyer at the ready in Durand, and her head slightly back on straight.

It had been a long, hard week. For much of it, Claire had been blaming herself for what Bruce had done. She should never have slept with him, but then, in quiet moments, she would remind herself that by the time she had slept with him, he had already had her husband killed. Whatever had been set in motion was not so much about sex, but rather about possession and his own greed.

She had treated Bruce like the honorable, generous man she had thought him to be while he was her partner. She would not have changed a thing that had happened between them. It was true she had loved him. Once or twice, she had even lusted after him, in that way that happily married people do, but she had never led him on. It had happened. And now it was over.

She had been interviewed several more times about the killings. Bridget had been called in, the forensic lab had verified what

Claire described; there seemed no question but that Bruce deserved a badge of honor and that Claire had been very lucky to come out of it alive.

Then there had been the funeral. Claire had worn a veil and dipped her head when she should have cried, but had remained remarkably clear-eyed through the proceedings. She had been supported on all sides by fellow officers. Then she found out that she had been listed as a beneficiary in Bruce's will. Claire thought it an odd way to be reminded that he had loved her in his own fashion. The fifty thousand dollars she would inherit would go right into a fund for Meg's college education.

Yesterday, she had called Darla and Fred and set up her appointment with them. In talking to Darla, she had sensed resignation and wondered what would come out of their meeting. The truth, she hoped.

Claire checked that the tape was in the recorder, then left the house. A scent of lilacs was in the air. Her crab apple trees had burst into bloom overnight. A cardinal was singing his two-noted love song. She stood by her car for a moment and breathed it all in. Spring spoke of such promise, if she could only begin to listen and trust this new song she was hearing all around her.

BRIDGET FELT ON top of the world. Actually, she was on top of her horse, and it felt great. The day had tipped over into eighty degrees, an early warm spring. She rode across the field and pulled Jester up before they entered the forest. The sun's warmth felt so good on her shoulders, she wanted to linger in it. She pulled off her sweatshirt and looked at the very slight bulge of her stomach pushing through her T-shirt. She was almost three months pregnant, according to the doctor, and she was beginning to get over the nausea.

Her visit with the doctor had left her feeling more in control. He said he saw no reason why she couldn't ride all through her pregnancy, or for as long as it felt comfortable. He told her that they had found that fit women delivered more easily. Of course, she should take it easy toward the end, but in fact a nice, gentle ride might even bring on the baby if for some reason it should go past term.

Then she could buy a Snugli, those baby carriers that fastened to your front, and go riding with the baby. It would probably put the little beast to sleep. Chuck was delighted he was going to be a father. He had stopped going over to his brother's to fix cars and was working on getting the room ready for the baby. She actually told him to go have a beer the other night, just to get him out of the house.

And Bridget had decided to take a cooking class. She had even bought a cookbook, the one her mother always used—Betty Crocker. She had cooked macaroni and cheese again, and even though it was a little burned on the top, Chuck said it was great.

Then, under her hand, she felt a movement, a slight thump. "Whoa," she yelled. "It's sending messages," she told Jester. Awful early for her to be feeling the baby; from what she had read, they don't kick until about the fourth month. But this was going to be one smart being. It had already begun to be part of her life in a way that amazed her.

She wheeled Jester around and sent him into the woods. The cool darkness touched her cheeks, and she welcomed the ride.

CLAIRE KNOCKED ON the door and heard someone say, "Come in," so she walked in. A middle-aged woman whom Claire had never seen before lounged on the couch. The woman stared at Claire, and Claire returned the stare, for this woman was a piece of work. She was tall and well-built, wearing a dress that showed off her cleavage. Her blond hair was swept back in an old forties-style hairdo. Claire kept feeling like she had seen the woman somewhere, but couldn't place her.

"Hello, I'm Dora." The woman stood up and formally held out her hand.

Claire shook the large hand and said, "I'm Claire Watkins, deputy sheriff."

"Yes, I see that. Nice to see a woman in uniform." The woman nodded Claire to a seat, as if she owned the house.

"Are Fred and Darla home?"

"Yes, they're doing something in the basement. They should be right up."

Claire sat and pulled out the tape recorder from her bag, then her notebook. Suddenly, she remembered where she had seen the woman before—she was the woman in Landers' photo. This was the woman who had signed, "Love to Landers."

"So you knew Landers?"

Dora nodded. "Oh, yes. I knew him well. I wasn't at the funeral because no one let me know it was going on. I was so sorry I missed it."

"So you were close to Landers?"

"Family, you might say," Dora said with a smile.

Claire couldn't figure out what Dora was doing here. Maybe she felt that she deserved something from the estate. But she seemed so comfortable. And Claire got the feeling that she was really enjoying this conversation. But then, she looked like a woman who enjoyed life in all its complexities.

Claire asked her, "Are you a friend of Darla's?"

Dora laughed, slipping a cigarette out of a pack and lighting up before answering. She blew a cloud of smoke up toward the ceiling and then said clearly, "Hardly. I'm her son."

"Whoops." Claire's arms rose, and her tape recorder, note-book, and tapes she had brought in went crashing to the floor.

Darla and Fred walked in as Claire was reassembling her material.

"So I see you two have met," Darla snapped. She did not look good today. She hadn't bothered to put on her wig, and her own thin hair was stick-straight and plastered to her head. She lacked her usual bounce and aggressiveness.

"Yes," Claire said. Claire looked at Dora and still saw a very attractive, large, middle-aged woman.

"At one time that person"—Darla pointed just in case there was any question about who she was talking about—"was my son. Now she's remade herself into someone I don't know."

"Or don't want to know," Dora added.

Fred said, "It's hard on your mom."

"Get over it, Dad. She always wanted a girl. She told me that all my life. Now she's got one. But you know Mom, never happy with what she's got. She always wants what the other person has." Dora turned to Claire. "But I think you have a reason for being here, and maybe we should get on with it."

"Yes." Claire turned on the tape recorder.

Fred sat down on the couch by Dora, and Darla sat on the piano bench on the other side of the room.

"Fred, you told me the other night that you saw Landers the night he got killed. Is that right?"

"Well, it was hard to see because it was getting dark out. I drove by his house. He was out in the yard."

Before he went any further, she Mirandized him. He lis-tened, but nothing seemed to move behind his eyes. "Do you understand all of this, Fred? I'm reading you your rights."

"Yes. That's why our son is here. I asked him to come."

"Okay, just so you understand." Claire felt sorry for the old man. He looked, as always, befuddled. She knew he was scared of her and hoped he would tell her the truth.

"Were you by yourself in the car?"

"Yes."

"Did you stop your car?"

Fred looked at Darla. She was staring down at the floor. He seemed at a loss for words. "I think I did."

Unsure why he didn't know what he had done, she went on to the next question. "Did you get out of your car?"

He grew more confident. "I did."

"Did you talk to Landers?"

"No."

"Did you hit Landers?"

"I'm not sure."

"Was Landers dead when you left?"

"I think so. He was facedown on the ground. I didn't check on him. I was scared."

"You know this is very serious, Fred." Claire looked at him. "Landers died because of an injury, and you could be tried for murder."

His face twisted up into a grimace, as if he were trying to hold something bitter inside his mouth. Fred looked at Darla again, then he said her name: "Darla?"

"Why did you hit him?"

Fred said, "I didn't want to hurt him. He was my brother. He helped me out a lot of times. He always stood up for me."

"I know that, Fred. Did you finally just get mad at him?"

"No, it wasn't like that."

Claire waited for him to go on. Sometimes she found she could be too directive in the questioning and miss what people really wanted to tell her. If she kept quiet once in a while, it gave them a chance to tell their story. But when the story started, it was Darla who broke the silence.

"Oh, this is a farce. That old fart had nothing to do with it."

Fred buried his face in his hands.

Darla continued, "He was there, but he didn't do a thing. I slugged Landers with the shovel. I'd been wanting to do that for more than fifty years."

Claire jumped in. "Darla, you understand your rights here. You may remain silent, and I am recording what you're saying, so it can be used in court against you."

"Yeah, yeah, yeah. Nothing's going to go to court. I'm not going to live that long. Look at me. You see a dying woman. What'd they give me, Fred? Another month or two, not enough time to pull this case together. Am I right?" She looked at Claire for confirmation.

Claire felt like this interview had gotten out of control. She stared at Darla, and now saw more than the signs of aging. Her clothes hung on her; her eyes seemed glazed, and her lips chapped and cracked. She was wasting away. Claire nodded in response to her question. "I doubt we could bring this to trial so quickly. But you're confessing to killing Landers?"

"Sure. Why not? I've hated the guy since he dumped me. He always looked down on Fred and me. Didn't think either of us was good enough for him. He wouldn't have had anything to do with us, but Fred was his brother, and in his own way he took care of us. What that meant was that we had to do whatever he asked. We didn't even own the goddamn house we lived in." Darla's voice shook, then she regained control. "He didn't think Fred could handle that. So he kept it in his name while we paid for everything. And when we finally had a chance to make some money on our own, get into this development plan by which we stood to gain maybe a couple hundred thousand dollars, he wouldn't let us. He said it wasn't a good idea."

"Mother—" Dora leaned forward, trying to stop the flow of words.

"Don't you Mother me, you mutant. You thought you knew your uncle Landers. He was always good to you. Well, you didn't know a thing about him. In fact, he was probably responsible for you turning into such a fairy."

Dora sat stunned and then fluttered her eyelashes. "My, I have one more thing to thank him for."

"He only liked you because he couldn't have kids of his own with his stupid wife. She was always such an invalid. Delicate, schmelicate. That woman was as manipulating as they come."

Dora drew herself up and spoke. "Landers was the only one in my family that stayed in touch with me. He even came up and saw my act a few times. I don't care what you say about him. He was a swell guy and a great uncle."

"How about father? How was he as a father?" Darla snarled.

Dora put down the cigarette and ran a hand through her hair. "What are you going on about, Mother?"

Fred raised his head from his hands and shook it. "Darla, do you have to? Can't you just shut up for once? Haven't you done enough damage?"

But there was no stopping Darla. She burned with rage. Fred's words only made her madder. "Landers got me pregnant before he left for the army. Why do you think I married Fred? I had to. Landers wouldn't even answer my letters. What could I do in those days? I didn't know anybody. My family wouldn't help me. Fred was the only one who was even nice to me. So we got married a few months before you were born."

Dora asked, "Did Landers ever know?"

"No, I never told him. He never figured it out. But a few

years ago, I decided to tell his idiot wife. I showed her a picture of me and Landers together. She had always wanted a child so bad. The idea that I had carried and raised Landers' child sent her over the edge. She held it against Landers and never told him. I loved it. He got back some of what he deserved, all right."

"So you killed him? Why, after all these years?" Dora had taken over the questioning, and Claire thought she was doing a good job. She just kept watch to see the tape recorder was still running.

Darla started to tremble. "Throw me one of those cigarettes. Doctor says I shouldn't smoke. Isn't that a laugh? Lung cancer as far gone as mine, and he's worried if I'm smoking." She grabbed the pack and pulled out a cigarette. Claire watched in fascination; she saw some similarities between Dora and Darla. With the cigarette lit and inhaled, Darla went on. "I didn't go over there intending to kill him. I was just going to talk to him and persuade him to sign over our property to us. But when I saw him bent down on the ground and the shovel right behind him, I was so pissed off at him, I grabbed it and swung. And he stood up. He walked right into it. The shovel hit his head, and he fell. Fred drove up, and I sent him off to pinochle. I left Landers lying on the ground. I didn't know if he was dead or not. I didn't care. I figured if he was dead, we would get the land for sure. I wanted Fred to get something before I died." Darla took a long drag on the cigarette and then pointed it at Claire. "But I'll tell you another thing. It makes me happy to think Landers died before I did."

MEG HAD RAMAH help her find his phone number. Then she dialed it by herself. After five rings, he picked up the phone. She said, "Hello, Mr. Pheasant Man." Then she started to giggle.

"Hello there, Miss Meg," he said seriously.

"I think my pheasant needs a bigger pen, and Mom doesn't know how to build it. Could you come over and help me make King Tut a better home?"

"Of course. When would be convenient for you?"

"Pretty soon. Could you come today?"

"I think I could arrange that. I'll bring my tools."

"I can help."

"I was counting on that."

"Good." Then she just hung up.

Ramah looked at her. "Why didn't you say good-bye?"

"Didn't need to. He's coming right over. That'll be good, because my mom hasn't seen him in a long time."

WHEN CLAIRE DROVE up, she saw that two people were busy constructing something in her backyard. She sat in her car and watched them for a moment until Meg saw her and began to jump up and down and wave her hands at her. Then she stepped out of the car. The spring weather had held, clouds floating above the bluffs in the clear blue air. A red-tailed hawk soared in the current off the bluff, and Claire felt her heart rise in her chest. To fly like that would be incredible.

She hadn't seen Rich since the night they had had a drink together. He was wearing a red flannel shirt with the sleeves pushed up and jeans. He raised a hammer as she watched him and drove a stake into the ground. It looked like King Tut was getting a new pen.

"The royal kingdom expands?" she asked as she walked up.

"Rich said I was right, that King Tut needs a bigger place outside. We're going to make the walls high so no coyote can get him."

"Great. Does anyone need any lemonade?"

"Sounds good." Rich wiped his face with his sleeve and smiled at her.

The two of them followed her into the house about ten minutes later, after having put up the chicken-wire fence.

"He likes it better than the porch, Mom."

"How can you tell?"

Meg wrinkled her nose, then jumped around the kitchen on one foot. "Because he can peck at the real ground and get little bits of dirt and stuff. Rich says that's good for him. You know how you always tell me you need to eat a little dirt? Well, I guess pheasants really do."

"Here, take this lemonade and run outside and watch King Tut peck at the ground for a while."

Meg leaned into Rich's leg. "Do I have to go outside? Can't I stay with you guys?"

"Yes, you have to go. It's a beautiful day, and I would like to talk to Rich alone."

"Why?"

"Because he's my friend too."

The last statement made Meg laugh, and she went running outside.

"Can I ask you a few questions?" Claire sat down at the table, and he followed suit, sitting across from her.

"Of course. Is this in the line of duty?"

"Yes. Sort of."

"Ask away."

"Who do you think killed Landers?"

"Well, the one person capable of it is Darla."

"Why didn't you tell me that?"

"It's pure speculation, and you never asked."

"Did you know that Darla's son was a transvestite?"

"Yes."

"Why didn't you tell me that?"

"Didn't think it was pertinent to anything, and you didn't ask." Rich wasn't saying it meanly, just matter-of-factly.

"Anything else you think I should know about this case but I haven't specifically asked you about?"

"Yeah, Darla's pretty sick. I'm not sure, but that might make a difference in what has happened."

Claire leaned back in her chair and took a good look at this thin, well-built man sitting across from her. His face pleased her; it was so angular and full of character. He looked like he worked for a living and spent a lot of time outdoors. He also looked like he was good with his hands, and she knew he could keep a secret. "I want you on my side from now on, okay?"

"What does that mean?"

"Well, let me tell you first that I met Dora today."

"How was she?"

"Fine, I guess. She found out that Landers was her father."

Rich screwed up his face in surprise. "That's one on me. Never guessed that."

"I think it made her kind of happy."

"I bet."

"She also found out that her mom only has a month or two to live, and that she killed Landers, rather on impulse. Darla wanted Landers' property. She did it so Fred would get the land."

"What're you going to do—arrest Darla?"

"I'm not sure yet. I don't think she's going anyplace. I have to go talk to the sheriff about this."

Rich sat and thought for a moment, then said, "You know what this means?"

Claire waited.

"It means that Fred doesn't get the land. According to what

you've told me and what I've heard, Landers died intestate. His next of kin is Dora. She'll inherit everything. I wonder if she'll sell me a chunk of Landers' property that borders on mine."

"So Darla doesn't get her final wish. I think that's good." Claire liked the way his mind worked. "So you'll be on my side?"

"Sure. What're we playing?"

Claire took a sip of her lemonade. Very sour lemonade. It made her mouth pucker. She had never done what she was about to do before. But she felt sure that it was her turn. So she asked Rich, "I was wondering if you would make yourself available for a date?"

Epilogue

C laire stood on the edge of the cemetery, watching a doe and two fawns feeding on the new grass. She had always wanted to be cremated until she saw this cemetery. On the side of a hill, cupped in a valley that went down to the lake, it overlooked a wildflower meadow. It was so quiet and peaceful, she actually believed that it might be a good final resting place. She was glad Landers was buried here.

As she stepped onto the grass, the deer stared at her and then turned gently and moved back into the forest. After they were gone, Claire walked slowly around the old gravestones and came to the new one, Landers' death date chiseled into the granite face. Not even a month ago, he had died. She had been meaning to come up and see him, but she had been so busy.

She bent over and placed a large bouquet of red flowers on his grave: *Tulipa greigii*. He had planted them last year and had been so looking forward to their blooming. She stood in front of his grave and said, "Thank you, Landers. You were right. They bloomed. Just like you said they would, they bloomed."